ALL I LEFT UNSAID

A LATINA'S JOURNEY TOWARD TRUTH

ROSY CRUMPTON

ISBN: 978-0-9908136-0-6

Edited by: Amy Ashby

Published by Warren Publishing, Inc.
Charlotte, NC
www.warrenpublishing.net
Printed in the United States

To my loving and supportive husband
who encourages and inspires me.

To my big, crazy, complicated family
that I would do anything for.

I love you all.

Table of Contents

Dear Kids,

Sigh. Where should I begin?

I can tell you that sharing this story has been
years in the making. There is so much to remember, so
much to share, and so much to re-live. It wasn't easy to
put this all in writing, but what really motivated me
was when I decided to write this for and to each of the
four of you.

Carrie, John, Celeste, and Amelia—the five of us
share a mother, and it's no secret that my relationship
with Mami has had its challenges. Over the years, you
witnessed uncomfortable interactions between Mami and
me that you were too young to understand. You may
have wondered why I was so obsessive about you four
always being by my side. You may only remember the
times when we lived at the Newberry Road house and may
have forgotten all the wonderful memories I cherished
with you before we lived there. The thought that you may
only remember our family from your teen years scares
me because I was a different person then. I was someone
who didn't always set a good example for you.

When I left our Newberry Road home, I did it because
I had to save myself. I made a selfish decision to
leave but it wasn't easy. I felt a weight of guilt come
over me when I left the four of you behind as I drove
away behind Raymond's white Chevy Blazer that Saturday
morning. You cried and watched me leave without knowing

why. I couldn't tell you why I left back then. Eleven years later, I'm ready to explain.

If I had shared this story with you years ago, it would've had a different tone and another ending. It wouldn't have been a story of growth; it would've been a story of bitterness, anger, and even rage.

I've learned so much over time and I want to share it with you. As you read this, please don't be angry at Mami, or Papi. And please don't be mad at me for keeping you in the dark.

I am so very proud of each and every single one of you. Each of you only one year apart and so unique. You've all grown up to be adults with unique paths. I love you more than any words can express. You're my world and always have been. I know you're not kids anymore, but you will always be my kids.

I love you today and always and I will be here for you no matter what.

Your big sis,
Olivia

CHAPTER 1

April 16

Months after the six of us should've moved out of the Newberry Road home, I still stared at the unpacked boxes lined up in my bedroom closet. The boxes were a reminder to me of how close we came to leaving once and for all. What hurt most is that I really believed it this time. The rest of you had already unpacked and settled back in, but I didn't mind rummaging through the boxes to get to my things every day. This was only temporary for me. I was going to leave one day.

The six of us had plans to move into a two-bedroom apartment not far from the Newberry Road house on April 16. You all would still go to the same school; we didn't want to disrupt your life too terribly if we could help it. The four of you knew of our plan to leave. For you all it only took months, but for me it took years.

Before the six of us deliberately arranged to move out, I had all intentions of moving out of that house, far away from him, as soon as I could. I was a college graduate and could afford a place of my own. It seemed like the *American* thing to do. But when I told Mami of my plans to leave, she couldn't understand it.

I told her I wanted to get my own apartment. I explained that although I wasn't married, I was of age. Most people I went to college with thought it was strange I still lived at home. They didn't say it, but I could see it on their judgmental faces. I had always maintained at least one full-time job and multiple part-time jobs. I had saved up enough money to quit the seafood restaurant I had worked at all through college and started my career using my psychology degree, serving people with disabilities and mental health diagnoses. I had done everything right. It was my time to be free and independent—FINALLY. But Mami didn't want me to leave her. She told me she was ready to leave Papi, but she couldn't do it without me.

Packing up to leave the Newberry Road home was probably the first time you remember Mami wanting to leave him, but trust me, she had done this before. I had heard this for what seemed like a hundred times and I couldn't take her seriously anymore.

"What now?" I asked. She explained his irresponsibility with managing finances, how he continued to drink and refused to go to church with us, and how she believed he was cheating on her yet again. She pleaded for my help to get out of there.

I hated that she asked. I hated her for putting this responsibility on me. Why couldn't she do this on her own? Why couldn't she be independent? She had a hold on me I hadn't been able to shake.

"If you're serious, then I'll help you," I said. I was down to one job at the time, but now as the primary breadwinner of our six-person family, I would have to go back to working multiple jobs. That's how Papi had been able to support us. That's all I knew how to do.

With my pride wounded and against all my desires and dreams, I asked for my job back at the seafood restaurant and was hired for the second time without a problem. I was yet again working two jobs.

I didn't want to work there again. I didn't want to work my full-time office job to then go straight to work forty hours at the restaurant. Mami only worked the one job *I* drove her to and picked her up from Monday through Friday and then went home to take care of you all. Why couldn't she get another job? I didn't want this to be my life. But I did it for the four of you, not for her. I was finished with her. On my first day back at the seafood restaurant, I cried in the parking lot before walking in. Little did I know how much worse the job would be this time around.

Another employee called out sick one night, so the manager ended up closing the restaurant with me. He was unsuccessful in finding a replacement and was not happy about working longer than he wanted to. Closing with the manager meant I did all the cleaning while the assistant manager, Mr. Williams, counted down the money and took it to the bank. I was in a hurry trying to get all of the cleaning done and left the bathrooms for last.

I was in the ladies' bathroom cleaning the fingerprints off of the mirror when Mr. Williams walked in. He startled me. I thought he might have something to tell me, but he didn't say anything immediately. I looked up as I saw him lick his lips in the reflection before me. Very nervously, I smiled.

"Those khakis look really good on you," he stated as he walked slowly toward me. He flashed his smile, his gold front tooth stood out greedily among the white ones. I took a deep breath as I finished up.

"I just have the trash left and I'm done," I said. He now stood directly in my way, hanging one-handed from the beam that connected the single stall to the wall.

"Aren't you going to say thank you?" he asked as he cornered me. I stood still, facing the mirror in utter fear.

"Thank you," I whispered. *If I comply, he'll go away,* I thought. Before I knew it, he had one hand around my waist and drew me to him. My butt pressed against his pelvis. He moved my head to one side and licked and kissed my neck. I could smell stale gum on his breath. I stood frozen, too weak to stand up for myself.

"I'll see you tomorrow," he whispered as he let go of me. "Don't forget the trash."

Dodging him at every chance, I worked there for a few months, saved up some money, and leased a two-bedroom apartment under my name. Mami didn't have good credit. I knew this and applied for credit cards that helped pay for back to school clothes and supplies for the four of you. We had a move-in date of April 16 and a deposit already down on our soon-to-be apartment. We told you all we were moving without Papi and that we couldn't tell him. The four of you suspected this and knew the situation between Mami and Papi was obviously not functional or loving. You each packed your things and boxed them up. Mami had always been clear that it was always us six. Although we all lived together, Papi was always separate and an outsider. None of you were upset about this decision. We weren't ever attached to him emotionally, only financially.

Two days before our anticipated big move, Mami changed her mind and decided to stay with him. Papi told Mami he was going to buy a new dream house in a nice neighborhood in the suburbs and this house was going to be nicer and better than any we had ever lived in. This news distracted Mami from the real reason we were leaving. She was miserable and had been planning to leave Papi for over a decade. She dreamt of a bigger home and thought about the two-bedroom apartment that awaited us. She chose the dream of her house. She chose him. Again.

By this time, I'd had more than enough with the both of them. I decided I was moving out despite her decision to stay. I had lost my hard-earned money on the deposit and I was exhausted at her cowardice. Why could she not leave the man who made her so damn miserable? Everyone I knew who had graduated was trying to live independently, starting their own lives, having fun with their friends and going out, while I had to tell people I lived at home because of our Hispanic culture. It was embarrassing, but saying I couldn't move out until I got married was much easier than explaining our ridiculous situation: my mom didn't want me to leave her and her four kids with the man she chose to marry.

Sometimes seeing the boxes in my closet made me angry because we didn't leave on April 16 as planned, but mostly it kept me driven.

"Come with us to the new house," said Mami, still fantasizing about the bigger house Papi had promised. But I decided I was moving out and I was going to follow through, unlike her. I would never live in that new dream house he'd promised her.

I yearned to leave the Newberry Road house every day. Each time I showered, I'd watch over my shoulder, afraid Papi would come in. I'd sometimes sleep in the living room because from there, I could hear when his bedroom door opened while you all slept in your rooms. I'd have sleepover movie nights in my bedroom where I could keep an eye on the four of you all night and hear if he ever came in. I lived in total paranoia. Papi had lost my trust a long time ago.

Mami had lost my respect.

The situation at home was insufferable, and I was extremely unhappy. I had started to resent Mami and Papi; especially Mami. I felt stuck. I wanted our parents to be a single unit separate from me and I didn't know how to express it. I wanted them to be responsible and loving. I didn't want or need the responsibilities I had. I wanted to be a "normal big sister;" I wanted to live the lives my peers lived. Instead, I had done everything our parents always wanted me to do. They didn't understand; what I was doing was normal for them and our "work hard and hustle" culture. But I wanted to live my dreams. I wanted to be on my own.

Although I loved you guys with all my heart, I didn't want to be the one responsible for adjusting my work schedule to take you to doctor's appointments, dentist appointments, orthodontists, to chaperone class field trips, volunteer at your school, attend parent/teacher conferences, e-mail your teachers when you were absent, etc.—all while going to school and working multiple jobs. As much as I enjoyed being there for you, I didn't want the weight of that responsibility.

It was my responsibility to take Mami to and pick her up from work. I took her to her medical appointments that were frequent since she'd had her first stroke during my sophomore year of college and developed epilepsy. Amelia's doctor's appointments were just as frequent with her epilepsy, too.

All of this weighed heavily on me while I tried to work and go to school over the years. I would do anything for our family and I did, but I had reached my limit and no one understood, especially Mami. Through my eyes, Papi was getting off easy by not having to participate in his kids' lives, and Mami was grateful but saw these tasks as my family responsibilities. By this point, I was tired and I felt like I was missing out on things I really wanted to do.

I wanted to live my life. I wanted to leave. I had put in my time.

The summer after we didn't move out, Mami told me that Papi's mom, Grandma Veronica, may be moving in with us because she was sick and getting older. The memories I had of her were all negative ones and I knew I had to make my move fast. I wouldn't live under the same roof with her again. Surely, I would be asked to care for her and I refused to care for someone who didn't even accept me as her own granddaughter. I knew this because she told me so. I secretly began to look for my own apartment.

I was in a new relationship during that time. I had just started dating Raymond and during a conversation about apartment searches, he invited me to move in with him. Normally this would have been a crazy thought in a new relationship, but I accepted his offer. We had been dating for six months. Although he didn't want me to contribute financially, I insisted on paying fifty percent of all the bills combined. Once we agreed on my terms, we made plans for me to move in that Labor Day weekend, exactly 139 days after April 16. It genuinely felt like the right thing to do.

My best friend, Saheli, had a hard time understanding my decision. She was my most trusted friend, practically family, but even she didn't know all my reasons for leaving. She hadn't met Raymond yet, but only because we lived in different states. She felt I was making an impulsive decision, and she was looking out for my best interest. I was the good Catholic girl; Saheli was the good Hindu girl. We held each other accountable to be safe and responsible at all times.

I packed up the remainder of my things without telling Mami and Papi. I sat the four of you down and told you of my plans to move. Very strategically, without revealing too much information, I told you to pay attention to anyone who may want to harm you. I reminded you that your body parts are private, and told you all to tell me of anything that made you uncomfortable at any time. And I told you I would be at the Newberry Road home within minutes if you called me. Thinking back on that conversation now, I must've scared you all a little. I wanted you to know I was serious, but I couldn't tell you exactly why I said those things. You were too young to know the truth about him, but I wanted you to be aware of danger and know to call me if you ever felt it.

By this time, you knew how to take care of Mami and Amelia when they had seizures. You all knew to call me while I was at work and I would walk you through what to do. I assured you I would be around when you needed me, even if it was every day. I asked you to keep my move a secret from Mami and Papi until I told them, and all four of you did. I was packed and ready for that Saturday morning, but it did not go exactly as planned.

The Friday before I planned on moving, Mami got sick. She had one of her bad seizures and ended up going to the hospital that night. The doctors increased her medications and she was released to come home after overnight monitoring. She didn't know of my plans, but of course she always found a way to ruin them.

Because of her hospitalization, I had not been able to sit down to tell Mami and Papi that I was planning on moving in with Raymond. I wanted to tell them of my plans that Friday night and had been dreading the conversation all week. They found out a little more abruptly that Saturday morning as Raymond was on his way to pick me up.

Papi arrived from the hospital with Mami that morning. He had stayed with her at the hospital during the night like she asked. It's so many years later, and I still can't understand what spell he had over her. She couldn't let him go.

I texted Raymond to come get me as soon as they pulled in. I wanted this to happen and I wanted it to be fast. Knowing he was on his way started the countdown for me. My new life was waiting. Living in sin with my new, sweet boyfriend was somehow more comforting to me than staying in this home for another minute. Like a bandage, I let it rip as soon as our parents walked through the door.

"I'm sorry I couldn't tell you last night like I had planned, but I'm moving out," I said. "Raymond is on his way to pick me up."

"What?" Mami whispered in disbelief.

I knew at that moment she was fine. I also knew she was getting ready to use her illness to guilt trip me into staying. I *knew* her. She knew exactly how to get me. She knew her epilepsy had kept me in that house longer than planned and she was arming it to use against me.

"I'm moving out," I said adamantly. I was afraid and mustered courage from the pit of my anger.

"Olivia Rose, I just got here from the hospital! You haven't even asked me how I'm feeling."

She squinted her eyes as if she were in some sort of pain, begging for sympathy and used my first and middle name to assert authority. *There she goes*, I thought. I wasn't going to let her win this time.

"Raymond is on his way," I said calmly. It didn't come out as firmly as I had hoped, but my statement was true. He was on his way, all my things were packed in my room, and my decision was made. I was going to finally move away and start *my* life.

"Is that the boy I met not that long ago?" Papi asked.

"Yes. And I'm sorry but I have to go." I began to gather my things. I was anxious and so close to leaving. It was really happening this time. I was *finally* going to escape. Mami became angry at this point. She raised her voice at me in an attempt to keep me in her nest.

"You're not moving! Are you crazy? I don't know this boy! *You* don't know him!" she shouted in Spanish.

"I'm still going to take you to work and pick you up. I'm

still going to take care of the kids. I'm still going to make sure they have everything they need…"

"No, you're not," she interrupted. Papi rolled his eyes and headed to his bedroom. This was typical of him—absent and disconnected. Mami carried on with her yelling. I knew she was fine.

"How are you still going to be here for us? How can you leave us like this?" She shouted.

I headed down the stairs to my bedroom where I found you girls. You looked worried and Celeste was crying softly. Celeste was always the first to cry. I've always admired her sensitive and vulnerable spirit.

"It's okay," I said, trying my best to comfort all of you.

I heard the roll of the tires and saw the shadow of Raymond's truck pull into the driveway.

"C'mon, will you help me bring my things to the car?" I double tapped Carrie on the knee. As the oldest of the four of you, I saw her as the next one in line to set an example. She immediately came to help me while Mami continued to yell.

"I can't believe you're leaving me!" she cried. "I can't believe you're leaving us, your family!"

"I'm not leaving you. I'm literally seven minutes away! You'll see me every day. I just can't live here anymore," I said, moving as quickly as possible.

Mami stormed upstairs and joined Papi in their bedroom, leaving the five of us behind.

In a hurry, I greeted Raymond at the back door with a handful of my belongings. He was clueless of the dramatic happenings only moments before. I had thought about asking him to pick up my things the night before while Mami and Papi were at the hospital, but I thought it would be disrespectful to do so before talking to them.

I didn't bring many things with me. I only brought my

clothes, books, toiletries, and important documents, which had already been pre-packed. Within three minutes, my bedroom had been cleared out.

"Don't forget what I told you," I said to all of you. "If you need *anything* or if *anyone* tries to hurt you, you call me! Got it? I'm right down the street. I can get here in no time."

You all nodded while we hugged. Your tears broke my heart. But if I didn't leave now, I didn't know if I ever would.

"I'll see you tomorrow, ok?"

I waved, blew you guys a kiss, and drove away in my car, following Raymond. I knew I was doing the right thing for me, but I didn't feel like I was doing the right thing for you.

CHAPTER 2

Sabanitas

Our origin, our roots, our background are from the beautiful, prideful, and culturally-rich Republic of Panamá. The four of you have been there. Carrie and John, you were too young to remember when you first went, but trust me when I say it's beautiful. Some parts of our hometown of Sabanitas look run down, and some areas, poverty stricken, but the happy, humble people remind you that it's about being rich in spirit. The chipped paint on buildings and the chaotic traffic is deceitful, as the people are proud, vibrant, and cheerful. Although you were not born there, this is where you're from—where we're from.

The town of Sabanitas is in the province of Colón. *Sabanitas* translated means 'small savanna.' The town's name accurately describes Mami's and my tropical childhood home.

I lived the first three years of my life in an apartment in the inner city of Colón before I lived in Sabanitas with Mami's side of the family. I don't have very many memories of my time in that apartment, but the few memories I have include Mami and my biological father, Iban. Mami and Iban were high school sweethearts who married a few years after graduation. Mami got pregnant with me immediately after they got married. They were following the traditional and expected path of a young couple in love.

The three of us lived in a fairly nice apartment in the center of Colón. Mami and Iban had very good jobs. Mami was an administrative accountant for the Colón Fire Department, an esteemed government career she landed while still in college. One day while making a transaction at her bank, she had been paid a compliment by a bank employee who suggested she apply for a job at her husband's office, the fire department. According to Mami, the teller was impressed with her graciousness. Mami explained she was a student, but after some thought, she decided she could use the extra money. She landed the job and ended up working there for nine years. Iban was a technical operator at the France Field airport in Colón. This was also a very admirable position to have, especially for someone so young.

I was enrolled at the best private school in Colón at the age of three. Mami and Iban wanted the best for me. I enjoyed going to school and looked forward to it every day. Mami told me I loved my classmates so much, I claimed them as my own and so I called them my kids. "*Yo quiero ver a mis niños*" I told them both every day. I was an only child despite my hopes for brothers and sisters. My classmates were like brothers and sisters to me. Mami and Iban's marriage fell apart, they divorced when I was four years old, and she and I moved to her mother's house in Sabanitas.

≈∕☺≈

Mami loved her family like I love her and all of you, but she didn't enjoy visiting them often while we lived in the city. When I was older, Mami told me she married young to leave her house and get away from the chaos. Mami lived in the city and consumed her life with work, young motherhood, her marriage, and her closest friends from high school. And although it was not far at all, while we lived in Colón city we rarely made the trip to the countryside of Sabanitas.

The public bus dropped Mami and I off at the bottom of the dirt hill that led to our grandmother, Mamacela's, property. On the top of the hill there was a fork on the road and the left fork lead to Mamacela's house. The right fork winded down a curvy dirt path to Mamacela's sister's property. Our Great Aunt Mercedes lived with her extended family in multiple homes on the same property. Down the left of that fork, on Mamacela's property, there were two homes—Abuelita Minerva's home and her eldest son's home. Tío Manuel, his wife Ester, and their two children, named after each of them, lived in that home just a few yards away from Mamacela's house. In Panamá, it is common for a family member to build a home on the family land when they get married. But this wasn't for Mami. She wanted a different life. After the divorce, Mami swallowed her pride and moved us back into the house she had grown up in and desperately wanted to move from when she got married only a few years before.

In that one-level, three-bedroom home lived our grandparents, fondly nicknamed Mamacela and Papou, our teenage tíos, Marcos and Mateo, our pre-teen Tía Mia, and our beloved great grandmother whom we adored, respected, and feared, Abuelita Minerva.

Abuelita Minerva was the most knowledgeable woman we all knew. I'm not sure why we called her Abuelita Minerva because her name was Marianna, but we didn't ask questions. In fact, the children my age barely dared to speak in her presence because as Abuelita Minerva said, "*Los niños hablan cuando las gallinas mean.*" As any children our age would, we took her expression literally and went outside to watch the hens until they peed so we could speak.

Our cousin, Ester was only eight months younger than me. Her younger brother, Manuel whom we called Manny, was our companion. Ester and Manny became like a brother and sister to me and they lived only a few feet away.

Ester and I played from the moment the rooster woke us up—yes, we had a rooster—until dusk when we went into our separate homes just five large steps away. We played with jacks, dolls, stuffed animals, sticks, mud, and just about anything we could find in the yard and get our hands on. Ester and I ran in the rocky front yard, leaving dust clouds behind us. We were barefoot, holding hands, and filthy from the dirt. We were both so happy to have a new sister in each other that we could barely stand to be apart. We played pretend games and would sneak off into our own made up adventures.

One day, we decided it would be a good idea to sneak off into Tía Mercedes's property. The adults had no idea what we were up to. They thought we were within eye's reach in the yard as usual, but we both knew we were scheming. Ester knew a shortcut to the far-away property—or at least it seemed far to us. We climbed through the brushes and trekked until we finally arrived. There it was, Tía Mercedes's colorful cement home with the rusty tin roof.

"Shhhh…they'll hear us and we'll get in trouble," I said.

After all, no one knew we were there. This was further than we were supposed to be. We giggled and hid in the greenery as we heard our aunts' voices. They were outside hanging clothes to dry.

"Look," Ester said, while pointing. "We can use these to cook with."

I grabbed the abandoned oxidized pots and pans and took off into the jungle to head back home with my clunking treasure in hand.

Later that day we used our new pans to make mud hamburgers. After careful measuring and forming the mud into perfect circular burgers, we placed them in the sun to dry and then later pretended to eat them. We giggled at the fact we actually tried to eat them and then moved on to the next adventure.

We had new adventures every day after school. Some adventures included Manny, but we decided he was too young for others, since we felt so much older and more grown up. We were only three years older than him, but this made a very big difference to us. We often found sticks and would ask Tío Manuel to tie a string to each end of our sticks to make a bow and then take another stick and use it as an arrow. The fresh branches from the Guarumo tree had a slight curvature and U-shaped ends that made it the perfect tool for pretend hunting. We lurked in the yard for our prey and ran barefoot until sundown. Manny enjoyed the hunting pretend game with us.

❧ ⑨ ❧

"Mami, Mami, Mami" I tugged at Mami's shirt one day, desperate for her attention. I was interrupting her conversation with Mamacela.

"Mamiiiiii," I whined.

"*Que hija?*" she replied attentively, ready to answer my desperate pleas.

"*Se me olvidó lo que iba a decir.*" In truth, I hadn't forgotten what I was going to say. I didn't have anything to tell her at all. All I wanted was for her to pay me some attention in between my playtime with our cousins.

"*Alguna mentira?*" She asked playfully. Mami liked to suggest that when I had forgotten what I was going to say, then it meant I was going to tell a lie.

"*No era una mentira, Mami,*" I assured her.

She leaned my head over on her hip just as I knew she

would and gave me a side squeeze before I ran off to continue playing, completely satisfied with my hug.

≈ ⑨ ≈

In Sabanitas, we loved it when it rained. At the first sign of a rainstorm, our family ran to the back of the house to make sure our two rusty iron bins were turned over so that the rain water would fill them up. I'm not using the term 'rusty' loosely either. I mean these bins screamed tetanus! I'm not sure how old these bins were or how we managed not to get any infections, but they served their purpose.

The iron bins were big enough to fit a large person in them standing up and they could store a lot of water. After the rain, we would use this water to bathe with since we didn't have running water at the house. After we made sure the bins were positioned, we grabbed a couple of bars of soap and went outside to shower in the cold rain while we laughed and enjoyed the water as a family. We then put on our pajamas, wet, worn-out towels draped over our backs and shoulders, and went back outside under the covered front porch to enjoy the rainbow that appeared over us into the nightfall. I sat on Tía Mia's, Tío Mateo's, or Tío Marcos' lap as one of them combed out the knots from my wet hair. The rainbow never failed to appear.

On our property we had dogs, cats, pigs, hens, a very mean rooster named Mario, snakes, exotic birds, and mango-stealing monkeys in the trees right behind our house. If you wanted a mango, you simply went outside, climbed the tree, grabbed it, and ate it. You could also use one mango to throw and make more fall so you could share the fruit with others. When you heard a sudden, loud bang on the tin roof, you knew it meant a mango had fallen off the tree on its own. That's when we all stopped what we were doing to run

outside and find it. Whoever got to the fruit first could eat
it. This wasn't a casual thing either; we literally raced. The
mango was a true treat.

~ 9 ~

I have very special memories of Abuelita Minerva. I wish
all of you could've met her. I only knew her for the six, almost
seven years I lived in Panamá, but in that short amount of
time, I understood how meaningful she was to all of us.

Abuelita Minerva had three daughters, whose names all
start with the letter M, just like Mami and her siblings—
Marcela (better known as Mamacela), our Great Aunt
Mercedes, and our Great Aunt Marta. Abuelita Minerva
lived with Mamacela all of her life after our great grandfather
passed away at a very young age. Abuelita Minerva raised her
three daughters and all of their children while the daughters
and their husbands worked.

You've heard Mami tell tales of how strict Abuelita
Minerva was to her and all of her cousins growing up.
Mami, our tíos, and tías still recite the expressions Minerva
would say and tell the stories of how she would chase them
into the yard and line them *all* up for a beating if *one* of them
misbehaved. They tell their endless tales of childhood stories
that all end with a beating, or *un cocotazo*, to the head from
her cane, followed by laughter and a comment about how
much they loved and appreciated her.

Years later now that they're all grown up, they still tell
stories of Abuelita Minerva from when I lived in Sabanitas.
She screamed blasphemies to our aunts, uncles, and
Mamacela as she limped around the house in her white
see-through mumus she wore with no panties. She cooked
most of our meals while Mamacela and Mami worked and
everyone else was at school. Abuelita Minerva was the only

person in the house who spoke English, Spanish, and Greek. Everyone else spoke only Spanish. She was of Greek descent. Her eyes were the color where green and blue meet. She had pale skin and was a blond in her younger days. I only knew her when thin, white and light brown hair covered her head.

Everyone knew what it felt like to get a beating from Abuelita Minerva, except for me. When I was not playing with Ester or Manny, I was with Abuelita Minerva.

"Olivia!" she would yell for me to come to her. "Come help me collect eggs."

I would skip behind her as she showed me how to do each task.

"You see, you have to trick the hens or they won't lay the eggs."

I listened to her as she explained the role of the single mean rooster we owned that roamed freely on our land.

One day, Abuelita Minerva called me in from playing. It was time for me to water her plants as I did daily for her. She had a door in her bedroom that led to the side of the house. I fetched the container I always used, poured water in it, and went right outside her door. I leaned in to water the plants and as I was almost finished, I felt a sharp pinch on my right butt cheek.

"Ahhhhhh!" I shrieked in pain.

Abuelita Minerva limped as fast as she could to find the rooster right behind me. After that day, Mario wasn't allowed to roam freely. Abuelita Minerva tied him to a tree using a faded blue braided rope around his neck. She purposely tied him in sight of her bedroom. The rope was long enough that he was reminded of why he was tied up as he saw me watering her plants every day, but just short enough he wasn't able to dare bite me again. It was a true Minerva punishment and that is how we became the only family that had a rooster tied up like a dog. This became a running joke with our whole extended family.

Another rooster bit me one other time not much longer after that. The second bite was from Tía Mercedes' rooster. Tío Manuel and I walked down the long gravel pathway to her house one day to pick up a tool. The sight of our Tía Rosario killing a hen had distracted me. She grabbed it by its neck with her bare hands and rang it in the air carelessly while holding casual conversation. The rooster came up behind me as I watched her remove the hen's feathers in awe. I still remember where that old bird got me right in the meat between my thumb and pointer finger on my left hand. Boy was our family angry when I came home crying that day.

Abuelita Minerva often pulled me from my playtime to teach me life lessons. She enjoyed my company and I loved hers. One day as I handed her clothes to hang on the clothesline outside, I looked up and saw a flock of big black vultures circling above us.

"Why are they doing that?" I asked.

"There's death near us," she said, and I believed her.

I didn't ask any other questions although I had so many. Everything she said was truth and wasn't questioned by anyone in our family circle.

One day while helping Abuelita with chores around the property, we came across a big black snake coiled up in our path. I remember being startled when it flicked its tongue at us. She placed her arm over my chest as to shield me from the leathery, slithering creature and to raise my attention. She then began to explain in a low voice that my uncles would likely kill the creature with a machete, but she wouldn't. The snake would surrender to her and she was going to teach me how. She stared the snake directly in its eyes and soon enough, the snake left our path and was no longer a threat to us. I remember being so impressed with her skill. I had never seen anything like it.

❧ ⑨ ❧

Sometimes all of us got together and played the first version of hide and seek I ever played. We hid for our lives, anywhere in the house or however many feet from the house we all agreed upon. The seeker carried a belt. If you were found, you were hit with the belt. Although the spankings were playful, I tried my best to not be found. Tía Mia taught me how to hide. She taught me to put my shoes behind the closed curtain to trick the seeker into thinking I was hiding behind it. I enjoyed watching the seeker get fooled from afar in my actual hiding spot.

One particular time, Tía Mia was the seeker. I picked the perfect hiding spot just like she had taught me. I even chose a location she hadn't shown me before. She had been looking for me for a few minutes when she walked into the room I was in. She seemed tired of looking for me and began to call out, "Olivia, where are you?" I immediately responded, "Here I am," as I walked out of my hiding spot. It was a trick and I fell for it. Tía Mia laughed at me as I ran into her arms not fully understanding the reason for her loud laughter. She was so amused, she didn't beat me with the belt.

❧ ⑨ ❧

Our tíos would pick me up, toss me around, and spin me upon request. I was loved and had everything I needed. We spent our evenings in Sabanitas as a family. We watched television as a family, with our own wire-hanger version of an antenna that had aluminum foil at both tips. I was told that this gave the clearest picture.

Abuelita Minerva watched all of her *telenovelas* while cleaning and straining the raw rice and dry beans with care during the day as we played outside. When the telenovelas were finished, we could watch whatever we wanted. Some of my favorite TV shows at the time were *Strawberry Shortcake, the Care Bears, Jem and the Holograms, Heidi: Girl of the Alps,* and *Punky Brewster,* which all aired in Spanish. But the evenings were when Mami and Mamacela came home from work and they liked to watch the news.

One time as we all gathered around the single television in the living room, a bat flew in through a screen-less open window. This happened frequently as the house was made of cement and its windows were only big rectangular holes formed in the walls. The big, black bat flapped its wings and flew all about the room. We screamed and ran behind the couch as we always did when bats flew in. I hid in Tía Mia's arms as the bat continued to fly around. Mami's screams filled the room.

Someone yelled, "Cover your necks! It's going to suck your blood!" I wrapped my hands around my neck as instructed. Mami's quick bursts of sharp screeches caused Mamacela to laugh, and Mami kept screaming and laughing at herself. Abuelita Minerva hollered, "Someone get the broom!"

Tío ran to get it while his girlfriend at the time, Sofia, began to jump up to grab at the bat with her bare hands. The rest of us laid low. Sofia missed and kept trying while Tío ran into the living room, swung it down with the broom, and beat it to death. Sofia grabbed the dead bat with her hands and threw it outside while scolding Tío angrily, "You didn't have to kill it! It wasn't harming anyone!"

Sofia was from Darien, a more indigenous part of Panamá. Anytime a bat flew in the house after that first time, Sofia took care of it while the rest of us ran away from it covering our necks.

Mami and I were living at Mamacela's house when Sofia came into our lives. We were all gathered around after dinner when we heard a knock at the door.

"Who is it?" multiple people whispered loudly.

"I'm not expecting anyone," someone responded.

"Shhhh they can hear you," Mami said.

Our family was not used to many visitors.

"Hide the food, it's probably our cousin, fat Rosario," said Tío Marcos.

The loud, brief chaos came to a halt as Mamacela walked over to the door. I ran up next to her as she opened the door and saw a pale, strange man wearing a straw hat and a white button-down shirt. A young, thin, pale girl with long, straight brown hair stood beside him with a horse behind them. Mamacela told me to go inside and get Mami. I didn't know what was said at the door during their conversation, I just knew Sofia lived with us from that day forward.

I learned later that the strange man was Sofia's father. In their town, children did not receive an education past elementary school. He wanted us to take her in and let her help us around the house in exchange for her going to school in our town and living with us. Sofia helped take care of Ester, Manny, and me. She also helped with the cooking and cleaning. She and Tío Marcos became boyfriend and girlfriend sometime after that.

≈ 9 ≈

As you know, Mami is deadly afraid of slipping and falling. This has always been the case. I remember the day I learned about her fear when we went to wash clothes at the creek.

"*Vamos a lavar ropa en la quebrada,*" Mami instructed out loud.

The room broke out in laugher.

Mamacela said to her, "You? You want to go to the creek? Did you forget about the muddy hill?"

"My brothers will help me," Mami responded, as if she had something to prove.

Mamacela noticed my puzzled look. "Your mom is scared of hills," Mamacela explained.

The family headed down to the creek. I quickly learned that Mamacela was right about Mami's fear of falling. The muddy, slippery downslope was a little challenging to navigate while holding your balance. It was even harder to do so while holding the clothes we had to wash. Everyone made it to the bottom while Mami screamed the whole way down, even with Tío Manuel's help. Everyone laughed at her screams.

"*No se rían de mi!* " Mami hollered down at us, even though she was laughing at herself, too.

Mami crossed her legs so as not to pee on herself from laughing so hard. You can imagine the laugh, her happy laugh where her eyes are almost closed and her eyelashes appear as a single black line below her eyebrows—and you can see all her teeth and gums. We all couldn't help but join in and laugh, too.

When Mami reached the bottom, we all got in the creek. The water was clear, a little cool, and flushed quickly all around me. Big, gray, smooth stones outlined the sides and bottom of it.

"Be careful in here, Olivia. I cut my toe open down to the bone once in the lake. Your tío had to carry me home. Watch your step," Mami warned me.

"What's that?" I asked, pointing to the flashes appearing all around me in the water.

"Those are fish," Mami responded.

After bathing and playing in the creek, Mami, Tío Manuel, Tío Marcos, Tío Mateo, and Tía Mia showed me how to wash our clothes with the wooden washboard and stones that lined the cool creek.

Although Mami often expressed embarrassment about our living conditions whenever a friend of hers would visit, times like these, she really seemed to enjoy being back at the home she grew up in. She didn't seem to miss her married life in the city.

The De La Cruz family lived on this property and we lived happy, humble, and normal lives.

CHAPTER 3

We're Going to Meet Santa Claus

I vividly remember the day I met the man we all call 'Papi.' He was introduced to me as Andrew, the Magician. I was standing in Mamacela's living room when he came in and sat on our old gray and brown couch across the room by the front door.

It was a typical evening at Mamacela's house. All of us children had finished our homework and we had all eaten the dinner our beloved Abuelita Minerva prepared with Sofia's help. The television was on, although no one could hear it over the cheerful chatter, and a cool breeze flew in every once in a while through our windows.

Mami sat beside Andrew with her hand on his lap while most of our family surrounded the new couple. She wore bright makeup with her dark brown hair in big curls that night. She laughed at what he said in an exaggerated manner. Her nose crunched up as she flashed her gums in laughter. Her upper body bent over into her torso and she belted out her laugh. She looked around the room at all our faces for approval. Her red lipstick outlined what was left of her thin lips as her laugh slowly turned back to a smile and she looked at him. It was genuine.

Mami's brothers and sister and Mamacela were infatuated with him. He was funny and made Mami happy. Abuelita Minerva, on the other hand, stood at the opposite side of the room, cane in hand, threatening him and cursing under her breath as she normally did with most strange visitors.

"Disgusting, bastard," she murmured.

I stood beside her, leaning my head on her legs and quietly questioning the rest of my family's trust. Mami invited me over into the living room to see his magic trick performance from up close. I hesitantly walked over and stood in between Mami's legs and faced him.

Andrew said to me, "I can make things disappear."

A little distrustful but still eagerly, I shouted out, "Show me!"

He pulled out a cardboard matchbook from his back pocket and ripped out a single match.

"You see this match? I'm going to make it disappear."

"Now close your eyes," he instructed me. "This match will be gone by the time you open them."

I closed my eyes, anticipating the magic. *Can he do it?* I wondered.

When I opened my eyes, the match was gone just like he said. I gasped. My eyes were wide in amazement. I was naively impressed. I had never seen anything like it. I looked around for it, but the match was nowhere to be found.

For his special trick of the night, he told me he could make me disappear. This was surely impossible, I thought. We counted to three out loud all together (except Abuelita Minerva who had retired to her bedroom) and all of a sudden, the family could not see me anymore. I tugged at Mami, I ran over to our uncles, and not even Mamacela could see me.

Andrew had bought himself into my six-year-old heart with his magic tricks and my innocence that night.

Andrew came around a lot after that evening. He often came by to eat dinner with all of us or simply to spend time with Mami. Mamacela, Tía Mia, and our tíos all seemed to really like him. Whenever I earned a perfect score on tests, he always brought me a bag of Peanut M&Ms, which he knew were my favorite, so he was all right with me. Abuelita Minerva never did grow fond of him. *He should bring her M&Ms, too*, I thought.

I began to see more and more of Andrew and less and less of my dad, Iban. Iban only visited me at our house for a limited time and then would leave. Mami told me she didn't like the fact Iban liked to ask me a lot of questions about her and Andrew while I was with him. Truthfully, Mami asked me more questions about the time I spent with my dad than Iban asked questions about Mami. Mami would prepare me on what kinds of questions he might ask me and would make me practice what my responses should be. After my time with my dad, she would interrogate me on how it all went and demanded details.

I once had a homework assignment in which I had to practice writing full sentences in cursive. The assignment was to write my relatives' names along with my relationship to them. For example: My mother's name is (insert full name)…and so on. While completing this assignment, Mami instructed me to write Andrew's name as my father's name in place of Iban. The sentence read: "My father's name is Andrew Butler." I filled in a full page worth of cursive. Mami then told me to show Iban my beautiful handwriting when he came for a visit. Iban cried after I proudly showed him my cursive writing skills and I remember feeling confused and not knowing why he cried. His visit was short that day.

I saw my dad one last time, the day before we moved to the United States with Andrew, the Magician. Andrew was from Panama but had a lot of family who lived in the United States, including his mother, Veronica. Mami had called Iban over to Mamacela's house. My dad and I began walking and sat at the cement table and bench our uncle had built. It was the nearest, shadiest spot on the property under the big mango tree next to the house. I was proudly showing my dad the good grades I made on my report card, when I became fascinated at a lizard crawling on the tree.

"Papi, what's that?" I asked.

"That's a chameleon. They change colors sometimes. It's their superpower."

"I want that superpower!" I cried.

We quietly watched it crawl away as not to scare it. Then Iban lifted me off the table and twirled me down slowly.

"C'mon, let's keep walking," he said.

The both of us walked around the property and talked as we usually did when he came to visit. We never went too far.

"*Paletas, paletas! Cinco centavos!*" we heard in the distance.

"Do you think we can catch him?" my dad asked.

I ran down the hill as fast as I could toward the popsicle salesman. I ran faster than my dad while squeezing the nickels tightly, one in each hand.

"Two lime popsicles, please," Iban ordered in Spanish and paid the man.

Lime was my absolute favorite flavor. I looked up at him and I squinted as the rays of sunshine above blinded my vision. All I could see was the dark shadow outline of his body. He was so much taller than me I remember thinking. My eyes drifted to the clouds.

"Do you see how far those clouds are?" he asked.

"Yes, very far," I said and licked on my popsicle in total bliss while still looking up at him.

"*Te amo hasta el cielo*," he replied, as he pointed to the sky.

I laughed in quiet comfort and continued to eat my popsicle, but I didn't say it back. Not because I didn't love him. I just enjoyed hearing him say it to me.

We walked slowly back to the house while sucking on our ice-cold treats and playing a game we played often. We pointed at clouds and told each other what we thought they looked like.

"That one looks like a truck," I said.

Pointing at a different cloud, my dad said, "Hmm… I think that one looks like a heart."

And we carried on.

We walked up the dirt road that felt so long to my thin brown legs. Then we finished our popsicles, said our see you next times, gave each other kisses, and he left as usual.

Unbeknownst to me, that was the last time I'd see him for a very long time. Later on, I was told he knew he would never see me again and he didn't even give me a proper goodbye.

That night I saw Mami crying. She was going through pictures and cutting them up. I sat on her lap to comfort her. She was cutting my father out of all of the pictures she had in her hand and I didn't understand why. I leaned my head into her chest, didn't say a word, and watched her cut him out of our memories and lives.

That same evening, Mami and I packed to move to the United States. Andrew had moved there a month before and was waiting for us. I remember that night very clearly because I had never seen our grandfather, Papou so angry.

"He's married! He has four kids with three other women!" Papou yelled. "Who are you going to live with? Do you think his mother is going to welcome you with open arms?" he carried on in Spanish.

"You're one to talk, just stay out of it!" Mami shouted, defending herself and the love of her life.

Mami had dreams to be with the one other man she had ever been in love with. She wanted to start a new life, away from certain people who judged her and frowned upon their relationship. She wanted a better life for her and for me. Although Mami was a good daughter and always helped her mother with her brothers and sister, she was a rebel. She always wanted more. She wanted to stretch her wings and fly away.

Papou didn't want us to go. They yelled at each other as Mami continued to pack. I didn't have any idea what was happening or exactly where we were going. All I knew was Mami and I were going to meet the Magician where he lived and Mami said he lived near Santa Claus. Andrew was going to introduce me to Santa Claus and I could tell him in person what I wanted for Christmas that year. I was on board with packing in order to make that happen.

Abuelita Minerva remained in her room while we packed. She didn't say anything to Mami, at least not that I witnessed. I slept in Abuelita's bed with her that night. As I drifted off into sleep, she began to pray, *"Qué Nuestro Señor las bendiga, que la Virgencita las protejan y Los Ángeles las acompañen...."* That was the last time I ever spent with her.

≈ ◎ ≈

The very next day, all of the De La Cruz family came with us to the airport except for Papou and Abuelita Minerva. Our aunts, uncles, their significant others, and our cousins came along to say goodbye to Mami and me. It wasn't until we had to say 'goodbye' that I realized what was happening.

"What do you mean, they can't come with us?" I asked. "Don't they want to meet Santa Claus? Ester wants to see Santa Claus! Why do I have to say goodbye?"

I cried desperately. I begged Mami to stay. She didn't want to leave, either. I could tell. Her face was red from all the crying. Everyone cried. Mami ripped me from my dearest Mamacela's arms and dragged me through the airport to board the plane that would take us to the United States. We went down the stairs at the airport and found a place where we looked up and saw our family standing on a glass bridge still crying.

"I'm not going!" I told Mami, but of course I didn't have a choice in the matter. I began to throw a temper tantrum. Mami grabbed my thin brown arm, pulled me toward her, and told me to stop crying.

She asked me, "If I buy you something, will you stop crying?" I straightened up and nodded my head, 'yes.' She acknowledged our agreement as we walked to find a store so she could keep her word. She began singing a familiar song we both liked that I had heard play at home many times— The Bangles "Eternal Flame."

"Close your eyes...give me your hand, darling...." We both sang along in our accents, both humming the parts of the song we didn't know.

The song distracted me from crying.

We boarded the airplane shortly after and I sat in my seat, wiping my tears quietly with my new teddy bear and Minnie Mouse stuffed animal in hand. The flight felt endless to me, but I eventually stopped crying. Surely, I would see our family again. Mami told me we were going to see Santa Claus and a whole new family would be waiting for us. I started to look forward to the arrival.

The flight made Mami very sick. She got up to use the bathroom on the plane so much that I spent most of the time alone in my seat. I remember eating mashed potatoes alone while Mami's food got cold on the tray in front of her seat. My two stuffed animals kept me company—after all, these were now my only toys. I had to leave all of my toys behind in Panamá, because we didn't have enough room to pack them. At the airport, I had asked Ester to take good care of all of my stuffed animals and dolls. She promised me she would until I came back for them, and I trusted her.

Little did I know at the time, but the reason Mami was so sick on the flight was that she was three months pregnant with the oldest of you—Carrie.

CHAPTER 4

Not la Academia

We touched down at John F. Kennedy airport in New York, our Ellis Island, that evening in early June of 1990. It had been a very long and emotional day. It was dark and Mami dragged me around the airport, walking for what seemed like an eternity. We finally reached a hallway and she told me, "Our new family is just behind those doors." I found the energy out of thin air to run down the hallway and meet our new family. I remember the carpeted, windowless hallway was eerily empty and dark.

The doors opened and I saw *hundreds* of people. I quickly scanned the room. It was loud, some people held "Welcome" posters, some were young, some were old, and they were everywhere. Right in front of all those people was Andrew the Magician.

I looked back at Mami with wide eyes in excitement and asked, "Are all of these people my family?" Mami laughed and ran to Andrew. We had arrived in the United States safe and sound.

Two faded leather suitcases and Mami's small black plastic tote contained all of our current possessions. That and my two new stuffed animals were all we had to start our new life in the United States.

We pulled up to a big, yellow house in Long Island: Grandma Veronica's house. This would be our new home for the next five years, and the first house the four of you ever lived in. This house had stairs, which was different from Mamacela's house. A lot of people lived in this house, just like in Sabanitas. Andrew introduced Mami and me to his mother, Grandma Veronica. Grandma Veronica then led us to the bedroom the three of us would share in the middle level of the home.

"Señora Veronica, do you have pillows we can use?" Mami politely asked.

"You brought clothes, didn't you? You can rest your head on those," she replied.

She walked away and returned a minute or so later with an empty pillowcase.

"This is what I have. You can put clothes in it and that can be your pillow." She laughed as if our mother had made an unreasonable request and walked away.

I put on my white cotton nightgown with tiny rainbows on it and skipped into the kitchen where Mami was. I told Mami I was hungry and wanted *leche con conflei* for dinner as I often had at Mamacela's house. Mami went over to pour my bowl of cereal but Grandma Veronica stopped her.

She disapproved of my dinner of choice and mumbled words in English with a Caribbean accent that neither Mami nor I understood.

Grandma Veronica made me a plate of what she had prepared for dinner that evening and told me I was not to get up from the table until I finished what was on my plate. I looked down on my plate and saw vegetables. I didn't eat vegetables. It smelled terrible.

"Poor children eat out of dumpsters for food you know," she said.

This was not going to be anything like my life as I knew it. *I miss home already,* I thought. The lights were turned off and I remained at the kitchen table alone with cold, untouched food on my plate. As stubborn as I was, I refused to give in and I fell asleep at the table. Mami snuck in after everyone fell asleep. She gave me some cereal, cleaned up after herself, and that remained our little secret until now. I went to sleep in my new bed. Mami and Andrew slept on a twin bed, and I slept on the trundle below them.

Weeks of avoiding Grandma Veronica during mealtimes went by. I was trying my best to get used to what my new days were like. I had new cousins who liked to watch TV, but I couldn't understand what the characters were saying, so I played alone instead. One day, the Magician had promised me a lime popsicle when he got home from work.

"Mami, what time is the Magician coming home?" I asked.

"I don't know, Olivia. I hope he gets home soon."

"Me too." I said.

"Olivia, come sit with me."

I ran in between Mami's legs.

"Do you want to call the Magician, 'Papi?'" she asked.

I smiled at Mami's sense of humor. "He's not my Papi, Mami. Papi isn't here."

"I know your Papi's not here, but Andrew is your *new* Papi. We live in a new place, so you have a new Papi now." I listened quietly as she continued. "And besides, I call him Papi. Don't you want to call him Papi too?"

"Ok," I agreed, doubtfully.

After work, he brought me a net bag of colorful icees instead of the lime popsicles I was used to. Although, not the same, I still ate them.

I was enrolled at Fairview Road Elementary School a month and a half after arriving in the States. This was the closest Elementary School to our house and I was placed in the second grade, even though I was midway through third grade in Panamá. Mami and Papi (I was starting to get used to addressing him this way) drove me to school and walked me to my classroom.

My teacher knelt down and introduced herself to me, or so it seemed. She spoke English and I didn't. I sat down right smack in the middle of the classroom in an empty seat. Mami and Papi waved goodbye and I was left alone in a classroom full of strangers who stared at me. Tears rolled down my eyes as Mami and Papi walked away. I didn't know these people.

The student sitting in front of me handed me a stack of papers. Instinct told me to grab the stack. The student behind me tapped me on the shoulder and reached for the papers, so I handed them to him. He took the papers from my hand and gave me one of the sheets from the stack. A task as simple as this was entirely new to me. The teacher then began to recite words. I looked around and students seemed to be writing down the words she was dictating. This was a new concept to me. I was in school, but I wasn't wearing my blue, white, and black, pleated uniform that reached down to my knees. And where were all the nuns? Who would whack our hands if a student tried to write with their left hand instead of their right hand?

Sometime later, I was brought to an indoor cafeteria where students formed lines with trays and chose food that was behind a glass. The food was slapped on plates by a person wearing a hairnet. At the end of the line was another person who took money. I observed this transaction. Some students exchanged words instead of money for which the person by the cash register would check something off a list.

Fortunately, I didn't have to get in line because Mami packed my lunch. I sat there and ate my crust-less cheese sandwich (just the way I liked it) as I continued to observe. There were pastel-colored plastic bins in the middle of each table in the cafeteria. I looked around at the endless rows. Students seemed to be using the pastel colored bins to throw their leftovers in and some were making a mess on their trays. They mixed their leftover food with their chocolate milk as they laughed and dumped it into the bins. I didn't understand the humor. *Where are the nuns?* I wondered again. *I miss Ester.* This was about the time we'd walk together and share a bag of cheese curls we bought for a nickel in the courtyard.

La Academia Santamaria was a lot different from this. In Panamá, I was used to wearing a uniform I wouldn't dare get dirty. Mami and Mamacela worked hard to keep my uniform neat, and pleated perfectly. We were surrounded by strict nuns whose hands were ready to whack knuckles with their yardsticks at the sight of a misbehaving child.

One of my teachers once grabbed a classmate by his ear and flung him to the cement wall for writing the wrong date on his paper and smart-mouthing her. I will never forget La Señora Gloria. Every day, the first thing we did was write on the first line of our notebook: *"Hoy es…."* Then we wrote out the day, month, and year in a full sentence. La Señora Gloria is the reason my script is so perfect; I did not want to get flung into a cement wall.

The teacher here didn't write in cursive, she wrote out each individual letter in print on the board. This was so strange to me because in Panamá, we only learned to write in cursive. Writing in print looked ugly and seemed lazy.

At Fairview Road Elementary, students came up to my face and yelled the numbers at me in Spanish. *"Uno, dos, tres,"* they screamed, as if talking louder made it possible for me to understand them better. They had strange accents as if they spoke with something in their mouths. I figured out later they just wanted to communicate with me, but numbers were the only words they knew in Spanish. The only English word I remembered from my English class in Panamá was 'milk.' A student brought me a small milk carton to appease me.

It wasn't long before I was transferred to another school that was further away but had an English as a Second Language program. At Elmer Avenue School, I came a long way. During my first few weeks at the school, I thought I made a friend. We held hands at recess like Ester and I did when we walked the property back in Panamá. The kids called us lesbians and laughed at us. After that, Maria didn't want to hold my hand anymore and didn't want to be my friend. I didn't even know what a lesbian was. I was desperately trying to replace my cousin who was a sister to me.

I learned a lot at that school and more than I even realized at the time. Mr. Grant, my ESL teacher, was amazing. I credit him for teaching me English and basic American culture. Mr. Grant did not speak any Spanish whatsoever, but he made me laugh when he tried. I attended classes with my main teacher, but was pulled out of class for hours to go to Mr. Grant's class. I loved it when he had waffle and pancake day. He would bring in batter and we ate what he called a typical American breakfast in the classroom. I didn't know it then, but he was teaching us more than the language. It was about the culture, too—or maybe he just liked waffles.

And so, day after day in my first year of second grade in the United States, I stood when my teacher commanded and all of us students faced the American flag that hung on the top corner of the chalkboard. The other students placed their hands over their hearts and recited words they all knew. Francisco—another ESL student—and I looked at each other, shrugged, and proceeded to mirror the others. We murmured through the words until a word came along we knew. Then we said that word louder as we mumbled the rest.

Mr. Grant would sure enough teach us what to say, and what it meant in due time. I had an idea of what this routine was, because we did something very similar at La Academia in Panamá. Each morning before going to our respective classrooms, all of the students from Kindergarten through twelfth grade lined up outside on the paved courtyard. We stood by classroom and by height, in perfectly straight lines. The lines were so obsessive-compulsively straight that we looked like a professional marching band. All the students knew not to make a mistake, because the nuns would get us if we dared to fool around. We then stood tall as we saluted the giant Panamanian flag that waved in the courtyard before us. With our hands straight at the corner of our foreheads, like tiny soldiers, we saluted and sang, *"Alcanzamos por fin la victoria en el campo feliz de la unión; con ardientes fulgores de Gloria se ilumina la nueva nacion..."*

But not today, not anymore. Today I sang, "My country 'tis of thee, sweet land of liberty, of thee I sing...." and made a pledge to a flag that was new to me.

Not long after this ceremony each day, there would be a knock on our classroom door. It was Mr. Grant's assistant to escort Francisco and me to our ESL class. The only times we were not in Mr. Grant's classroom was during art, gym, and music. These were different from classes in La Academia, too, but I didn't mind it one bit. I was just happy I didn't have to go to sewing class like we did in Panamá. It would take me the entire class period to thread my needle. The nuns in sewing class would shake their heads at me in disapproval.

A nun hit me once during sewing class. None of the students had done well on this particular day and the nun decided to hit all of us. When I came home and Mami saw the red mark on the outside of my hands, she was upset. She showed up at the school and used words the nuns and the school director did not expect to hear. She knew I was playful and overactive at home, but she had taught me to behave at school. So, when Mami showed up in the fire department vehicle (a perk of her job) demanding explanations for why I was hit that day, the nuns never thought to hit me again.

≈ ⊙ ≈

At home in the yellow house, I watched *Sabado Gigante*, *Chapolin Colorado*, and telenovelas with Mami on the spanish channel. It didn't take long before I started flipping over to *Tiny Toons*, *Growing Pains*, *Family Matters*, *Full House*, and *Blossom*. I understood them. I sat on the same couch where I'd sat days after I'd arrived, but now I watched, laughed, and understood what characters were saying.

This was the same couch I'd laid on when I took eggs from Grandma Veronica's refrigerator and laid them around me on the couch. Abuelita Minerva had taught me that eggs needed to be warm to hatch. I hadn't seen hens in New York, so I took it upon myself to keep the eggs warm. The refrigerator was cold. I just knew the eggs would hatch by morning. Needless to say, Mami woke me up to find cracked eggs all over me and the couch the next morning.

During this time, I also developed a love of reading. I discovered the library was full of interesting books and stories, and so I lived there. I loved to read, I loved understanding what I read, and I loved to teach it to Mami, Papi, and eventually you guys. Best of all, that reading helped me with my English. After two years of ESL classes at Elmer Avenue School, I knew enough English to graduate from ESL. I went back to Fairview Road Elementary in fourth grade after I'd learned a sufficient amount of English to be integrated with my peers. By this time, I walked to school with my neighborhood friends, and lived a typical American life as I knew it.

I spoke English. I made friends and even had play dates and the occasional sleepover—after I explained to Mami that sleepovers were normal. I could communicate well enough with neighbors to participate in school fundraisers. I'd go door to door with catalog in hand to sell gift-wrap, knick-knacks, or whatever our school asked us to sell. Spelling tests no longer made me cry, and Saturday morning cartoons became a part of my routine.

Although I was embracing the new country and new culture, there were still things that made me feel a little different than my peers. I was always a picky eater and I didn't like the food at the cafeteria at school so Mami packed me leftovers for lunch every day. No other student packed a bowl of cold rice and asked their teacher to warm up their lunch in the teacher's lounge. At first it didn't seem to be a difficult thing to ask for and so I did for a while until it started to become embarrassing for me to be different from my friends.

When my classmates and I spoke about our weekend, my experiences were always so different compared to theirs. Our family did the same thing every Sunday—and it was an all-day affair. Mami's side of the family has always been very religious. We were born and raised Catholic with a family priest and the whole family attended the same church. The same priest who baptized young cousin so and so, also married Tía you know who, and so on. We were part of church processions, partook in live nativity scenes, and participated in processions of Jesus on the cross.

Back in Panamá, Tío Manuel had been a deacon at the church, and our family came from a long line of altar servers and proud Eucharistic ministers. Mamacela always impressed me with the fact she could tell you what saint day it was any day of the year, followed by what that saint was known for. Mamacela prayed the rosary every morning, followed by additional prayers to Mary, Jesus, and various saints. I joined her when she asked me to. Our church in Panamá was not easy to get to which only made the experience that much more significant.

Every Sunday our entire family would put on our 'Sunday best' outfits. Some of the ladies covered their heads with lace scarves as a sign of respect. Mami always put me in a colorful dress. I wore my best white dress socks that folded over once to show off their ribbon bows, and my shiny patent leather shoes were the finishing touch. If I had scuffed my shoes, then I'd brighten them up with a little dye. I didn't mind doing this. I liked the strong paint scent it gave off because it made me feel like I was wearing new shoes.

Once we were all dressed, we'd walk to the bottom of the dirt hill to wait for the bus. We'd ride over to the closest bus stop to the church, then walk for about thirty minutes while we prayed in unison as a family. After mass, we'd do the same thing in reverse.

Until we figured out the public transportation system in New York, our trips to church were similar. Mami and I walked to mass on Sundays while Papi worked. It took us approximately two hours one way down the highway. Even after the four of you were born, we continued this ritual. We all adjusted into our new life and our own version of New Yorkers.

Mami and Papi were impressed at how quickly I picked up the language. They were proud of me and bragged about me to our family in Panamá. *"Los niños aprenden tan rápido"* they would say. I learned from each awkward experience and explained to our parents any time what they had planned did not seem like the "normal American" thing to do.

Speaking English better than Mami and Papi was quite an advantage, as well as a lot of pressure for me as a child still in elementary school. I wrote my own letters to excuse my absences from school—only with our parents' permission, of course. I translated letters that teachers sent home for Mami to sign off on. I interpreted what teachers had to tell Mami and Papi about me on parent/teacher conference nights. (Lucky for them I was a good kid.) I earned excellent grades at school, and was never in any kind of trouble.

Mami and Papi relied on me for many things due to the language barrier. They relied on me for any basic English needs. I was their pocket translator, human spell check, and accent verifier. I assisted them with anything they needed to read and write for their jobs. In a short amount of time, I had gone from a scared child who spoke no English, to a fluent speaker in this new, strange country.

My new life was becoming comfortable and safe. Although it could be chaotic living in a house full of people, our family had developed a routine. I went to school then came home to our loving Mami who cooked our favorite cuisines. I played with our cousins and with Carrie. Every now and then Grandma Veronica moved us to different areas of the house, but other than that, everything was predictable. I have all sorts of memories in that house, but by far, the most memorable was our second Christmas in Grandma's attic. That night changed my life forever.

CHAPTER 5

Christmas in the Attic

We had worked our way up from a bedroom in the middle level of the house to living in Grandma Veronica's attic after about a year and a half of living in the U.S. This was an upgrade. We had earned and proven our financial potential and were loyal tenants. A worn-out hunter green carpet led up the narrow stairway to our private quarters.

The attic had a small, finished bathroom– a luxury for us—and two rooms on either side of the bathroom. To the left of the stairs was the bedroom we slept in and to the right side was everything else. A tiny hallway in front of the bathroom connected both rooms.

The other room was our living room/kitchen/dining area. The multi-purpose room had a sofa we'd inherited from the neighbor's dump pile and, eventually, a small television. Mami tried to make the attic seem as much of our own as possible, so she improvised. We didn't have a kitchen, but somehow Mami cooked all of our meals on a one-burner Oster cooker, and a two-pilot portable stovetop. She made my favorite meals in that attic, the Panamanian meals I was so fond of. I ate white rice with butter and ketchup, lentils—which, as you know, are my favorite—and all of the fried bologna sandwiches I could ask for. One of our favorite after-dinner treats was white bread with butter and sprinkled sugar on top. This might sound disgusting to you now, but it was what we were used to and all we could afford. I also ate cereal for dinner if I wanted to without Grandma Veronica telling Mami not to give it to me. After dinner, we would wash all of our dishes and utensils in the bathroom sink.

The attic, in my opinion, was so much better as it was the most private living area in the house. We didn't have to go through a house full of people to get to our living space. The stairs that led up to the attic were right by the entrance of the house. We didn't have to share our food, and, best of all, we didn't have to share a bathroom with the rest of the house.

The attic was a fun place to live for a child, and there were only a couple of downfalls. I had to be quiet in the attic or else Grandma or Tía Bertha would use their broomstick to bang on the ceiling below us and yell. This usually meant I was being too loud or walking too hard and they would give Mami and Papi a hard time about it later. Besides it being a small living area for us to share, we made the very best of it.

"Bidi bidi bom bom... bidi bidi bom bom... bidi bidi... bom bom... bidi... bidi... bidi bom." I'd sway my hips from side to side along with the beat, singing along to the hottest artist at the time—the very talented Tex-Mex queen, Selena. Using a broomstick as my microphone, I'd sing with emotions I couldn't yet understand. The mic suddenly became my dance partner as I used it to turn my body from one side and then the other, singing loudly as I did my Saturday morning chores.

Selena was my idol. She was beautiful, kind, fashionable, *bilingual,* and so very talented. Mami and I watched her every concert on Univision and followed her career on TV.

I'd continue to sing passionately, *"Mi corazón se enloquece asi cada vez que lo veo pasar y me empieza a palpitar... asi... asi... bidi...."* My concert would come to sudden halt with the sound of banging and yelling below me. "Stop making all that noise *niñita—callaté!"* So, I'd obey and stop immediately.

Up in the attic, the ceilings hung low close to the walls, so you had to be careful and watch where you were going. There were a total of five screen-less windows that afforded us a view of the outside, and they were great on hot summer days. Sometimes Mami even let me climb out onto the roof and look over the whole street, but not during the icy winters.

We truly had it made in our own private little space.

≈๑≈

It was December of 1991, a typical cold, New York winter. It was our first Christmas in the attic and the first time we could put up a Christmas tree—a "real" artificial small Christmas tree. Papi and Mami had purchased ornaments from the thrift store. It was an exciting time with a lot for us to celebrate.

We had spent our first Christmas in the States living in Grandma's basement only a year before. We celebrated with a small tabletop tree I made in art class that was made from cardstock paper with green pompoms glued to it. I got a small stuffed animal that year, the one I had been eyeing at the thrift store next to the restaurant where Papi worked. I thought Santa must've been watching me.

≈๑≈

Over the past year, Papi had worked himself up from a busboy to a line cook. Mami had several homes to clean and was paid well. She was also busy keeping children for single moms. Carrie was not even one, and Mami's swollen belly was starting to show again. She was hoping for a boy.

The radio was tuned in to the Spanish radio station playing low in the background. Mami was humming along to the songs, even though I knew she knew the lyrics. She pressed her lips together and squinted at the tree in complete concentration. Our box of colorful ornaments laid on the floor within Mami's reach. She walked around, examining the branches as she held each ornament and tried out its placement before committing to it. Christmas was Mami's favorite time of year, just as it is now.

I was sprawled out on the couch, not too far from her, with one hand in the box of silver tinsel. In Spanish, it's called *lagrimas*. Why *tears?* I always wondered. Tears symbolize sadness and Christmas was a happy time.

"You're falling asleep, Olivia. Go to bed. I'll finish up."

I fought her for about thirty minutes and finally gave in to my sleepiness.

"There are clothes on your bed I have to iron. Go lay down with Papi. I'll move you over to your bed when I'm done."

Mostly asleep, I walked straight ahead, zombielike, into the large queen size bed that took up three-quarters of the bedroom. My twin bed and the crib took up the rest. I blew baby Carrie a kiss. Her four limbs were sprawled with her empty sippy cup not far from her half-way open right hand. Her face was turned to one side with her mouth slightly open. Her small, round tummy expanded with every breath as she slept peacefully. I crawled into bed with our snoring Papi and drifted into sleep almost immediately. My next moment haunted me for the next two decades.

I was dead asleep when I felt his rugged, calloused, hand caress my inner thigh. My head rested on one side, facing Mami in the other room, my face opposite of his. He couldn't tell he had awoken me (at least I don't think he knew I was awake). I inhaled quietly as his fingers ran upward to my eight-year-old vagina. He reached it, and kept going. I held my breath and felt my chest tighten up. He stuck his fingers inside me as I laid there, watching Mami in the other room just a few feet away from me, yet too far. She was still humming carelessly to the fainted sounds coming from the radio.

Should I scream? Should I move? Should I run? What is he doing? Why is he doing this?

He continued to insert his fingers inside me under the covers. It felt wrong. I didn't like it and I wanted it to stop. He grabbed my hand and positioned my fingers around his penis. He gripped his hands around mine and maneuvered them upward and downward still under the covers. I felt it swelling in my hand.

I cried for Mami in my head.

Mami, please help me. Look at me. Come in the room. Think of something you need. Come check on Carrie. Come check on me. Please look at me. See I'm awake. See I'm uncomfortable. Look at me! Something is wrong!

She never came in. I pretended to be asleep until it was over.

I was only eight years old at the time and didn't understand what had happened that night. I only knew I didn't like it and it was wrong. There was an unspoken understanding that I shouldn't speak of it. Papi communicated this in ways I understood without him having to bring up that night. He told me that him and I could keep secrets. He told me he could trust me. He bought me snacks I liked and told me we could hide them from Mami under the bed. When I seemed to drift away in thought in his presence, he would snap me back and smile at me. He'd pat my head and tell a joke that would make me smile. He randomly bought me stuffed animals and told me what a good girl I was to encourage me to keep my mouth shut.

More than anything, I wanted my life to carry on as normal and pretend like that night hadn't happened. Papi, your dad, and my stepdad, was the breadwinner of our growing family. Mami loved him. Sharing this awful secret would affect our lives. So, I suppressed it—or I tried to.

Over the years, I thought I could go on through life, thinking what he did and made me do to him wouldn't affect me. Boy, was I wrong.

CHAPTER 6

The Yellow House

Y ou four were probably too young to remember living in Grandma's house. The yellow house was a three-level home with a chain link fence that outlined the property. The front was plainly landscaped with two bushes on either side of the door. A metal clothesline took over the small backyard and was where all the yellow-house families hung our clothes to dry. The house sat on a calm, well-established street a few blocks from several busy intersections. It looked peaceful from the outside, but inside was always intense and dramatic.

You entered the home to find yourself in the middle level. Upon entering, you were in the living room, which shared a wall with the kitchen. To the right of the kitchen was the bedroom Mami, Papi, and I shared for the first couple of weeks we lived in New York. Next to that bedroom was Grandma Veronica's room. Down the hallway to the left of the kitchen were two more bedrooms. All of us shared one of those rooms at some point.

The more you could afford to pay in the yellow house, the better your living conditions were. You see, in the big yellow house there lived Grandma Veronica, Tía Maria, Tía

Bertha, and her husband Oscar with our two cousins Lilly and Oscar Jr., and their two dogs Bonnie and Clyde. Tío Adam, his wife Isabel, and his growing family lived in the house, as well. They had a daughter when Mami and I first moved in, but had three daughters by the time our family moved out. Tío Alvaro and his family of five lived there at one time, and Tío Felipe, his wife, and their three kids also lived in the house for some time. Tío Max's ex-wife, their daughter, and son lived there temporarily. Papi had a very large family. The longer we lived in that house, the more people moved in.

Going to the bathroom was one my most uncomfortable memories of living in that house. There were only two bathrooms in the home. One bathroom in the attic that attic tenants used and the other on the main floor that everyone else used. Grandma Veronica was thrifty. I didn't know it at the time, but I understand now if you live in a house full of people, you need to cut back where you can. At any given time, there were anywhere between twenty to twenty-five people living in the yellow house. As a child, I believed Grandma Veronica was evil. Our showers were timed because you could not use up all of the hot water.

In Panamá we didn't have hot water, so I didn't know what the big deal was until I experienced a New York winter. You were not allowed to lock the bathroom door while you showered, because someone might have to use the bathroom while you were in there. The shower doors were sliding glass doors that sat on top of the tub and the view of the inside was distorted, but still visible. And then there was Grandma Veronica's famous rule; you could not flush the toilet unless you did number two. After all, we had to pay for that water. Multiple people's urine sat in the toilet until someone had to go number two. We were encouraged to pee while showering to save toilet flushes. None of these things made sense to me at the time, but Mami told me I had to do it, so I did. "Nothing is free, Mamita," Grandma Veronica would say in her thick Caribbean accent. She sounded so old and frail, even back then.

The big yellow house also had an unfinished basement. The basement was where we stored canned goods for the household and where the washing machine and clothes dryer were. I hated going down to the basement—it was the scariest place in the whole house. When Mami went downstairs to wash our clothes, she would always ask me to go with her. She didn't like going down there alone, either. It was cold, creaky, and dark. Grandma Veronica thought it was ridiculous that we were afraid. Sometimes she would ask me to fetch a can of something she wanted to cook and I did, but dreaded it. I would walk down the stairs, looking around just in case something was down there waiting to get me. I then turned the corner to where the food was stored. I'd grab the can of whatever our grandmother needed off the wire rack shelf and race back up the wooden stairs as fast as I could. I was relieved to have gotten this far, so all I had to do was get back to safety. Sometimes there was no time to shut off the light—I could do it later—I just had to get out of there. I'd slam the basement door to trap all the scariness down there, and then, out of breath, I'd give Grandma Veronica her can.

Grandma would turn her hand to open the can with a handheld device (we didn't have this in Panamá—Abuelita Minerva opened cans with a sharp knife while banging the handle with another can). Grandma Veronica would scold me with each stroke of the can opener. "This is the last time I tell you not to run up those stairs! Go turn that light off before you run up my bill!" To this day, it's imprinted in my brain to shut off a light when exiting a room to conserve energy. Thank you, Grandma Veronica.

Trips to the basement only got worse after our cousin Jason and I found a mirror in the basement. We had gone on a brave basement-exploring excursion one day when he told me a story about a so-called "Bloody Mary." I said her forbidden name three times in front of the big round mirror behind Tío Alvaro's liquor bar. Our imaginations allowed us to see Bloody Mary's face appear in the reflection, and we screamed like McCauley Caulkin in Home Alone and ran up the stairs.

Mami, Papi, and I ended up living in that cold, dark basement not too long after that incident—in a room just past the room with the mirror. (This was before our growing family earned the prized attic living quarters.) Grandma Veronica had a new tenant she was putting in our room, so she told us we had to move to the basement within hours while Papi was at work. Our pregnant Mami rushed as fast as she could. She was only a few weeks away from giving birth to Carrie. I tried to help as much as a seven year old could. Our new room in the basement only had two beds, one for me and one for our parents. That basement wasn't meant to be lived in; it was only meant for storage, yet there we were.

Living in that basement was a humbling experience. Our little family wanted so much more than our small living quarters, and that cold, dark, unfinished basement made us yearn for more. There was a better life to live and we wanted and needed it more than anything.

≈·9·≈

Working hard was a concept that Mami and Papi taught me at a very young age. I learned so much about work ethic by their mere example. They taught me you always arrive at a job on time, you work hard, you do the best you can at the task you are given, and you excel if you can, because hard works pays off.

During the time we lived in New York, Papi became a busboy at an Italian Restaurant called Pasta Boutique. I didn't know what a busboy was at the time, but I knew he came home with a lot of cash tips. Mami and I often counted the dollars Papi came home with late at night and she used this money to pay our bills.

Papi came home one night very excited to tell Mami and I that he had been promoted to be a line cook. He had been paying attention to their cooks and had expressed interest, and now the restaurant owner was going to train him on how to cook Italian food. I was happy for him; I understood a line cook was paid better than a busboy.

Every once in a while, Papi took us to Pasta Boutique for dinner. The restaurant owner would give us a pizza to share as a family. I was against trying pizza since it was still so foreign to me, but Papi gave me some fresh made cookies and cream ice cream that he made at the restaurant and I devoured it. He always liked to gratify and reward me with food.

Mami cleaned houses for a living and she relied on business through word of mouth. The American women liked how she cleaned houses, so these women would tell their friends. Papi often dropped Mami off at the houses she cleaned, but when he couldn't, she would ride the bus or train to get there and back. She often traveled to other boroughs to clean homes. The three of us coordinated our schedules between their jobs and my school so someone could always take care of you guys at home.

≈ා9ා≈

"Mami, can I go to work with you today?" I asked one day. "I don't want to stay home with Papi."

"Sure! You can help me finish faster." She smiled at me half-jokingly.

I liked going to these homes with Mami just to walk around and look inside them. They were so much bigger than the yellow house—and I thought our house was big. The homes Mami cleaned had a machine that washed dishes in the kitchen, big shiny refrigerators with smiling family pictures stuck on with magnets, wooden floors, and fluffy blankets on the beds. I'd walk around the entire house, letting my fingertips softly glide across the furniture. I did this in every room while Mami cleaned.

"Olivia! Olivia Rose Batista come here!" she hollered out in Spanish one day as she cleaned a house. I knew I was in trouble, because she said my *full* name. I ran down the wooden stairs as fast as I could, sliding on the freshly polished floors and into the kitchen where she was. I ran so fast, I nearly slipped.

Out of breath, I explained to her, "I wasn't going to break anything or mess anything up."

Mami looked at me puzzled and then asked me to read a note the homeowner left. Relieved, I explained to Mami that the lady was going to be on vacation for a week and wouldn't be home. Mami asked me to write the homeowner a note back acknowledging that she'd gotten the message.

In addition to cleaning homes, Mami also became a babysitter for neighborhood children. This was a job I think Mami did not expect to have for as long as she did, but it was quick cash. It started out with a Salvadorian woman who lived across the street from the yellow house. She was a single mother who worked and needed someone to watch her baby. Like us, she lived in a house with multiple families. She rented out a room in her house, too. (This so-called 'baby' was the biggest baby I had ever seen. He was bigger than Carrie, who was a tiny and delicate newborn. He had a big head, and he cried a lot too.) I figured babysitting was another business you got through word of mouth, because Mami started watching another child. This time the boy was one year younger than me. His name was Sergio and he was my worst enemy at the time. His mother was pregnant and, just as I expected, Mami watched his youngest sister too when she was born.

Sergio was seven years old and was not happy about being an older brother. He also liked to tell lies, which I wasn't a fan of. I didn't like him one bit, but when his mother, Erica, told me she was going to name his new little sister my middle name, Rose, the flattery made me want to tolerate Sergio just a little bit longer. So, I did my best (as if I had a choice in the matter).

Around this time, I also made friends with my new cousins, relatives of Papi who lived in the yellow house we all shared. Our cousins were just a few years older than me, but we managed to get into some adventures and trouble.

Our cousin Jason and I liked to go up to the attic and climb on the roof. Mami was okay with it, until Jason had the bright idea of bringing four-month-old baby Carrie out there with him one day.

"Look, she can fly!" he said as he waved her in the air on the roof.

Mami saw him and ran to him, yelling in panic and distress, "She no can! She no can!" She didn't know how to speak English very well, but was trying to tell him the baby could not fly.

I once convinced our older cousin, Oscar, that I spoke baby language. I told him I could easily communicate with baby Carrie and he asked me to prove it.

"Let's go," I said.

We ran up to where Carrie was. She was sitting in her car seat babbling away as she always did. I babbled back.

I told him, "She just said that she's tired and wants to take a nap."

"Yeah, right," Oscar said.

I babbled some more back and forth with Carrie and then said, "She said she can hear you and that I'm telling the truth."

Oscar was amazed. "No way! Ask her if she knows my name."

I babbled at her. Carrie babbled back. "She said it's Oscar, duh."

"Whoa," he reacted in astonishment.

Oscar later figured out my scheme, but I had fun with it while it lasted.

Our older cousin, Nora, taught me how to ride a two-wheel bicycle after many scrapes and scratches down the uneven pavement. She also showed me how to discreetly feed the dog my vegetables.

Our older cousin, Lilly, taught me what a 'Your Mama' joke was—and not to take them literally—and walked me home from school sometimes. Lilly was two grades ahead at the same school as me. She was in the sixth grade when I was in fourth. We only went to the same school for a year before she graduated. I looked up to her. I was so proud to have her as my cousin and I wanted to let everyone know.

I was in class one day and told my teacher I needed to ask my cousin something very important. She was in the classroom just down the hall, so my teacher let me. I knocked on the door of her classroom. When Lilly's teacher opened the door, I said, "I need to speak to my cousin," as if everyone knew whom that was. Lilly and I did not look anything alike.

"Well, who's your cousin dear?" she asked as she slouched over. I pointed at Lilly. Lilly looked surprised and embarrassed at the same time as she got up in a hurry. She walked out in the hall with me and the teacher shut the door to give us some privacy.

"What's wrong with you?" she asked.

"Are you going to walk me home today?" I asked.

"Yeah, why wouldn't I?" she asked, annoyed.

"I don't know," I said, naively.

"Get out of here," she said with a smile on her face.

I smiled as I walked away. She loved me.

Lilly always pretended to be ruthless like her mother, Tía Bertha, but she was sweet to me. Lilly and Tía Bertha argued often, loudly, and in front of everyone. Anytime Mami and I witnessed their arguments, which sometimes ended with a slap to Lilly's face and curse words being said, Mami would say *"La ropa sucia se lava en casa."* I asked Mami what that meant once, and she explained it was a common saying in Panamá that meant some things are just private matters and shouldn't be discussed outside the home. This would be like saying, 'we don't air out our dirty laundry.' We didn't talk about what happened in our home to anyone who didn't live there.

I always sympathized with Lilly; Tía Bertha was mean. I never had any kind of positive interaction with her. She was short with me and wore a mean expression all the time. The only time Tía Bertha hit me was justified—at least according to Mami and Papi. I ran to her in excitement to show her my loose tooth as I was showing everyone else. Unexpectedly, she punched me in the mouth! Only the staircase braced my fall to the ground. I laid in shock, speechless, holding my bloody mouth and fallen tooth as she laughed at me. I couldn't imagine having her for a mother. I didn't understand how this was justified according to Mami and Papi.

꧁◉꧂

The summer of 1992 in the yellow house was even more crowded than the previous two summers. All of our cousins were home from school with nothing to do. Our brother

John was only born a month before. Celeste and Amelia, you two weren't born yet.

"Mami, can I take swimming lessons with Nora this summer?" I asked one day.

"Swimming lessons?" she asked.

"Yes, Nora said they're offering lessons this summer at the high school." I handed her a slip of paper with information.

She looked it over, pointing to the cost on the sheet.

"Is this how much it costs?" she asked.

"Yes," I replied.

"*Ay, Dios mío.* This is expensive, Olivia! This school is far. We pass it on the way to church," she said.

"But I want to learn how to swim." I gave her my best "please, Mami" look hoping she would say "yes."

"I wish your *padrino* was here. Your godfather taught everyone in our family how to swim in Panamá. We all learned how to swim in Gatun Lake." She continued her story, comparing the U.S. and Panamá as she often did. "He walked us over to the lake, tied a rope to our waist, and threw us in the alligator-infested waters. We didn't have a choice but to learn to swim if we wanted to survive. The rope was only as a last resort to pull us up if he needed to. Everyone your uncle taught how to swim is a perfect swimmer—except for me. I'm a scaredy cat." She carried on with exaggerated hand gestures.

"These lessons are in a pool…" I interrupted.

Mami thought it over some and then said, "You can take the lessons. I want you to learn because I never did."

That summer, Nora and I walked to the high school three times a week for each lesson. Mami and Papi had paid for my lessons with their hard-earned money and I wanted to make them proud. There was a ceremony on the last day of class in which parents were invited to see their children show off their skills. Mami and Papi came with Carrie and John.

Nora's class went first and she did well. She swam across, did her stunts, and the crowd clapped. It was my turn to go. My class, the beginner class, only had to do one thing. We had to jump from the diving board and swim across the pool. Everyone from my class had done it without a problem. I was the last student to go out of all the classes. I climbed the steps to the diving board and looked down at a drop that seemed further than life. My teacher saw my hesitation and jumped in the pool below me to encourage me.

"Come on, you can do it," he yelled. He waved his pale, old, hairy arms at me.

The crowd cheered me on and I told myself it was just one little swim across the pool. *It's not a big deal. I can do this,* I thought. I stalled for a few seconds, playing with my teal bathing suit straps and re-positioning my swim cap. I smiled at the crowd and looked out at our family. Mami stood alone and proud, cheering me on and Papi sat next to her along with the rest of the crowd. Carrie and John played by themselves.

I leaped in feet first, against what I was taught. *Why did I jump in this way?* I thought on the way down. I was instantly submerged, surrounded by bubbles from the non-dive move I had made. I opened my eyes and looked up only to see myself sink. I panicked and couldn't hold my breath any longer. I became limp under water. *Come up, Olivia!* I told myself. *How do I make myself come up?* Had I learned anything in this class? After what seemed like eternity, my instructor rescued me and carried me by one arm on his side. My limp body and head rested against his hairy, wet chest. I coughed the water out of my lungs and mouth. The crowd now cheered for my rescue. I felt so humiliated. The lessons were all for nothing. I was embarrassed for Mami and Papi and felt bad for wasting their money, but after some time, it became one of the funny stories we told.

During the five years we lived in the yellow house, we moved to different areas and rooms. Mami and Papi were doing their best financially when we upgraded to the attic. We were downgraded when we couldn't afford the rent. The attic was always the reward.

Summers in the attic were extremely uncomfortable— it was very hot. The heat only bothered Mami and Papi at bedtime, so we bought a white, three-speed box fan. It was still uncomfortable and sticky. The fan only felt like it was blowing the same hot air back at us. On really hot nights, Mami and us kids would wait for Papi on the front steps of the house because outside was cooler than our attic. When Papi got home, he would take us for a ride in the car with all the windows down just to feel the breeze for a bit before going to bed. Mami also had the bright idea of buying a big blue storage container that one would normally use for storing clothing or seasonal decorations. Mami filled it up with water from the showerhead and let us take turns sitting in it to cool off. I pretended it was our pool.

The attic was freezing in the winter time. Again, Grandma cut costs where she could. She only cut the heat on when she was home. She did not get home until after 6 p.m., and she would leave at 6 a.m. This meant that the house was cold throughout the day—and the attic was colder.

Papi went out and bought a space heater and one day, when Grandma Veronica visited us upstairs, she noticed it. I remember her telling Mami and Papi they had to pay more rent because the electric bill would go up with a space heater. Our parents knew we needed it, so they bit the bullet and gave up more of their hard-earned money. Papi paid her back the difference in increments, but Grandma Veronica had to teach us a lesson and downgraded us back to a room on the middle floor.

Grandma Veronica always thought she was teaching us a lesson, but moving around the house was our new norm.

I learned to not get attached to my living space. There was always a new tenant whom she seemed to favor. She often welcomed our uncle's illegitimate children, hence all the cousins who lived there. Mami always used to tell me that she didn't do it to be kind. Grandma Veronica enjoyed *chisme*. She thrived in the center of the gossip and drama in her children's lives. Pretty soon, it caught up to Papi. The newest faces that arrived shortly after our latest move to the middle floor of the house, were by far the most surprising.

CHAPTER 7

Pretend Surgery

It was an ordinary summer day in the yellow house when the doorbell rang. I remember it being a Thursday, because it was Papi's only day off from work. Tía Bertha immediately got up; she was expecting company. The rest of us were not. At the door stood a tall woman with two children. Tía Bertha smiled and greeted the stranger and she was invited into the house with her suitcases. The woman was tall, medium built, with nutmeg-colored skin, and stood grim in thought as she looked around the room where Mami and I sat on the couch across from her with young Carrie and newborn baby John.

The two children stood at each of her sides with tired, somber faces and sad eyes. The girl was taller than the boy. She was clearly older than me, her hair short and disheveled. The boy was slender and young. He had short, shaved hair, and clung to his mother's pants.

I had met these children before; we had shared a ride on a merry go round together when Mami and I lived in Panamá. Mami and I went to a carnival and met the Magician there where he was with these same two children. Mami recognized them too and immediately called Papi into the living room.

The woman began to scream at Papi as soon as he entered the living room. I didn't know who she was. Mami and Papi knew, but they were clearly not expecting her or the children at our house based on their facial expressions.

"You're unbelievable!" Her voice quivered as she accused Papi in Spanish. Grandma Veronica walked over to greet the children, while allowing the disruption in the tight square living room to continue.

The woman at the door was Papi's wife. He had run away to start a new life with Mami, their love child, Carrie, and me in the United States. According to the angry woman, he abandoned his family for us. She pointed at me and Mami animatedly and cursed. He didn't acknowledge her at first, but greeted the children instead. The two kids were discouraged from greeting him back. He instructed them to go with me. Papi remained calm, unlike the strange woman.

Tía Bertha forced a surprised expression and wrung her hands in pure enjoyment of the dramatic happenings that made everyone else in the room feel uncomfortable. Mami was uneasy and quiet, which concerned me. Tía Bertha had dropped a grenade in the room and walked out—but not so far that she couldn't enjoy watching things explode. Tío Felipe, Papi's older brother, intervened and asked for Grandma Veronica's support. They invited the woman whose name was Priscilla upstairs to the attic for a private conversation with Papi.

Papi went to follow and Mami told him he wasn't going to talk to Priscilla without her. The adults went upstairs and left Priscilla's two kids, myself, one-year-old Carrie, and two-month-old John alone in the living room on the main floor of the house. The room stood quiet except for the distant shouts upstairs.

"I'm Olivia… this is my sister, Carrie and my brother, John," I said timidly but invitingly in Spanish.

"I'm Alejandra. This is my brother, Drew," the sister replied.

Alejandra proceeded to speak over the shouts above us to tell me they had just moved here from Panamá. They had just arrived today. I knew what that felt like. I had moved to the States only two years ago. I wanted to make them feel welcome, so we talked as we heard the grownups continue to argue upstairs. We weren't sure what was happening, but we knew not to interrupt them.

John soiled his diaper after some time went by while we watched TV, so I had to change him. I invited Alejandra and Drew to help me and in order to make it fun; I made a game out of it.

I told them my brother needed surgery and we had to take him to the operating room as I walked them into a bedroom of the house. Confused at first, they followed me.

At this time in the yellow house, we stayed in one of the bedrooms on the middle floor. We walked down the hall into the room we all shared. I instructed Carrie to make "beep-like" noises, as if John were hooked up to a machine. Carrie did as instructed and began to make the sounds. Carrie was cheerful all the time; she admired me and did what I asked her to do without question. She was my play partner and was used to my pretend games.

Carrie mimicked the heart monitor noises and smiled at me in between. I gave her a thumbs up for approval. I pointed at Alejandra and Drew and appointed them as my nurses. "I'm the surgeon and I need you now more than ever," I encouraged them dramatically.

I laid John on the bed, removed his clothes from the waist down, and uncovered his diaper to discover the mess he had made. He was grinning up at us and kicking his little legs playfully. I had to move fast before he shot pee up at me like he sometimes liked to do.

I began to call out to my nurses, "Scissors, I need scissors!" Alejandra looked at me like I was crazy. I pointed at the wipes. "Scissors!" I demanded. She handed me a wipe. I called out, "Cotton balls! Towels! Pins!" and continued to request random objects I imagined I'd need in an operating room. Alejandra and Drew handed me wipes for every item I called out. I cleaned up our little brother as I had been taught to do, rubbed rash cream on his bottom, and taped his diaper shut. He was clean and recovered from surgery safely. We all giggled.

After the surgery, the five of us had bonded. We played and talked for hours with the toys I shared while we took care of each other. The adults came downstairs after several hours and Alejandra and Drew left with their mom and Tío Felipe.

Alejandra, Drew, and their mother moved into an apartment building twenty minutes from the yellow house. They lived with a family friend for some time before getting an apartment of their own in the same building. We often picked them up in the conversion van our family owned at the time. Papi would try to find a parking spot in front of the building—or at least on their street. He would call Priscilla to let her know he was downstairs, and she always asked him to come upstairs alone. Mami hated it; it really pissed her off. She often tried to get me to go with Papi, but he always told Mami it would make Priscilla mad and that Priscilla didn't want me in their apartment.

≈⊙≈

After Alejandra and Drew came into our lives, I learned that Papi had two other children with two other women. Zoila, who was the oldest of his children and Dennis, who is in between Alejandra and Drew's age.

Zoila was the daughter of Papi and his high school sweetheart, Ramona. Ramona and Zoila lived in Colón, Panamá. You haven't heard many stories about Zoila, since she was mostly around when you all were much younger. She was welcomed into the yellow house and stayed with us in the attic for a couple of years.

Zoila was sent to live with Papi by her mother when she became too much to handle. She dropped out of school in the seventh grade and was always up to no good. She stole money from Mami, Papi, and Grandma Veronica. And I don't mean a few dollars from their wallet (which she did, too). She stole checks, forged signatures, and withdrew money from their bank accounts. She often snuck out of the house, practiced voodoo, and ran up the phone bill to thousands of dollars with no intention of paying the money back. Those are just a few of the running list of items on her criminal résumé.

Mami and Papi paid money to enroll Zoila at the local community college so she could finish her high school education, but she didn't show up to her nightly classes. She eventually resorted to prostitution for money. She even gave herself an abortion with a wire hanger.

Zoila didn't grow up; she simply got older and lived her life carelessly and destructively. I often stuck my tongue out behind her back. When she caught me once, she told me she was going to slap my back and that my face would get stuck that way.

I tolerated Zoila when she lived with us. She was pregnant at the same time Mami was pregnant with Celeste. She and her son, only one month older than Celeste, both stayed with us in the attic for a while. Mami and Papi slept in the bedroom, and the rest of us slept in the multi-purpose room. When her son cried in the middle of the night, she would throw something at me to wake up and tend to her crying baby. I didn't mind and eventually she didn't need to prompt me. I fed him, burped him, changed him, and soothed him back to sleep. I had seen how she carelessly handled him. She didn't like to be bothered by him. She always hit his head against the mattress to calm him down. He eventually learned to bang his own head to soothe himself.

Our brother Dennis, is one year older than Drew. His mother, Mikaela, and Papi dated briefly while he was married to Priscilla. Mikaela was much older than Papi and apparently didn't want to be committed to him at the time. She was content with her only child, Dennis, after years of trying to get pregnant. Papi and Mikaela ended their relationship while Papi carried on his cheating life, but they remained friends over the years. Mikaela married someone years later and her husband adopted Dennis as his son. Mikaela was always grateful to Papi for the gift of her young son and Dennis maintained communication with him. Mami didn't mind Mikaela. She wasn't a threat to their relationship like Priscilla was.

Priscilla was Papi's legal wife. Mami was the mistress. Priscilla was willing to do anything to salvage her marriage and she was going to stick around for as long as she needed to. Her plan was to get her husband back, and move back to Panamá to live a happy life with her family.

Mami had left her career, her family, and her whole life for Papi. She had given him two children and had hopes of living her American dream.

Priscilla was not making life any easier. She grasped at all straws to get her husband back. She once called Papi from a payphone outside of Pasta Boutique, where he worked. She stood on the opposite end of the restaurant across the busy six-lane highway with Alejandra and Drew at her side. She threatened to tell them to cross the intersection if Papi didn't come outside to get them. He ran outside in a panic to save his children.

She'd call the yellow house, demanding to speak to Papi. When he answered, she would cry and beg him to leave immediately. She would tell him she had locked up Alejandra and Drew in their bathroom and that she refused to feed them until he came back.

Priscilla continued to make her grand demands of Papi—and it was working. Priscilla even dared to call and ask to speak to Mami. Tía Bertha would hand Mami the phone and watch as Mami's world crumbled at the sound of Priscilla's voice. Papi ran to Priscilla's rescue every single time. Mami believed he had made his choice and she'd had enough. Mami's first attempt at leaving Papi came shortly after that.

CHAPTER 8

White Van

We earned our way back into the attic a few weeks after learning that Alejandra and Drew were our brother and sister – just in time for the peak of that summer. The windows remained open and we waited desperately for a breeze that never came.

It was early in the morning, the midday heat hadn't reached us yet, but it would. I was awake watching cartoons on television and heard Mami and Papi yelling at each other from the bedroom just a few feet away. I had heard them argue many times before. We shared tight spaces so they never had privacy. I continued to watch TV.

"Tell your Papi, goodbye," Mami demanded of me as she walked to where I was sitting. "You're never going to see him again, tell him goodbye!" she yelled louder.

He sucked his teeth dismissively.

"You're not going anywhere. Where are you going to go? You have nowhere to go!" he replied, his voice heavy with condescension.

"I won't be here when you get off work. You'll see!" she cried.

"With what money?" he threatened.

"Tell him goodbye," she yelled louder.

"Bye, Papi," I said obediently.

"Give him a hug!" she said, her words short. I hesitated. "Aren't you going to miss him? You're not going to see him again."

I walked over to give him a side hug with my eyes still locked on Bugs Bunny, then I hurried back to my show. There was more yelling followed by a door slam and angry stomps down the stairs.

Mami mumbled under her breath before she demanded my attention.

"Olivia, help me pack. We need to leave," she said.

I realized she was serious when she grabbed the box of black trash bags from our makeshift pantry and told me to start throwing our things into it. She turned the television off and frantically yelled out demands. Then she hurried to the secret stash of cash she kept hidden from Papi. Mami and I saved money by digging through the couch for loose change that had fallen out of Papi's pockets; dug through the car for forgotten cash; took some of Papi's balled up tip money he hadn't yet counted; and Mami secretly babysat children and cleaned homes she sometimes wouldn't tell Papi about. Plus, she'd have me ask him for weekly lunch money I didn't need because I had free lunch. Mami saved the money and when there was enough collected, she sent it to our family in Panamá via Western Union. She knew how much they needed it back home, but we needed the cash this time. She unzipped a pocket in my stuffed animal, reached inside, and pulled out all the dollar bills in between the white soft cotton filling.

"Pack everything. I'm only leaving behind his clothes and this stack of bills!"

Mami paced quickly, at first scattered and angry, but then she became determined and organized. As I did as she asked me to, I heard her in the other room on the phone. I couldn't tell who she was talking to. She spoke low at first but was starting to raise her voice. She was asking someone for money to put me in private school—I didn't know I was going to a private school. We were in the middle of summer break. I continued packing.

She called me in the room. She was upset; I don't think the person was going to give her the money.

"Iban wants to talk to you," she said with an angry expression. *"No le digas nada,"* she whispered, motioning a zipper over her lips.

Iban? My father, Iban? The one whose name cannot be said? Anytime I asked about him, Mami told me not to bring him up. I thought about him often, but dared not say so. Mami told me Papi was my new dad. Papi took care of me and provided for our family. She said Iban didn't want anything to do with me and I hadn't spoken to him since we moved to the U.S. So many emotions ran through my mind in the short five seconds before I picked up the phone—shock, nerves, confusion, fear.

Mami's jaw tightened. Her lips puckered and her eyes opened wide. It was the face she made while we were in public and I was doing something that was embarrassing her. It was her threatening face. It was like her eyes were yelling at me.

I hesitantly accepted the phone from her.

"Olivia, ¿cómo estás? Habla Iban, tu papá."

Mami pressed her face next to mine while she held the phone to my ear.

His voice was cheerful and warm. I acknowledged his greeting with a smile he couldn't see and a tiny sigh.

He carried on in Spanish. "Your mom tells me you're doing well in school; she's proud of you. I'm proud of you, too."

Mami continued to press her ear to the phone, hearing his every word to me. She shook her head in disapproval. She mocked him silently, moving her hand mimicking his speech.

He paused to await a response I didn't give him.

"Olivia, I miss you…."

Mami ripped the phone away before I could hear the rest of his sentence.

"She doesn't want to speak to you," she told him and shooed me back. Why did she lie to him? I wanted to talk to him. I missed him. They spoke for only a short minute after in which it was clear he wasn't going to send Mami money for private school.

Mami and I managed to pack up everything she wanted to take with us. We didn't own very many things, but we cleaned out the place. We took food, our clothes, diapers, the playpen, the stroller, and our favorite toys. At this time, only Carrie and John were born.

"Aren't you going to take your stuffed animals?" Mami asked. "Just because I'm mad at Papi doesn't mean you can't take the gifts he's given you."

I knew what the stuffed animals signified. They were rewards for keeping my mouth shut about *that night*. I grabbed a couple of them as not to alarm Mami. This secret would follow me forever, wherever I went.

Before I knew it, a white van had pulled up outside the yellow house.

"*Vámonos*," Mami instructed me.

We went outside to greet the strange man. He was a short, Hispanic man, a little older than Mami. He was wearing loose-fitting khakis, a light button down white shirt and black wispy hair just barely covered his scalp. He introduced himself to Mami and opened the back of the van for us. He seemed pleasant, but he was still a stranger to me. Mami was overly friendly to the stranger. We loaded up the van and the strange man took us to Tía Samantha's house. Tía Samantha is Mami's cousin and her only nearby relative.

Tía Samantha lived in a house in Queens about thirty minutes from the yellow house by car. The house she lived in was a blue single-family home. Tía lived in the basement; Russian tenants lived in the rest of the house. The basement had its own entry door separate from the house. And from the way Tía greeted us, I don't think her tenants knew we were moving in. We quickly got Carrie and John out of the van, unloaded our things, and settled into Tía's family's space.

Tía's basement was one bedroom that had a door and a connecting bathroom, and an open space for a living room and a kitchen in the back area. Tía lived in this basement with her husband and our cousin, Thomas. We had visited Tía's house before and often went there on weekends. Mami and Tía Samantha were close. They shared a grandmother—our beloved Abuelita Minerva—family stories, and their affection for our beautiful Panamá.

We settled nicely in the space. I continued my summer break in Queens, accompanying Mami to look for more houses to clean. We always stopped at the Catholic church only a few blocks from Tía's house to pray. I remember going to this church every single day with Mami while we lived in Queens. She knelt beside me and prayed quietly. I remember kneeling beside her but not praying. I didn't know what to pray for.

I had just turned nine years old when the Summer of 1992 was drawing to a close. My birthday in the United States meant it was almost time to go back to school and this time I would be enrolled at a new school in Queens. I was set to begin classes there in just two more weeks. I remember Mami apologizing to me for all the recent changes, but I didn't feel a thing. I wasn't attached to the yellow house, the people living in it, the school I went to, the people I had met there, or anything really. I had zero feelings about starting at a new school. I felt completely indifferent. I had

Mami, Carrie, and John and so everything was alright. Tía
Samantha and her family were good people. She didn't slap
her children. She didn't yell. She didn't bang on the ceiling
when the upstairs tenants were loud. I felt loved in that space
even though I did threaten to call Child Protective Services
on Tía once.

My tooth had been loose, so she told me she could knock
it out without it hurting. She tied a string to my tooth and the
other end on her bedroom door. She slammed it shut and blood
filled my mouth. I threatened to call CPS, and before long,
Mami and Tía threatened to give me a reason to call. I had
to explain to them that I had learned about Child Protective
Services at school. They never let me live that one down.

~⊙~

One day while we were all watching TV in the living
area, we heard a loud knock on the window.

Thump! Thump! Thump!

Someone kicked on the glass above. The location of the
basement hopper windows on the top of the staircase did not
allow the viewer to see us.

Thump, thump thump! They continued to kick the glass.
Mami and Tía told me to shush and be quiet.

"I know you're in there, Marcela." "C'mon. I came to
bring you home." He confidently declared in Spanish.

Tía gathered Carrie and John in her arms and carried
them to her bedroom. She whispered at me and told me to
follow her and she shut the door.

Later that day, we packed up all our things and moved
back into the yellow house. Our Papi made Mami angry, but
at least he came to look for us. Iban still hadn't come to get
me and take me back home to Panamá.

Mami was still angry at Papi when we moved back into the attic. She was upset about his wife being in our lives. Mami stayed unhappy and more erratic from that point forward, and she found a friend in me. She told me that Priscilla would dress up in sexy nightgowns and greet Papi in them when he picked up Alejandra and Drew on the weekends. That's why she always requested he come up alone and threatened for him not to be able to see his kids if he didn't do as she said. Each time we waited in the car, Mami became furious if it took longer than she expected. I listened to Mami vent. She always ended the conversation by asking me to not act differently toward Papi. Mami was too pre-occupied to notice, but I was already distancing myself from him as much as I could. When he was home, I locked my eyes on the television, played with you all, or found a reason to leave the space we shared. Mami wanted me to be on Papi's good side. She wanted Papi to be in a good mood on his days off when he was in the yellow house. She wanted him to choose us, not Priscilla. But sometimes, her actions were conflicting and confused me.

Their arguments continued. Mami and I would wait up for Papi to get home from work since she was so worried and upset every night. She knew the restaurant closed at eleven on weekdays and one on Fridays and Saturdays. She also knew it took Papi twenty minutes to drive home. If he wasn't home within thirty minutes, she began to call every hospital in the phone book to make sure he hadn't been in an accident. I'd lay beside her on her bed while she made the calls.

When Papi got home, Mami would tell him what she did to make him feel guilty for worrying her—and they would argue again. Papi always tried to explain his reasons—"We had customers walk in late." "Chuck [his boss] wanted to have a beer with me." "We had to do inventory tonight." "The kitchen was a mess." "Someone called out and left me alone to do everything." "I got caught in traffic behind a car accident." Papi always had a reason and Mami never seemed satisfied with it. She always accused him of being with Priscilla or another woman.

≈ 9 ≈

One day, while playing in the multi-purpose room that I now shared with Carrie and John, Mami asked me to call Papi for her. She really needed this favor. I walked over to their bedroom across the hall.

"I need you to tell a little lie for me. I need to see how much he loves me."

I listened to Mami and did as she asked me to do. She told me to tell Papi that she had swallowed a lot of pills and that I had found her on the bed unconscious. She handed me the phone and even said she would dial the number for me. All I had to do was ask for Papi and tell him what she had just said. If he asked questions, just repeat what she said and don't give any more details.

I did as she asked. Papi *did* ask me questions and sounded panicked. I repeated myself and he told me that he would be home soon.

When we hung up, Mami told me to tell her exactly what he said. She then told me to be sure to stay in the other room with Carrie and John when he got home.

Shortly after hanging up the phone, Papi came home in a panic. We heard him pull up to the house and rush up the attic stairway. Mami rushed me out their bedroom to set the stage. He opened the door to the attic to find me on my bed watching Carrie and John sleep. I pointed to their bedroom without saying a word. With their bedroom door still open, I watched him shake and wake up Mami as she pretended to come back from her unconscious state. He hugged her and, shortly after, shut their door. Mami and I didn't speak of this night again.

Mami had become pregnant with Celeste just a couple months after we moved back into the attic. John was still a baby with four deadly little baby teeth; he loved to bite Carrie on the shoulder or arm when she wasn't paying attention. Poor Carrie was always surprised and wailed every time. Just as I was Mami's best friend, Carrie was my best friend; we did everything together. I forced her to play dolls with me and I would talk to her about all the happenings at school each day. Carrie was my soundboard and smiled up at me in her complete innocence.

"Olivia, I need to tell you something. Papi and your brother and sister are going to go to Panamá without us," said Mami one day, referring to John and Carrie.

"Without us? Why?" I asked sadly.

"Papi has to take care of some business in Panamá. He has to do some paperwork so that he and Priscilla... well, so that he and I can get married. He's taking Carrie and John for the family to meet them."

"I want to go too, Mami!" I cried. "I want to see Mamacela, and Abuelita Minerva, and Ester, and Tía Mia, and Tío...."

Mami interrupted. "I want to see them too, Olivia, but we have to stay here with each other. If we leave, we can't come back."

I didn't understand why Mami didn't want to leave but I knew there must've been a good reason.

"And besides, Carrie and John have to get baptized," she added. "We haven't done it here because I don't know anyone and they need godparents."

"I thought babies got baptized when they're little. Carrie is not a baby anymore." I noted.

"Well, *la llorona* isn't here," said Mami.

"La llorona?" I asked. "Who is that?"

"I haven't told you the story of la llorona? There's a legend of a weeping woman who lost her baby."

"What happened to her baby?" I asked, feeling somewhat concerned.

"The baby died. It's a sad story," explained Mami. "La llorona desperately wants to soothe her broken heart, so she wanders the night looking for an unbaptized baby to steal and fill her void."

My eyes were wide in astonishment.

"She almost came for you once," Mami added. "You were six days old, and soon to be baptized, but not for another week. I heard her run her fingers across the wooden bars of your crib. I ran in the room to get you and we baptized you the following morning."

Mami shivered in horror as she completed her story. "*Ave María Purísima*." She made the sign of the cross over herself and instructed me to do so, too.

CHAPTER 9

Dream House

One day when I was about nine years old, Mami called out to me in anger.

"Olivia! Did you cut your hair?" She looked at me with disbelief in her eyes, her jaw clenched tight.

"No, Mami!" I cried. Mami had just come home from a long day of cleaning houses.

"Well, if you didn't do it, then who did?" she asked.

I shrugged my shoulders at her. She stared at me waiting for a response. Half of my long thick hair flowed down my back. The left side hung to my shoulders.

"I woke up this morning and it was like this, Mami." I told her.

"You really expect me to believe that?" she asked, raising her brows.

I was lying through my teeth. I had played all day with Carrie and John and got bored, so I decided to cut half my hair off. No one was there to stop me. The truth sounded so stupid to admit; I didn't realize the lie sounded much worse.

"Are you going to take communion this Sunday with that mouth?" Mami continued.

She got me with the Jesus guilt. I had to come clean.

"I'm sorry, Mami. I did it," I said, frowning.

"Okay. We'll make some time to go to confession before Sunday," she said, calmly.

"Yes, Mami." I was so embarrassed and ashamed.

"Go get the scissors. Now we have to even it out."

Thick locks of my straight hair fell to the linoleum floor around me. I stood there, quietly listening to her tell me about her day. Here she was, our pregnant, hard-working mother doing the best she could to support our family and all I had to do was take care of my sister and brother and behave. I had cut my hair out of whim and boredom. I had inconvenienced her and I had lied to her. I promised not to do it again.

Living in the yellow house was not a forever plan for our parents. They had dreams of moving out and being able to afford a house just for our growing family. More and more people moved in and out of the house and Grandma Veronica continued to make us feel unwelcome, especially Mami and me. By this time, she had made it clear I was not a Butler like her and Papi. And I was not her grandchild. Alejandra and Drew were Butlers.

Mami and Papi began to discuss plans for moving out after Papi got into a new argument with one of his brothers. Tío Felipe now sided with Grandma Veronica and accused Papi of not taking care of his children- Alejandra and Drew. Tío Felipe threw a punch at Papi. Mami was pregnant with Celeste at this time and she got in the middle of it to try to protect Papi. She fell back and landed on the stairs, but luckily wasn't hurt. I watched the whole thing quietly. Tío Felipe threatened to call immigration on Mami and me to force Papi to choose a family. Although not everything our tío claimed made sense to me at the time, I knew better than to ask questions. I knew Mami would tell me and we would pray about it later.

Papi made us pack that night and we lived out of our conversion van while things blew over with our tío. I have memories of eating hot dogs straight out of the packaging and leftover food from the restaurant Papi worked at. We used a cooler in the van to keep food cool. Mami was such a neat freak, we even had a broom and cleaning products to make sure the van was always tidy. I remember sweeping out the van every day as my chore. Mami and Papi told me not to tell anyone at school what was going on at home because, again, *"La ropa sucia se lava en casa."* We moved back into the attic two weeks later. After that, however, Mami and Papi couldn't take it and began to plan our exit strategy to escape the yellow house once and for all.

≈ ♪ ≈

Mami and I were a team when it came to tending to the kids, secretly hiding money from Papi, and when Mami needed a person to talk to. Mami, Papi, and I *had* to be a team as our common ground was that we all wanted to leave that dreaded house.

Mami and Papi worked hard to save money so that we could eventually move out. My job was to take care of you afterschool as always. By the summer of 1994, Amelia was born, bringing the total count to seven of us sharing the attic space. By the summer of 1995, our family finally moved out to never return. But not before Mami let all the Butlers know that she was there to stay.

"We're getting married tomorrow," Mami told me with a smile on her face. She seemed happy as she looked through the clothes in her dresser. She pulled out a pair of white, cotton pants and a white t-shirt with a powder blue vest attached to it.

"What do you think Olivia?" she asked.

"It looks good Mami." I nodded.

"This is a good thing. *Tu papá nos puede pedir.* You know, for our papers. We can become U.S. citizens!"

She looked at me, waiting for the excitement to reach my face.

"You have to be there. No school for you tomorrow," she added, hoping that would peak my interest.

❧ ⑨ ❧

The following morning Mami and Papi drove the five of us to the courthouse in Nassau county to get married—with Papi's boss as their witness. The eight of us waited in a small waiting room until Mami and Papi were called. Mami, Papi, and Mr. Chuck went into a room behind two large wooden doors while us kids sat patiently in the waiting room. Celeste and Amelia were asleep in the stroller and there was a bowl of colorful lollipops that the rest of us helped ourselves to. Before we could finish the candy, the three adults walked out of the room. And so late that afternoon, Mami officially became the new Mrs. Butler and I became the only person in our family with the last name "Batista."

❧ ⑨ ❧

We had one vehicle that Papi drove to work. When he worked and Mami was off, Mami and I ran errands and took all of you to your doctor's appointments using the bus or train—or we just walked. Mami was always afraid of getting robbed, so she'd tuck some cash in each side of her bra, different pant pockets, and in her socks. She'd ask me to do the same. Her logic was that if a robber asked us for all of our money, we would pull the cash out from one of those locations and they'd assume that's all we had.

Mami would tell me stories of how in Panamá, the robbers would yank off your jewelry and keep running. "They will rob you at gunpoint," she'd say. "Leave your jewelry at home." The only jewelry I had was a gold saint medallion necklace from Panamá. I knew it was real gold because Mami said that if you bit the metal and your teeth marks wouldn't show, it was real. I didn't want anyone to steal this valuable piece from me. "Ok, Mami," I complied.

Mami, the four of you, and I went everywhere together. Mami and I packed Celeste and Amelia in the big stroller since they were the youngest, and Carrie and John walked. Mami and I took turns pushing the stroller and holding the older two. We did it all. The six of us went everywhere. If one of us had a doctor's appointment at the clinic, we all went. And clinic visits were the worst!

Trips to the clinic felt eternal. We were a low-income family and received WIC, food stamps, and the four of you got Medicaid benefits. The local clinic was always packed with people, it was hot and stuffy, and each visit was an all-day affair. Mami needed me to complete the forms and to interpret what the clinic staff asked of her, and we all formed a line at the counter. Patients always formed multiple lines before being seen by the physician. Then we'd sit in the waiting room with no personal space until a name was called. Once we were called back, we navigated our way down several narrow hallways to one of the small patient rooms in the back of the building.

On one particular afternoon, we all went to the doctor to be seen. Mami had managed to schedule an appointment for Carrie, John, and I all on the same day. It was time for my routine vaccine, so Mami asked if I could set an example for the younger two. I have never been a fan of needles and the idea of setting an example was not going to change my mind about it. In my mind, needles were bad and I did not want you kids to be exposed. As the nurse prepped the needle, I took a deep breath and got a whiff of the alcohol from the swab she had just opened. I looked over at Mami who stood to my right, nodding to encourage me. Past her were our two youngest sisters; Celeste was asleep, and Amelia was awake and looking at me with her big round face, brown eyes, and rosy cheeks. Of all of us, she resembled Abuelita Minerva the most, with her lighter hair and fair skin. The stroller blocked us all into the tiny, square room. Carrie and John walked in circles, looking at me and smiling. I saw a window of opportunity in the millisecond I had left before the nurse pricked me and as loudly as I could, I yelled *"Ruuuuun!"*

I shot up off the chair, grabbed the stroller and took off as Carrie and John ran behind me. Celeste woke up and the four of you laughed as we gave the nurse and Mami a run for their money. You four thought it was a game. We navigated through the crowded halls, escaping every adult we came across. It was quite a sight to see an eleven-year-old pushing a twin stroller and being followed by a three- and four-year-old who were squealing the whole way. Just a few steps behind us followed an angry nurse, a confused security guard, and a fuming mother who was trying not to laugh and pee herself while chasing us all.

"Ven acá, carajo! Te voy a matar!" she threatened and laughed while cursing in Spanish. She laughed, but not because she thought it was funny. It was the laugh we all heard when any one of us did something to embarrass her, and it meant she was going to get us when we got home. It was her "I'm going to laugh to keep me from killing you" laugh. *"Ave María Purísima,"* she cried in prayer for help. That nurse eventually caught me and gave me my shot.

Mami held me down as the security guard stood at the door. I didn't have much of a choice then. John and Carrie got their shots, too—but not without putting up a fight. I got in a lot of trouble after that.

≈ ⑨ ≈

We'd ride the bus or walk to do our errands and shop for clothes, shoes, or any items we needed. Mami taught me to slip past the driver while mounting a public bus. There was yellow tape around the silver pole as soon as you got on the bus, and if your height was above the tape, you had to pay. When I got taller than the line, Mami showed me how to scoot low and fast and slip through the crowd so we wouldn't have to pay.

One day while shopping for clothing, Mami and I became distracted while picking something out for the youngest two girls. Carrie walked away from us, though still within eye's view. I looked up and saw a strange man who was standing uncomfortably close to Carrie. I remember he was wearing dirty brown clothes and a navy knit cap. Carrie just stood there in her pink dress looking up at something that caught her attention. Mami saw me watching and turned to see what I was looking at. The man reached over and placed his palms on Carrie's bottom for a second, then immediately walked away.

We called Carrie over to us. She was ignorant of what had just occurred and I was unsure myself, but I knew I didn't like it. With Carrie safely at our side, Mami and I made eye contact with each other. Our eyes half squinted and our lips tightly shut. Mami whispered *"Cochino,"* or "Pig," under her breath and we left the store.

≈◎≈

Mami was a proud mother. Although we received medical and financial government assistance, she didn't want to and she certainly didn't want anyone to know about it. As a child, I didn't understand why.

During one of our trips to the grocery store, I happened to spot one of my teachers in the aisle. I was so surprised to see her as if she were only allowed to be at school. I ran over to her with excitement.

"Hi, Mrs. Destin," I said, and waved with a big grin on my face.

"Hi, what are you doing here?" she asked.

I began flipping through the blue slips of paper Mami had asked me to hold. "We're buying milk, cheese, juice, cereal..."

Mami yanked the slips from my hand and gave my teacher a fake, embarrassed smile. She waved goodbye and pulled me away. I didn't understand what I had done wrong. She proceeded to explain that we didn't tell people about our slips of paper because it meant we were poor. I still didn't understand how the two were related, though I took her word for it.

The slips told us exactly what to buy, how much to buy, and when to buy it. We always came home with boxes of Kix and Cheerios cereal, more gallons of milk than we could drink before it went bad, blocks of cheese, and gallons of apple juice. We always had so much that Mami shared it with neighbors and housemate family members. I was glad she did because I could only drink so much apple juice and eat so much Kix. From time to time, Mami bought us Froot Loops, Cocoa Krispies, or Cinnamon Toast Crunch off-brand cereals for special treats.

Our parents struggled financially, but wanted us to enjoy our childhood, so they took all the opportunity they could to purchase items they knew we liked. Going out to eat was always very expensive. Still, they took us out to Roy Rogers from time to time—usually to celebrate an accomplishment or a birthday. When we went grocery shopping at the local Compare Foods, Mami would sometimes buy me a cassette tape of Merenhits of that year. 'Merenhits' was a composite of the famous merengue songs that year and vendors always stood outside Compare selling cassettes and t-shirts. I liked to dance to my merengue tapes as I cleaned the house on Saturday mornings. I'd use my favorite blue feather duster while wearing the special cleaning apron that Papi and Mami bought me at the thrift store.

Saying that Mami and Papi worked hard is an understatement. I always admired them for their hard work. I was there when we arrived at JFK airport with two suitcases in hand after they both left their country, their careers, and everything they ever knew to take a gamble at something better. So, when Mami and Papi told me we were moving to a new house they were building just for us and no one else, I knew this was the dream come true—and I was willing to do anything to make that happen.

≈ ⑨ ≈

We had a routine. We ate the food Mami prepared for us, we played, we watched television, and we did so quietly so Grandma Veronica wouldn't come upstairs. You four were everything to me. You were my kids, my siblings, and my friends. I changed your diapers, potty-trained you, bathed and dressed you, fed you, and taught you each how to feed yourself. I even combed your hair daily and learned how to tame Celeste's thick, tight curls. I taught you how to tie your shoes, how to read, and everything you can think of while our parents worked and worked hard.

You four listened to me talk about my day and the kids and teachers at school, and I taught you what I had learned that day. During the summer, I played school with you. I wanted you to know everything I knew, and I wanted you to get ahead of other kids in your class. The five of us were close. We were all we had and we even ended up sharing a bedroom. Mami and Papi moved our beds into the attic's multi-purpose room so they could have a little more privacy, and the five of us shared two twin beds. We were so close; I didn't know anything different.

I especially didn't mind the new sleeping arrangements, because I used our beds as a means of transportation. I would climb from the couch to the beds to get across the room, and I taught you four to do it, too. Of course, we turned this into a game. The more we stayed off the floor, the less noise we made, so Grandma Veronica and Tía Bertha wouldn't bang on the ceiling.

≈ ⑨ ≈

Building a house in the United States was a much more complicated process than it was in Panamá. I have a memory of riding in Tío Manuel's truck to buy cinder blocks when he was building his house in Panamá. A neon pink sign advertised the price on the side of the road. Tío pulled over, bought the blocks and loaded them onto the pickup truck. He and his friends later got together and built the house on our family's property where we watched everything. The process was simple – it took months to build, but no paperwork was involved, to my understanding. Things were a lot different in the U.S.

The day our parents closed on our dream house in the Poconos was a true celebration. It symbolized freedom from Grandma Veronica. It meant the threat that immigration would take Mami and me away from the four of you was all going away. It meant new beginnings.

Mami and Papi brought us five kids to the house and all I could do was run. I ran throughout the house—up and down the stairs, inside every bedroom, in the dining room, in the huge kitchen—in and out of every single room, completely free, without a care in the world about the noise I was making. Our kitchen even had a machine that washed your dishes just like the houses Mami cleaned.

The four of you watched me and followed behind with your little feet. We held hands and stumbled, tripped over each other, laughed, got back up, and ran some more. Mami and Papi just watched and laughed at us. We were so happy to have a space of our own.

We closed on the Pennsylvania dream home in February of 1995, however, I was only a few short months shy of graduating from the sixth grade. I told my teacher the great news and she asked our parents to hold off on moving until I graduated. We didn't understand what the big deal was; we had moved much further before. Moving mid-year was not a big deal to our parents or to me, but they listened and we trusted my teacher. Mami and Papi decided to let me finish my school year in New York, even though they were anxious to start our new life in Pennsylvania.

They still had to find jobs and get all of us enrolled in school. They explained this to me, and although it was hard, we made the best of it. Mami, Papi, and the four of you moved to Pennsylvania in February, while I continued to live in the attic in New York until I graduated. Mami would cook enough food for me to last all week and instructed me to freeze it. I knew to un-thaw it during the week and heat it up in the microwave when I got home from school. On weekends, all of you would come pick me up and I would spend the weekends in our new home. I would go back to New York on Sunday evenings to get ready for school.

Grandma Veronica checked on me occasionally throughout the week. I distinctly remember one of the times she came upstairs to visit me. I was watching television and had already done my homework and eaten the dinner Mami had prepared for me. I was enjoying some popcorn from one of those big tin cans you see mostly around the holidays. She came and knocked on the attic door. I ran to answer it and she walked in. She saw the open tin can of popcorn by the couch and asked me if that was what I was eating for dinner. Of course *this* was when she came and checked on me. Why couldn't she come check on me while I was doing homework or eating my well-balanced meal? I explained that I had already eaten. "Okay, Mamita," she said, with a disapproving tone. She went back downstairs. Graduation could not come sooner! I couldn't wait until I graduated so I could live in our dream house all together as a family—or so I thought.

≈☙≈

I didn't realize back then how difficult it would be to live with Papi and to carry the uncomfortable memory of that night in the attic. What would happen when I became a woman? Would he notice? Would he do it again? According to Mami, my day was soon arriving. She hinted at it with joy and laughed at my discomfort in not knowing that 'it' was much more than avoiding the 'birds and the bees' talk. I feared Papi finding out I was becoming a woman and wished that day would never come. I wanted to tell Mami, but I couldn't. I didn't know *how* to tell her.

I finally joined you all at the dream house four months later, and well, my dreaded day arrived about a year after that.

Americanization

My world had been turned upside down and inside out when we first arrived in the United States. Everything was a new concept to me. The language, the food, the weather, the people, the architecture—it was all very different from what I knew. Even as an almost seven-year-old at the time of our arrival, I felt it.

The older I got, the more I felt *Americanized*. By the time I was in middle school, I thought I knew exactly how to be an American. I could hold a conversation with a classmate about the latest movie. I could communicate with my teachers and peers effectively. I made good grades and was often recognized for my academic achievements. I had learned everything I had to learn to be an American – or so I thought at the time.

I always held my Panamá near and dear to my heart and still do. I still held on to all of my memories of living in Colón and Sabanitas and I collected the letters Mamacela and our aunts and uncles had written over the years. I even kept them in their original white envelopes with the blue and red lined trimming around the edges. There was something special about knowing that I held the paper they once touched before they sent it to me. It made me feel connected to them.

I had a tape recording of our cousin, Manny, singing his favorite song that I listened to frequently. At the end, he told Mami and me how much he missed us. I missed his sweet little voice. Every opportunity I had over the years at school I did a project on Panamá or the Panama Canal or my memories of the Panamanian Invasion of 1989.

On December 20, 1989 the U.S. Army, Air force, Navy, and Marines invaded the Isthmus of Panamá under the Operation "Just Cause" in efforts of capturing Manuel Noriega, the Panamanian military governor. After a massive manhunt, hundreds of dead and wounded civilians, town destructions, and utter chaos, Noriega finally surrendered to the U.S. military on January 3, 1990. Noriega was taken to the U.S. immediately as a prisoner of war. He was later tried on eight counts of drug trafficking, racketeering, and money laundering.

My memories of the Panamanian Invasion are few and choppy, but I've held on to a few recollections. One of my memories of those two weeks is being at home in Sabanitas. Mamacela was worried because she spotted U.S. soldiers outside our house and Tío Mateo wasn't home. He was at his friend's house playing basketball. She knew he would be home any minute and she didn't want the soldiers to shoot him. Mamacela panicked and paced around the house nervously. I didn't know who the soldiers were, though I understood they were bad guys because they had guns.

Mami told all of us children to stay down on the ground, but I was curious. I poked my head up to look out the window and I remember seeing several soldiers in their camouflage uniforms pointing long black guns toward us. They were spread out and hid behind trees that were at the front of our property. Mami instructed Esther and me to be quiet. Then, out of nowhere came Abuelita Minerva with her cane. She opened the front door of the house and started yelling at the soldiers. She was yelling in English. Mamacela and Mami grabbed her and told her they were not trying to take our chickens and told her to be quiet.

The other memory I have of the Invasion took place in Colón. I was in an apartment building on the second floor where we were visiting Mami's friend. Again, my curiosity intrigued me as I watched out the window. The city was in complete disorder; fires blazed everywhere, sirens were going off, alarms were blaring, and people were running down the streets. Broken glass from windows lay all around as people looted department stores, sprinting with appliances and electronics that did not belong to them. Mami opened the window and yelled to a person she recognized. They exchanged some words and he continued to run with a television in his arms. I didn't know what was going on at the time, just that one day, the soldiers were gone.

≈ 9 ≈

Growing up, I'd always smile when I thought of Panamá. I thought about my biological father, although his name was forbidden in our house. I never knew what to call him the few times he came up in quiet conversations between Mami and I. Usually Mami and I would just whisper his first name as to not offend Papi. Papi would never learn about the *one* time I spoke to Iban while in the United States. In fact, even that seemed long ago even though it had only been three years ago.

I often thought about our family in Panamá and all the beautiful memories I had of them. As I embraced American culture, I tried not to let go or forget where I came from. I spoke English at school and spoke Spanish at home. I excelled in academics at school and participated in Spanish community spelling bees. I watched MTV and BET music videos during the day and telenovelas with Mami on Univision at night. It was a balance I was comfortable with. I thought I had it all figured out, but I was still different. I didn't feel normal. I still didn't quite feel like my peers.

As the four of you got older, I remember wanting you to never have to struggle with the insecurities I did on a daily basis. I never wanted you to be bullied about being different. I wanted you to be "cool," because that was important to me at the time. I wanted you to wear fashionable clothes. I wanted John to cut his hair in a fade—that's how all the cool boys wore their hair—so when I learned to drive, I took him to the barbershop every two weeks for his trendy haircut. I styled you girls' hair in butterfly clips, and gelled it to the side because I wanted you to fit in with the latest style. I wanted you to listen to the popular music that was playing on the radio so you would know the lyrics and be seen as "cool" to your classmates.

I didn't feel cool. As an immigrant, I always felt different and out of place. I was made fun for not knowing things everyone else seemed to know. I didn't know the songs and artists my classmates talked about because I listened to different music for a long time. I was made fun of for the clothes and shoes I wore. They were always second-hand and never name-brand. I didn't want you to experience this like I did. I *needed* you to learn everything I learned. I wanted you four to *never, ever* feel like you couldn't speak up. I wanted you to have a lot of friends to back you up if anyone bullied you. I remember telling you guys to always speak up, and not hold back. As I dressed you in the morning, I'd tell you to be yourself—and then I'd tell you what kind of music to like. I wanted you to like the things that I learned were most American and wear what was most in style.

Looking back now, I realize it was somewhat hypocritical of me to tell you to be yourself—when I struggled so much with doing just that. I hope you know I always had your best interest at heart and as a child and teenager, I thought I was doing what was best for you. I didn't want you to feel foreign in your world like I often did.

≈ ◦ ≈

"He's not my dad!" I yelled emphatically and deliberately at our brother, Drew.

"I'm telling," he said softly as his face filled with rage and intent.

It was the summer we moved into the dream house, all nine of Papi's kids were together for the first time in our lives. I wanted to read my *Babysitter's Club* book collection and be left alone, but Drew wanted to play with me.

"C'mon, let's go outside!" he said.

"I don't want to go! I want to read. Leave me alone!" I hollered, annoyed at our brother.

"If you don't, I'm going to go tell Papi." That was all I needed to hear. I was purposefully hurtful when I said it: "Andrew isn't my real dad. *He's not my dad!*"

Later that night, Mami and Papi called me in their room. Drew had told them what I said. Mami told me I'd hurt Papi's feelings and explained how he *was* my dad because he took me in and raised me. I apologized to him and to Mami for being disrespectful.

≈ ◦ ≈

That year I was enrolled at Northway Intermediate School where I began the seventh grade. Carrie and John were enrolled in a pre-school called the Play House. Carrie was in Ms. Fanny's four-year-old classroom, and John went to Ms. Ellen's three-year-old class. This is where you met some of the friends you still have now. Celeste and Amelia, you stayed home with Mami until you were old enough to go to the Play House.

Our family was active in our new suburban life. We quickly got involved in the nearby Catholic church and made friends with the Latinos and non-Latinos in the community. We made friends with neighbors and schoolmates and were living the life our parents wanted for us. *"La ropa sucia se lava en casa,"* so no one had to know all the hard work it took for us to live the happy lifestyle we appeared to have.

I specifically remember my thirteenth birthday party. I had a sleepover party, which in itself was very American. Sleepovers outside of family members was an outlandish concept to us. I invited my two closest friends, Alejandra, Drew,—and, of course, the four of you. Everyone had finished singing "Happy Birthday" to me when Mami and Papi handed me a birthday card they wanted me to open immediately. When I opened the card, their credit card slipped out and fell onto the floor.

"What's this?" I asked.

"It's for you. You can go on a shopping spree," Mami said as Papi stood beside her in agreement.

With shock and joy in my voice , I asked, "Like the girls in the movie *Clueless?*"

"Yes. Take the credit card and you can go clothes shopping," Papi affirmed.

I thanked them both and hugged them. "Thank you, thank you, *thank you!*" I exclaimed.

The next morning, Mami and Papi said the shopping spree was just a show for my friends, and they took the credit card back. Isn't that just like them? I laugh about it now.

I helped Mami and Papi apply for jobs in Pennsylvania. Papi had to work three jobs to be able to pay the mortgage on the house. He worked a daytime job Monday through Friday, an evening job Monday through Friday, and an all-day weekend job. He was a cook at all three places. He was a culinary master and we were all really proud of him. Papi even liked to cook for us kids on the rare occasion he had a day off. His food was delicious. Mami and Papi would often instigate and try to get us to choose the better cook among the two. It was a running joke in our household.

Mami got a job doing what she knew how to do—cleaning the office for the company that built our dream home. This was a part-time job. She also cleaned houses for people in our new neighborhood, and even got linked up to clean new houses before people moved in.

This last job was not through the home developer's office, but through someone who was subcontracted. This man paid five dollars an hour and Mami got me a job with him when I was just thirteen years old. We called him *El Gordo*. It was not a creative nickname, but it was fitting. In addition to being heavy, he wasn't very kind.

Our job was to clean up after the construction workers and all the mess they left behind. We were responsible for picking up all of the leftover material that was lying around. We had to clean off white gum-like gunk from the new bathtubs, which was very difficult, and we had to remove all the sawdust, and polish all the trimming on the floorboards, doorframes, and doorknobs of the entire house. We vacuumed and made the houses spotless for the new owners.

I remember Mami telling me we had to work fast because the faster we worked, the more work El Gordo would give us. Mami and I walked away from these spotless homes with splinters in our hands and a twenty-dollar bill each. I would give the money to Mami; I knew she and Papi needed it to pay for the house, food, or gas. I didn't clean homes with her for very long since Mami needed me at home to take care of you guys. Eventually, cleaning homes was not enough. Mami began to babysit children again. It started out with just a couple of kids, but eventually it turned out to be a goldmine business. We lived in Northeast Pennsylvania where a lot of parents commuted to New York and New Jersey to work. The commute was two hours each way, which was short enough to be worth the suburban lifestyle, but long enough to require childcare arrangements.

The parents loved Mami. She ran her own afterschool care out of our home and started out watching one child, but there were times when there were over twenty children in our new house. Mami and I were teammates and were pretty damn good at managing it all. She would wake up as early as four o'clock in the morning to receive the children from their parents before they went off to work. I woke up when Mami did to help her pack lunches and get the house ready for the morning routine of getting everyone ready for school. The morning routine consisted of making sure everyone was clean, dressed, fed, had all school supplies, and made it to the bus stop safely and on time.

While all of us were at school, Mami cleaned houses. The elementary school let out after the intermediate and high schools. By the time I was in high school, I was always the first one home in the afternoon, since I was the oldest. My school schedule worked out for us; if Mami wasn't back in time from cleaning homes, I was already at home to get all the kids from the bus stop. I would get everyone fed with something Mami had already prepared, and get everyone started on their homework at the dining room table, kitchen table, and small plastic table and chair sets Mami had bought. Saheli was always right there with me to help. We had a system with afterschool snacks and homework, followed by dinner. We had different work stations for homework and divided up the different waves of children by age group. Parents began to pick up their children any time from six o'clock in the evening until eleven o'clock at night. We worked hard to make sure each child was fed and had homework completed by the time their parents came to pick them up. I would then work on my own homework and chores, then get ready for the next day to do it all over again. We made the best of it, and made up games all along to make it fun. We maintained this routine throughout my intermediate and high school years. The number of children we took care of varied as children grew older, parents' employment situations changed, and relationships grew apart for whatever reason.

We also had some negative experiences during our babysitting years. Some of the kids we took care of were not well-behaved and liked to steal, bite, or yell, though other times it was just kids being kids. Some of the kids were defiant and some were just plain annoying.

Occasionally, parents did not want to pay by the end of the week and ended up owing Mami a lot of money. They always had sob stories. Parents gave Mami IOUs and unkept promises that they would have the money the following week. Mami was so kind, she continued to take care of these children for free.

One time a mother dropped off her child and we didn't hear from her for a week. We called both parents several times, but neither one answered. Mami asked me to leave messages, telling them their daughter needed clothes and food, but we still didn't hear from them. We ended up feeding little Aisha, and buying her clothing, and even school supplies she needed that week. Her parents eventually turned up and told us they had gotten into a fight and both had gone their separate ways. Mami told me they were young parents and were immature, and to top it off they didn't pay us or reimburse us for the items we had bought their daughter.

After years of awful caretaking experiences, Mami decided she was going to cut back on the babysitting and work as a custodian at the local high school. She worked from three until eleven p.m. and would head into work as I left school. She would stop by my school bus to greet me by tapping on the window with the umbrella she always carried just in case it rained. I watched her as she walked into the building in her t-shirt, worn out pants, and low ponytail. Our parents were hard workers. I always admired them for that.

Young Lady

I was 13 years old when I got my first period, or when I "became a lady" as Mami puts it. I was in the eighth grade and my best friend Saheli had already gotten hers. Mami always described this moment as a beautiful surprise gift that would arrive and change my life. My best friend was younger than me by a little over a year and I thought I was doing a great job at prolonging the dreaded day from arriving. All the other women in the world could keep this present; I didn't want it.

It was a Saturday morning; we were all at home except Papi who was working. I went to use the master bathroom in our new home and there it was. I stared down at my pink-stained panties and I became instantly pissed. I knew exactly what it was. Mami had told me all about what to expect.

I called Mami's name while still sitting on the toilet seat with my head down, disappointed at myself as if I could've prevented this moment. She came over to the locked bathroom door.

"I got it," I announced.

"You got what?" she asked.

"I got my period," I huffed with a deep sigh.

You would've thought Mami won the lottery. She cheered on the other side of the door. I heard her pick up the phone to call Papi at work. She mocked my disappointed reaction as she shared the news and moved on to call the next person on her list. In between her proud conversations, she instructed me on where to find pads under the sink. I angrily squatted and scooted over, balancing my panties around my knees and reached in the big blue and green box for the little square wrapper. I already knew how to put it on. I had watched Mami do it multiple times growing up. She was not ashamed and often used the bathroom with the door wide open—only to pee, of course.

By the time I walked out of the bathroom, Mami handed me the white, bulky, rectangular cordless phone. The silver antenna nearly poked my eye out. She had called her mother, Mamacela, in Panamá to brag that I was a woman. Mami laughed at my agony of embarrassment and cheered in excitement. Our family in Panamá passed the phone around to different members as they all congratulated me. Why did this have to be such a big to do? I was close to my family and loved them all, but this was all too strange for me. I was humiliated and angry at Mami for putting me through that. "I forget you're American now," she teased me. "In Panamá, it's normal to talk about these things without being embarrassed," she carried on.

The eighth grade was a tough year for me as I discovered and tried to embrace the changes my body was going through. I wanted to start shaving my legs, but I was terrified to ask permission from Mami.

"Mami, can I ask you a question?"

"*Dime, hija,*" she invited me to talk.

I was afraid Mami would turn me down due to her conservative backgrounds and strict rules. My approach was dramatic. I'll admit that now.

"*Hija*, talk to me," she said.

"I forgot what I was going to say. Never mind."

"*Alguna mentira*?"

Mom's silly expression she always used in her attempt to catch me in a lie made me work up the nerve to finally ask. And so I shaved my legs like a *señorita* that day and I felt like a real, young lady after that.

I started wearing shorts to school to show off my clean, shaven legs, and I wanted to start picking out my own clothes, instead of accepting whatever Mami ordered from the JC Penney catalog or thrift store. I'd become interested in name brands like any other child my age, and wanted to buy the knock-offs if we could. I knew owning the real deal was not an option. All my peers were wearing name brands and I just wanted to look like I was wearing them.

I remember wanting a pair of FILA sneakers that year more than anything, and I was surprised when Mami bought me a pair. They were mostly white with a black velvet trim and a green and red logo. She said I deserved them and they were the *real* deal. That was the first name brand item I ever owned, and it was brand new. I loved the sneakers so much I chose to draw them for a sketch project in art class. I'd always have a memory of them that way.

Those sneakers and my curling iron were the most treasured items I owned at the time. Without that curling iron, I couldn't do the two small curls that framed my bangs, a popular style in the mid to late '90s.

I also became interested in boys. Eighth grade was the year of *Ramiro*. Ramiro was a short Puerto Rican with cinnamon skin, jet-black wavy hair, and the cutest smile with big, straight, white teeth. My best friend and I both loved him and Ramiro had no clue. He was one of the few crushes we shared—along with most of the other girls in our grade. I had just gotten over my first crush—*kind of*—

but only because I didn't get to see him as much as I did in seventh grade. Ohhh, Carlos... I thought I was going to marry him one day. I knew it the second we met at my new school in Pennsylvania.

I wanted my body to grow into itself so I could show off and get Ramiro's attention. On the other hand, I wouldn't know what to do with the attention if I received it. I just knew I wanted it. Still, the attention I sought was very selective. I was an ageist. I wanted *boys* to notice me; I wanted *men* to ignore me.

I had conflicting thoughts that year. I wanted to embrace my new body and take interest in my feminine side, but what happened that night five years ago was holding me back. I had to tell someone. The burden was too big to bear alone.

Later that year, I finally worked up the nerve to tell Mami of the memory that had haunted me since that Christmas in the attic. It was like a bad dream that I knew had really happened—and I couldn't seem to get out of my head. And all I ever wanted was to forget it ever happened. Still, the memories crept into my mind suddenly and without a specific trigger. Living with *him* set off my emotions. Maybe Mami could fix me.

"Mami, can I talk to you?" I looked at the ground in shame. I was fearful and nervous.

Over the past five years, I'd convinced myself that I was at fault. I'd thought I would get in trouble, or let Papi down for not keeping it a secret—or even let Mami down in some way.

Approaching Mami in this manner was unlike me. She knew that what I was about to say was to be taken very seriously. She led me into her bedroom with her hands on my shoulders, shut the door behind her, and we sat on her bed. I told her everything. I told her I still thought about it from time to time, I wanted more than anything to forget it ever happened—and I had tried, but I couldn't. The memory made me angry for not being able to put it behind me.

Mami cried—we both cried– and she apologized to me. She told me the incident should never have happened and she was sorry it did. That was when I learned something similar had happened to her when she was younger. She'd had to move on and forget it.

Mami spoke to Papi later that day when he came home from work. He admitted to my accusations and, according to Mami, cried and apologized to her. I didn't want to talk about it, let alone talk to *him* about it. I still just wanted to forget.

Mami explained that things were very complicated. She wanted me to be okay, but Papi had to continue to be a part of our lives. We needed Papi's financial income to help support our family; all four of you were born by this time, and we wouldn't be able to make it without him. A single, non-U.S. citizen mom and daughter, with four additional young children was not an attractive or favorable situation. Plus, our residency status was coming up and we needed Papi to stay in the country so we could continue to live our lives in the United States.

Mami further explained her own sacrifice. She was unhappily married and Papi was cheating on her with his co-worker. He often came home well after his shift had ended, and he had been doing so for years. This wasn't the life she wanted, but as long as we had each other, we could get through anything. Mami sniffled back her pain. She continued to pour her heart out and shared all her worries. Papi drank every day. He poured Bacardi in a coffee mug and brought it to work in the mornings. He drank at the restaurant bars where he worked, then came home and fixed himself more drinks. He was a functional alcoholic—never sloppy, always discrete.

Papi's ex-wife, Priscilla, was a troublemaker. Mami still worried about her trying to take Papi back, especially since Mami had invested so much in him. Child support and emotional support for Papi's four other children (from three different women) was taking a toll on her. It was all so overwhelming and difficult. Before I knew it, *I* was consoling *Mami*. Mami and I had always been close, but sharing our pain brought us even closer. To know that the most disturbing thing that had ever happened to me was an experience I shared with her brought me comfort in a strange way. I wasn't alone. She assured me that she got through it. Sharing that she now hurt for different reasons made me feel sympathy for her. We suffered together in different forms from pain caused by the same man, but we at least had each other.

The only positives according to Mami were that he always came home and he always gave her his paychecks from the restaurant. She did wonder about his cash tips and how he spent those, but she was satisfied with the paper checks.

Mami concluded that I could never tell anyone about my memory. If I did so, Papi would go to jail, and we didn't want that. Our family depended on him. I understood and didn't want him to be in any kind of trouble—as long as we didn't talk about it.

Mami asked me if I would be okay continuing our lives with him in it. I remember that question vividly, because she never asked me again. I lied to her that day and I regretted it for a very long time.

At the time, I understood the complicated situation we were in. How selfish would it have been to ask Mami to leave him? And was it truly my option? Did Mami really give me that power or did she only pretend to? But then again, if I'd just told her 'no' that day, what would've happened to us? Where would we be? What kind of lives would we have lived?

For years later, I'd fantasize about how different our lives might have been.

≈☺≈

As my body gradually changed with puberty, all I wanted to do was hide. I didn't want Papi to notice I was a woman. I purposely wore oversized clothing around him and hunched my body over to hide my small curves and growing chest. I sat and stood in unflattering postures. I avoided eye contact and him altogether.

What would he do to me now that he knew?

I began to worry that Papi might want to harm one of you. I became protective of you girls especially and I found myself getting angry at Mami as she didn't seem to share this burden with me. Although we had two bedrooms to spread out in, we began to have sleepovers in my bedroom so I could keep an eye on you. I stayed awake until I knew he had come home from work, drunk his rum and Coke, and gone to bed with Mami.

Mami and I didn't want to speak of what had happened to me ever again. After all, it wouldn't happen again and I was determined to forget about it. As people got older, they forgot things. I was counting on it.

CHAPTER 12

Our Secret

When we moved into our dream house in Pennsylvania, we didn't have doorstoppers. The doorknobs made holes in some of the walls of the house over time due to our carelessness, and the bathroom I used was one of the rooms with a small hole. It was a hole through the sheet rock that started out as a tiny slit from the lock on the door and, increasingly over time, became a little bigger.

One morning when I was sixteen, I was running through my usual routine to get ready for school. I walked into the bathroom, turned on the water in the shower, and turned on my radio. It was tuned in to my favorite radio station. I was in the hip-hop stage of my life and was rapping along to song after song. The water was piping hot just like I enjoyed it. I undressed, threw my pajamas on the ground, and entered the shower.

It was the only time of day I spent alone. I was the first to get ready for school and the only one awake. When I finished, I would wake up each one of you in age order to start getting ready for school. Mami would finish getting you ready. I took my time every morning as I wanted to look pretty for the boys who didn't know I existed. I always thought, *Maybe today will be the day they notice me.*

After my shower, I playfully danced to the music while I dried myself in front of the mirror. I took a moment to admire my young, naked, new womanly body in the steamy reflection. This was my time to appreciate the body I tried to cover up for most of the day. In the privacy of the bathroom, I attempted sexy facial expressions I'd seen women do in telenovelas and video vixens in MTV music videos—though I'd never do that out in public. How embarrassing would that be?

Which lip liner should I wear today? I wondered, while puckering my lips.

I reached for my neatly folded bra and panties that sat on the shaggy toilet seat cover and proceeded to put them on. Then I walked back over in front of the mirror to carefully comb out the knots of my long brown hair.

There was a pause in the radio reception and, in those few seconds, I heard a noise in the next room. It was a soft thump on the wall behind me. I immediately reached for my towel to cover myself. Maybe one of you kids were up?

A floor creaked outside the bathroom door. Someone was definitely out there. I opened the door, rapidly, expecting to see one of you looking for me. But it wasn't any of you.

It was *him.*

There he stood in his solid, navy-blue bathrobe exposing his thick, curly, revolting gray chest hairs. He stood within arms-reach from me and we locked eyes. He stood before me—taller, wider, and stronger—and his glare was full of guilt. Mine, I'm sure, was disturbed and defeated.

I closed the door and locked it, creating a barrier between us.

I immediately knew what he had been doing. I caught him. He was *watching* me. He had been watching me every morning, I'm sure. That stupid hole in the wall, the result of carelessly opening the door over time, now exposed, broken sheetrock, had become the perfect window for his perversion. Why didn't we ever get doorstoppers?

My hands shook in terror. My body, stiff in panic, grew cold. *How long has he been doing this?* I thought. *Why, why, why is this happening to me?*

I heard his footsteps fade away, and seconds later, there was a clanking of pots and pans in the kitchen. He was cooking something down the hall, not far enough away from me.

I stood tense in my cold sweat. *What do I do? I can't get out of here. I don't want to see him. I don't want to see him. I don't want to see him.* My hands in prayer pose and my eyes closed tight, I begged for answers. My eyes began to water. *Don't make a sound Olivia. He might hear you. He can't hear you cry.*

"*Maaaaaaaaaammmmmmmmiiiiiiiiiiiiii!*" my voice quivered in a soft whimper. My jaw was tight and vibrating. My hot breath seeped through the spider webs of saliva that formed between my lips. I wanted her to hear me, but I couldn't let *him* hear me. What would he do to me? Would he come back? Force the door open?

I whisper-yelled my distress again, "*Mami!*" The clanking continued down the hall as I fell to the floor under the hole on the wall.

I wanted her to see him. I wanted her to ask him what he was doing. I needed her to come rescue me, but she was asleep. How would I tell her? How *could* I tell her that this happened after the other incident? She had to see it for herself.

I wiped the tears from my soft cheeks and wiped the backs of my hands on the towel that still covered me. *She's not coming. I'm on my own,* I despaired. I shook my head in attempts to pull myself together and grabbed toilet paper to wipe the wetness that still covered my face.

If you can make it out this bathroom, you can go to school and you won't have to see him all day. Get it together, Olivia. You have to do something.

I covered the hole with toilet paper from inside the bathroom. Then I took deep breaths and threw my clothes on as quickly as I could. It was a good thing I brought them in the bathroom with me every day. The last thing I wanted to do was see him. I had to leave that house. I couldn't face him. I figured if I could get my clothes on and head for the front door, I wouldn't have to go through the kitchen. I could finish getting ready at Saheli's house. My book bag was in the living room on the way out and Mami could get the kids up and get them ready. She'd be up soon. The plan was set and played out perfectly in my head.

I was dressed, now it was time to bolt. I grabbed my pajamas and undergarments and balled them up in my arm, they'd fit in my backpack. I opened the bathroom door with all the bravery I could muster and walked rapidly and softly toward the front door. I grabbed my backpack, tossed it over one shoulder and reached for the brass doorknob.

"Olivia," he called at me in his deep, stern voice.

He caught me. This was it. I turned back, my head down, my shoulders caved inward as he knew me to stand.

"Here," he said, holding out a paper plate. On it, an omelet, an *apology* omelet.

I grabbed the plate from him, turned around, and hurried out of the house.

My heavy book bag swayed from side to side and slapped my back with every forward step. I crossed the main road that connected our homes and turned into my friend's cul de sac and her brown, two-story safe haven just up ahead.

I'd made it. I knocked on the door.

As I waited for Saheli, my thoughts raced. *Why did I grab the plate? Why didn't I throw it at him? Yell at him? Yell for*

Mami? Make a scene and wake the whole household? I should tell my school counselor when I get to school. I should tell Saheli's mom as soon as she opens this door. The police will arrive and take him away forever. Away from me, away from Mami, away from all of us!

Mrs. Baral greeted me at the door. She was surprised, yet pleasant. "You're early, Olivia. Come in." I was still in disarray.

"Can I throw this out please?" I asked, handing over the disgusting, symbolical plate. "Sure, is everything okay?" she asked as she took it from me.

"Yes." I smiled timidly and uncomfortably.

I ran up the stairs and followed the music to the bathroom my best friend and her sister shared. The door was open; they were finishing up getting ready. Saniya was singing and dancing to the Backstreet Boys with a brush in hand as a microphone. Saheli making fun of her dance moves only encouraged Saniya more. She swayed her hips to the drumbeats and carried on as if she were the sixth member of the group.

"Hey, Olivia. Are you okay?" Saheli could tell I was shaken up. She knew me so well. She only had to study me for half a second to know I wasn't myself, despite how hard I was trying to hide it. I was safe now. I just had to move on with my day.

"Yeah, Yeah, Yeah. I just need to get ready." I quickly dismissed her concern.

I took over Saheli's mirror and finished up as fast as I could before Mrs. Baral called us down for breakfast. I always ate breakfast at their house on school days, so she'd set the table for three. She didn't ask me why I hadn't eaten the breakfast I brought that morning. I appreciated her for that.

During breakfast, I did a really good job of pretending to act normal. I was proud of myself; I was moving on and was on track to forget. I followed along the conversations and laughed along with the silly things that were said. I was doing *well*.

On the way to the bus stop, Saniya walked ahead of us with her friends and Saheli and I hung back as usual. We were in no rush to get to the school bus. She knew something was wrong and asked me again. "Okay, what's going on with you?"

What if I told her and her parents found out? Would I get Papi in trouble? Would *I* get in trouble? Mami would kill me. Just minutes ago, I wanted to tell everybody just to make him go away. Now I had come to my senses and knew I couldn't tell anyone who would get him in trouble. Our family needed him.

We paused our walk and I looked at her dead in her eyes.

"Do you promise not to tell anyone? I really mean it, Seli. It has to be a secret."

Her eyes got wider and looked steadily back at me. "Yes, of course." I believed her. She was my best friend, my only real friend, and the one person I could trust.

I told her what had just happened to me and she listened to every word. I don't think she knew what to say, but, somehow, not saying anything was the right thing and exactly what I needed her to do. Only a few seconds passed before she broke the silence with something that always made me laugh.

"Look at Saniya and her stupid friends." She mocked their walk ahead of us. Saheli and Saniya loved each other, but made fun of each other constantly. Saniya was two grades ahead of us. She was popular, played sports, and had a social life. Seli and I had each other and loved to mock her since Saniya picked on us frequently.

My school day carried on as usual. And Seli came over after school to help me take care of you all as she always did.

I told Mami about the incident later that night when she got home from work. She made Papi patch up all of the holes that night when he came home. Patching the holes was supposed to give me peace that it couldn't happen again. It didn't. I was terrified. He couldn't be trusted. Had he been watching me every day since we'd moved here three years ago?

I became more paranoid. He could use a mirror to peek under the door. If he tilted it from the outside, he could see me for sure. I tried it. It was possible. I'd have to cover up the bottom of the doorway every time I showered. Every time I used the bathroom, really. I patrolled the bathroom door when one of you were in there. I even taught you guys the towel trick and told you it was to keep the bathroom warm.

I showered quickly after that day. The longer I stayed in the bathroom, the more time it gave him to see me. Even with the wall and shower curtain as a shield between him and me, I'd check behind the plastic curtain. *What if he got in and I didn't hear him? Did I forget to lock the door?* Of course I didn't, but I still checked.

I compulsively inspected where the hole once was. I tried to peek through at night and looked for any hint of light in the adjacent room. I felt over the plastered square to check for any signs of soft spots or signs that it would not hold up.

I was obsessed and thought he would find a way to watch me. This paranoia continued throughout all the years I continued to live under the same roof as him. It continued after we moved out of the dream house and into the Newberry Road home in North Carolina. I was terrified he would hurt me again until the day I finally moved out that Labor Day weekend with Raymond.

After that incident, the little physical interaction I may have had with him became non-existent. We greeted each other with a simple, verbal acknowledgement, but only when others who didn't live with us were present. We did this so as not to raise suspicion. We couldn't air out our dirty laundry.

We didn't have to put on this act for you four. You were too young to notice.

There was absolutely no touching or hugging, even when socially appropriate. He didn't give me 'peace' at church the handful of times he joined us for Christmas and Easter mass throughout the years. We always managed to act as if we ran out of time to acknowledge each other so the people around us wouldn't think it was odd. During academic ceremonies and even my high school graduation, I skipped him while hugging the entire rest of our family. While passing dishes around the table during holiday dinners, Mami was our buffer. I feared his finger may slide and touch mine by mistake. His mere presence brought on so much discomfort and agony that I grew angry at Mami. Why wouldn't she leave him? Couldn't she see how uncomfortable I was?

He disgusted me in every way. It was frightful and what he did haunted me every single day. I didn't look at him and avoided him every chance I could. The oversized clothing and blanket-wearing continued. And Mami? Mami knew all along how I felt, but she pretended like life was peachy. We were a loving family from the outside looking in.

Every day I was fearful of what else he was capable of doing. Was there something I wasn't thinking of? I had let my guard down in the bathroom, which is why I'd let that happen. I was always afraid of him getting into one of our beds. I told Mami of my fear of him hurting you four in any way. He was clearly not sorry. He was not better and it was difficult to live with him. Mami told me she would make him see a counselor and she thought I should see one, too.

Although Mami had good intentions about seeing the counselor, it was poorly planned as Papi had to drive me there. The car ride was incredibly uncomfortable to say the least.

Mami found a therapist far enough away from town that we wouldn't run into anyone we knew. The three of us rode in silence for the brutal forty-five-minute drive.

We all knew what was going to happen. *It* was going to be talked about. Out loud. I knew I had to talk to a stranger about it (not by choice), and that alone brought on major anxiety.

We pulled up to the counselor's office that looked like a regular gray and white house except it had a big white, gray, and red wooden sign in the front of it announcing to the world what I was walking into. The three of us walked in. The floors were creaky and wooden, the walls were white, and there were framed pictures adorning the walls. I wanted to fade and disappear into the hallway.

No one was in the foyer to greet us. We heard a voice from a back room, then a red-haired woman came out from the office and invited us back. Mami asked me to sit out in the foyer while her and Papi talked to the lady. I sat there feeling like something was wrong with me for almost an hour before Mami and Papi came back out. Papi walked straight out the front door and Mami invited me to walk back with her to talk to the therapist.

I sat down with Mami and the counselor and spoke, knowing the man we were talking about was just a few feet away somewhere outside.

The red-haired woman was polite, and asked a lot of questions. I answered only what she asked. I didn't tell her any more or any less. What if Papi was right outside the window listening to every word? At the end of the almost hour-long session, she spoke. I hated what she said next.

"You have to confront him," she stated simply.

WHAT? Is this woman crazy? I thought to myself. Had she not heard me say that all I wanted was for her to make me forget about all this? *Can't you hypnotize me,* I thought,

wave your pocket watch before my eyes, and make this go away?
I've seen hypnosis work on TV. Do that!

"You have to confront him to get the answers you're looking for," said the counselor. "I know it's tough," she added as she tapped my knee and leaned forward, trying to connect with me.

What did she know? What answers? I didn't have any questions for him.

I shut down even more. I was so disappointed. A part of me wanted this lady to convince Mami to get Papi out of our lives, but she didn't. Now two people knew outside the three of us and I was still going back home with him.

How could she have it all figured out after only one hour? I have been carrying these feelings for years! This was a waste of time, I thought on the long, uncomfortable car ride home. I didn't see the counselor again, even though we scheduled another appointment on the way out.

"A counselor and me are the only people you can talk to about this," Mami said later. "You can't tell anyone else, okay? This is our secret. *La ropa sucia se lava en casa.* Saheli doesn't know, does she?" she asked in fear.

"No!" I responded and lied through my teeth, annoyed. *All she cares about is who knows,* I thought. Saheli hadn't brought it back up. Had she even heard me tell her? Did she believe me?

My frustration, anger, and insecurities grew over the years. And as time went by, I began to direct this anger toward Mami. It felt like she chose being with him over our safety, over me, over us, despite how twisted and disgusting he was. Her reasons for staying with him no longer made sense to me the older I got. It began to occur to me that I would rather live somewhere else and struggle financially than continue living with him. We struggled even though he was in our lives, too. Our struggle was beyond financial.

CHAPTER 13

Black Hole

I was a Junior in high school when the thought of committing suicide crossed my mind for the first time. I didn't see any other way out of getting away from Papi.

I felt completely alone in carrying this thing that had happened to me. I felt like I was in a black hole, alone with myself and my thoughts. I had fallen into this emptiness and screamed with all my might, but when I looked up, no one could hear me. I wanted help, but how could I seek it when I couldn't talk about *it?* I was alone.

~ ◎ ~

One night I stood in the kitchen, chopping hot dogs into little pieces. Back then I cooked them in a tomato sauce and I'd call them 'frog legs,' because it made you all laugh so much. You knew they were really hot dogs, but we liked to pretend. I stopped and stared down at the silver blade in my right hand for a brief moment. The thought left me almost immediately and I continued to chop.

Later that night when everyone was asleep, I walked back over to the kitchen and pulled the knife out of the drawer. I held it in my hand. Where should I stab myself? My stomach? I'd bleed to death and feel relief as the wound slowly emptied me out. Should I slit my wrists? I held the blade inwards with a tight grip on the black handle, my eyes fixed on the rivets, then the thought of you four interrupted my dark thoughts.

The four of you brought me so much joy. You looked for me when you got hurt to make you sugar water, a sweet treat that took the pain away. We did our homework together every weekday. You loved the silly rhythms I'd come up with that helped you remember the toughest spelling words. Replaying how you danced to them made me smile. You comforted me when I wasn't feeling well. You tried to clean up my vomit the last time I had the stomach bug and made a mess on my way to the bathroom. You poured my medicine for me when I was too weak to do it myself. You were the friends I hung out with after school. You four were my whole world. I didn't want any of you to find me this way—lifeless, surrounded by a pool of blood.

And then I thought of Mami. She needed me. She had to work so much. She cleaned so many houses and office buildings, and now she was a custodian at my high school. She cleaned so much that the chemicals ate away at her hands. She cried about how badly they stung when she came home at night in her stained old t-shirts that no one had claimed from the lost and found bin at the school. She worked so hard and she needed me. I had to be there for the five of you. You five were my reason to keep going.

I released my grip and put the knife back in the drawer. I quietly went back to the room where you four were sleeping and went back to bed.

Although I chose to put the knife back in the drawer that night, I didn't let go of the thought. I often fantasized about ending my misery for all the years I lived with him. Mami was miserable, too. This couldn't possibly be the dream she wanted for herself. When she spoke to our family in Panamá, she shared only accomplishments. She told them of my good grades and the instruments I was learning to play at school. She told them of the four of you and how smart, sweet, and funny you all were. She described Papi as an admirable man who worked hard to provide for our family. She didn't tell them that she slept maybe four hours a night. She took care of us and the kids we babysat in addition to keeping up with her cleaning jobs. Papi was still unfaithful to her. He only contributed financially and it wasn't enough. Mami and I could raise you all without him, I figured. We'd be happier.

≈ 9 ≈

A few months later my dream of living without Papi almost came true.

"Olivia, I'm done with him!" Mami cried one day on my shoulder. She sobbed uncontrollably. I felt dampness on my t-shirt underneath her muffled wails. Her pain was my pain. I comforted her.

"Look at what I found in the closet!" she wept as she tossed a handful of Polaroids at me. A half-naked white woman posed proudly for the photographer. She was evidently proud of her curves and chest. She screamed of confidence, something I would never have. Something Mami did have but lost over the years.

The strange woman was thin, with long, curly brown hair that grew past her butt. She wore a tight, green velvet skirt and a black blouse that exposed her cleavage. Her makeup was done heavily—not like Mami wore her make up anymore.

"He doesn't come home many nights," she continued. "He claims to work late and says the commute from his job in New

Jersey is closer to his mother's house so he stays there. Those must be excuses! He's spending time with other women!"

Mami decided to confront him that night. This would be the day Mami left Papi for good. We would start a new life without him. We began to set their breakup stage. As Mami looked for luggage to pack our things, I placed the pictures on their bed for Papi to discover. Mami rehearsed out loud what she would say to Papi. She would have the five of us wait outside in a taxi cab that would drive us away. She colluded as I cheered her on, but it was not long before our bubble was burst.

I looked over at Mami and watched her slowing down. She was beginning to realize that we didn't have anywhere to go. At who's doorstep could a single mom and her five children present themselves? What would life be like without his financial support? The unknown scared Mami more than the anger motivated her to leave. As instructed, I collected the photos back. I gripped onto them, knowing that releasing the photos would mean letting go of the dream of living without Papi. I didn't have a choice. I placed the pictures in the shoebox that was buried back in the closet where Mami had found it.

I was defeated. Mami returned the few items she had begun to pack. "It's getting late," she pointed out as she instructed me to go to bed. I walked quietly to my room to not wake you all up.

CHAPTER 14

Teenage
Love Affair

Mami had very strict rules about dating, and by 'strict rules' I mean dating was not allowed. This changed after me.

You're welcome.

Something happened the summer between my elementary and middle school years. I walked around the hallways of my new school and it seemed like everybody was in a relationship. All of my peers were coupled up. They held hands and 'made out' in the hallways, despite threats of getting written up for public displays of affection. By the time I was thirteen, the only relationship I had even come close to being involved in was the one between our Tía Maria and her long-time boyfriend, Nathan. Tía Maria often asked me to write letters she dictated to me for her to give to Nathan.

Tía Maria used to live in the yellow house, was the same age as Mami, and had an intellectual disability. She and Nathan both worked for the same cleaning company. Tía rode the city bus to the company headquarters where they shuttled workers in vans to the different homes and office buildings they cleaned. Nathan had an intellectual disability, too. They saw each other at work sometimes, but spent the most time together on their days off when he was allowed to come over.

While they were away from each other, Tía asked me to help her write him dirty notes that she would slip to him at work. Tía could copy a phrase repeatedly on paper if it was written at least once for her, but she didn't know how to jot down the things she wanted to say that were in her mind.

≈ ◯ ≈

She had the same thoughts that anyone in their late twenties and early thirties had, and she shared those thoughts and feelings with me and asked me to write them down for her. She described in detail what she wanted to do to him physically, where she wanted to touch him, and how she wanted to use her mouth. She asked me to write the letters in Spanish and he only spoke English. I didn't know what I was writing half the time—and neither did he.

≈ ◯ ≈

In elementary school, a lot of the girls would giggle around me and secretly share with me who they liked in our classroom. I giggled back and agreed with them about who they thought to be cute at the time. Boys and girls got 'married' to each other during recess as other girls giggled about marrying the boy of their dreams. I only played along to fit in at the time. Truthfully, I wasn't interested in any boys as a ten-year-old, nor the idea of being married.

The one boy from elementary school who still sticks out in my mind was Calvin. Calvin was a bad boy. He made jokes during class, which classified him as a bad boy to me. He was

short, his skin was the color of light brown sugar, and his hair
was jet black and wavy. His facial features were strong. His
eyes looked like he wore eyeliner, and his eyelashes curled for
miles. *"Eh,"* I thought to myself, as I shrugged my shoulders.
He was cute, I'd admit, but cute did not mean anything to me.
When I thought of Calvin, I just thought of something funny
he said in class that made me giggle.

As I heard girl classmates talk about their crushes, I
started thinking maybe I was strange for not having one,
so I forced myself into liking a boy named Neil. Neil lived
around the corner from me, so I found it convenient to 'like'
him. Neil's sister and I walked to school every morning.
Neil always left after us because he was never ready on time.
I don't know if he purposely didn't want to walk with his
younger sister and I, or if he really was always careless and
could never be ready on time. He was certainly sloppy. My
memories of him are of his mom yelling for him to get out
of the house and him stumbling out with one book bag strap
over his shoulder. He even moved sloppily. His upper body
was always ahead of his legs like he was always rushing.

Every morning I walked over to Neil's house and waited
by the door for his sister, Monica. I always peeked in to get
a glimpse of Neil to see if I would feel a little something for
him. Neil was cute according to some of the girls in my class,
and he was biracial from what he explained. I never saw his
father, but I knew his mom and sister were both a darker
complexion than him. Neil was of pale skin and wore his
hair like many other boys our age. He had a high top like the
one Kid 'n Play wore from the *House Party* movies. My crush
for Neil didn't last as it was never real.

≈ 9 ≈

It wasn't until I was in the seventh grade that I knew what it felt like to have a real crush. That was the day I met Carlos. We had just moved to Pennsylvania and we were in Mrs. Lindburg's class when Carlos and I were introduced to each other. He was the dreamiest person I had ever seen. Carlos was from New York, as was I. He had just moved from Washington Heights in Manhattan, he was Dominican, and he also spoke Spanish. Carlos was the tallest seventh grader in the school, thin as an ironing board, with skin bronzed brown as mine. His eyes were dark and mysterious, and his lips were full and pale rose-colored. He had a tiny birthmark on his right cheek that bent as he smirked and introduced himself to me. Nothing else mattered to me at that moment but him and me. I pictured the world standing still. Everything around us became fuzzy and abstract, except for the two of us, almost as if we were some art piece. I pictured wind blowing in my face, waving my hair and making me look like a beautiful model and him just perfect as he already was. I shook my head, waking back up into my reality. I was wearing overalls, my hair tied back in a braid, looking like a freshly brought in immigrant child. I was speechless.

At last, I scrambled to find words. "Nice to meet you," I said. I didn't want to be introduced to anyone else. This is what a *real* crush felt like. Carlos and I smiled and waved in the hallways when we saw each other that year and I studied the back of his perfectly shaped head in the one class we shared.

My crush for Carlos came back strong in the ninth grade and lasted all the way up through the end of high school. He was convenient for me to like as Mami began to babysit his little sister and our moms became friends. I started to see him a lot more at school, and my feelings began to grow for him. The next two years were simply harmless, beautiful years.

I had a very innocent relationship with him, although it was never labeled as such. Carlos walked me to class, held my hand in the hallways, kissed me on the cheek, met me at my locker between classes, and we wrote each other letters to exchange in the hall (go ahead and laugh, we wrote letters prior to texts). The more I got to know Carlos, the more I fell in love. He was an artist and he had a mysterious dark side. He drew me pictures that I cherished. Sure, they were pictures of dragons and violent creatures, but he gave them to me so I loved them.

We had a lot in common. We were both Hispanic and we were both the oldest sibling. After school, we talked on the phone while we completed our chores of cooking for our families, cleaning, and so forth. We shared secrets with each other, and even pain we had endured. He had his secrets he carried, and I had mine. I didn't tell him about Papi, but he knew I wondered where my biological father was and how I dreamed of seeing him one day. He knew I wanted to be out of our house and he knew about my suicidal thoughts, but he didn't know all the reasons why. He was the only friend I confided in other than Saheli.

Carlos was a distraction from the secret I carried with me. Love songs were suddenly about him. He made me feel beautiful and quietly confident. And not lonely.

It was all very innocent and beautiful until one day in the eleventh grade when it ended. He had reached a limit with our innocent relationship and wanted something more that I wasn't ready to give him. Although I had never felt like this about anyone else before, I wasn't ready to 'prove it' the way he was ready to. In no way did he pressure me. I simply wasn't ready to experience this with him, not when I associated my body and intimacy with negative feelings and with someone else. Carlos was my happy, innocent place where everything was perfect. The extent of our love felt safe, happy, and every bit comfortable. I was still a girl. I found boys attractive, but my physicality was a dark place I wanted to keep suppressed. My two worlds couldn't mix. I wasn't ready.

There was no warning to my heartbreak. He just stopped one day. He didn't meet me at my locker. He didn't meet me at the end of English class to walk me to biology as he had done all year. He just stopped.

One morning during geometry class, I got up to go to the bathroom. The hallways were cleared because everyone was in class—except for two people at the end of the hallway. There he was with Virginia.

Virginia was the newest girl to move to our school and she was beautiful. She was Puerto Rican and had thick, jet-black hair that cascaded down her back. She wore tight jeans and fitted shirts every day that showed off her curves. I couldn't pull off those clothes. I was thin, but didn't have the Coca-Cola bottle shape she had. Carlos's 6-foot, 3-inch frame was hunched over her, whispering into her ear. His hands rested on her waist, like he'd held mine. She laughed at whatever he was telling her as her back rested up against the fire red lockers. I wondered if she felt what I felt when I rested in his arms. Did she melt at his touch like I did?

It took everything in me to walk past them as if it meant nothing to me. Inside it felt like I had been stabbed in the chest. I barely walked into the bathroom as tears poured out my eyes. I sobbed quietly and alone. I hoped they would be gone by the time I left. My nose was bright red from crying, and my eyes still watery and now puffy. He'd know I was crying. I couldn't let him see me. I couldn't let *her* see me.

Singing along to Son by Four's newest single, "Purest of Pain," on repeat in both Spanish and English became a part of my afterschool daily routine after that day. I felt I had lost so much with the end of our friendship. You four were surely concerned. I neglected you to tend to my heartbreak.

I'd trusted Carlos with my entire heart. It was the first relationship I had experienced that was pure. He didn't know it, but our relationship was so very meaningful to me. At that age, he was the only boy who had earned my trust and didn't let me down. My biological dad had rejected me. He never came looking for me and I often wondered why he never cared enough to try to contact me. Papi had lost my trust a long time ago. In losing Carlos, I lost total faith in men. The males in my life had failed me.

Virginia and Carlos didn't last very long. He dated a few other girls that year and the next, even dating one that rode the same bus as me. *Stab me harder, why don't you?* I eventually met another young man who filled the void of my broken heart. Still, Carlos held a special place in my heart, while I wish he didn't.

I didn't exactly have the opportunity to date boys or even have the guts to do so, especially after Carlos broke my heart. Dating wasn't even allowed in our home. Mami knew I would obey her no dating rule because I was always at home when I wasn't at school. Fortunately for me, at the beginning of my eleventh-grade year, our family was able to afford a computer. It was the first computer we ever owned and I learned to maneuver it very quickly. We even had the Internet, as many families were starting to. I surfed the Internet all the time. I created a screen name for myself when AOL Instant Messenger was the newest thing, and I entered chat rooms to meet people. This was my opportunity to be social while hiding behind my computer screen and taking care of you kids.

One day I went into a chat room and began to chat with a 17-year-old Dominican boy from Washington Heights. We exchanged safe and innocent pictures of ourselves and began chatting on a regular basis. Luckily for me, this was not a scam or a dangerous person. Nick eventually became my boyfriend for the next seven months—after a very reluctant first meeting. This was the beginning of the Internet dating era and although we were two seventeen year olds, we knew the potential danger.

The first time Nick and I met in person was at Port Authority in Manhattan. I frequented the city during my high school years and knew Port Authority very well. Alejandra and Drew, Jr. both still lived in Brooklyn in the same apartment they moved into when they moved to the United States with their mom. I liked to spend time with them and enjoy the city, so at least once or twice per month I rode the Martz bus from our town to Port Authority, which was only about a two-hour ride.

For this particular meeting, I had asked Drew, Alejandra, and Alejandra's big, muscular boyfriend, Walter, to be present just to be on the safe side. Nick must've had the same idea because he arrived with his cousin, Angel.

Nick looked just as cute as he did in his picture. He walked over to embrace me with his baseball player's build—tall and lean. His chest was solid underneath his white, round-neck t-shirt. He wore a Yankees cap with a slight tilt to the side that drew a shadow over his beautiful eyes and pointed nose. I tucked my head under his chin in complete comfort. I looked up at his handsome, hairless face as I pulled away from the hug. His teeth were a perfect solid straight rectangle as he smiled down at me. Instant attraction.

The six of us really hit it off and hung out in the city every other weekend for the next few months. We met up in the city, played pool, walked around at the park, played arcade games, and anything else fairly well-behaved teenagers could think of to do. Nick's parents met mine and talked fairly often.

About two months into our long-distance relationship, I finally told Nick my real name. Skeptical about the chat rooms, I had gone by the name Yesenia. Our brother, sister, and their friends played along with me. Nick and Angel couldn't believe I had kept the lie up so long, and we all laughed it off together. He wasn't even upset about it. He was amused that I had kept it going for as long as I did.

I broke Nick's heart that spring of our senior year. We had both been saying, "I love you" for months like two teenagers who think they're in love. One day I realized, however, that the "L" word was deeper and meant something I simply did not feel. I told him I didn't love him, and it broke his heart. The truth was, I still couldn't shake Carlos off my brain. I loved him and I simply didn't care about anything else. If *love* was anything, that was it.

Nick, Angel, our siblings, and I stayed friends, but only after a minor teenage feud on each of our sides. The six of us had a sweet friendship that none of us was ready to part from, so we all played nice—eventually. Nick was the first boy I'd ever kissed and my first real boyfriend. He was exactly what I needed to help me cope through my Carlos heartache.

≈⑨≈

My high school graduation came and went and I was getting ready for my big move to "the south" to go to college in North Carolina. My feelings for Carlos were still the same. It was summer and I couldn't stand the idea of not saying goodbye to the boy who still had my heart. Two weeks before our moving date, I called him out of the blue to say our last goodbyes; I was very bold and very dramatic about it. I knew how to get what I wanted. I wanted to see him and I had to make my move.

Carlos asked me to come by his house for one last hug. We both figured we'd never see each other again, after all. He was planning on moving to New York City to go to school, and I was moving to North Carolina.

In my heart, I knew this wouldn't be an innocent goodbye. This was a well-thought-out decision. I felt ready to have this experience with him, and this decision was entirely mine. I was in complete control. No one could take this from me. So I lied to Mami that summer afternoon. I asked a friend of mine to take me to Carlos's house and I told Mami I was going to the movie theater. I arrived at his house knowing I would lose my virginity to him that day—and I did.

CHAPTER 15

Cheerwine

Y ou four were all in elementary school when we moved from the dream house in Pennsylvania to North Carolina. Mami and Papi told you it was because I was going to college in North Carolina. This was true, but not the whole truth. You see, I didn't want to move to the south. I wanted to go to school in New York or New Jersey where most of my classmates were going. "Fitting in" was all I strived for and I didn't know anyone moving as far as we were headed.

The truth was, Mami and Papi had been forced to file for bankruptcy on the dream house when they could no longer afford the mortgage payments. They were in over their heads, and despite all of their various jobs, they simply couldn't afford it and all of us. Mami told me we were moving to North Carolina because the homes were cheaper there than in the north—and because her numerologist friend told her it was where our family needed to be.

Mami was very big into numerology back then and took on much of the advice that numerology led her to believe. She told me the name of the school I had to apply to, the reason being that her friend's sister's son was going there and had said it was a great school. Although I was angry and rude about it, I applied like an obedient daughter, while secretly wishing and praying that I didn't get in.

When I thought of life in the south, all I pictured were tumbleweeds in the desert and some farmer in the background with a straw in his mouth. This was not a life I wanted. When my acceptance letter came in the mail, I threw it on the table; I knew that meant I didn't have a choice. None of the acceptance letters to schools I actually wanted to attend mattered. We were moving to North Carolina whether I wanted to or not.

Two weeks prior to my first day of college, our family rented the biggest U-Haul available and we made the trek down Highway 81 South. Papi drove the big U-Haul with Alejandra, Drew, and I as the passengers. Papi drove and I fought for the window seat—not for the view, but because it was the one furthest from him in the confined space. The U-Haul pulled the red pickup truck Papi owned at the time, which was also packed with our things.

Toward the end of our time in the dream house, Mami's brother, Tío Marcos, his wife, and son had moved in with us from Panamá. They too wanted to start a good life and decided to follow us to North Carolina. Tío Marcos drove our family car, the white Ford Explorer, with the rest of our family in it and a few personal items that didn't fit in the truck.

Our family of twelve embarked on this journey all because I got into a college I didn't want to attend in the first place. We would all live together, except for Drew. He was only helping us move and staying for the summer, though even Alejandra had decided to start a new life with us in the south. We went in blind, yet once again hopeful of our future. We had a four-bedroom house waiting for all of us. We had our family and a roof over our heads and that's all that mattered as always.

So, on that July in 2001, the twelve of us made the twenty-three-hour road trip together. We drove slowly, cautiously, and made several bathroom and food break stops. Mami was always prepared and had packed the cooler with sandwiches and snacks to last throughout the trip. We slept as we all traveled to our new home on Newberry Road.

Our new house was quaint. It was a small, split-level single family home that we rented. The entrance to the home was in the midlevel, and when entering through the front door, you would be in the living room. The back entrance put you in the kitchen and dining area. There were six steps to the upstairs, which held three bedrooms and one bathroom. The basement was finished to be a bonus area containing another bedroom and a bathroom. You all probably remember this house the most as you lived there for six years.

Our family of eleven (temporarily twelve, including Drew) all lived in this four-bedroom rental home. We survived off inheritance money that was left to me from our Tía Adriana who passed away when I was eight years old. Tía Adriana had left me ten thousand dollars, which made a significant impact in our lives.

Tía Adriana was Abuelita Minerva's stepsister and had lived in upstate New York for most of her adult life. She lived the American dream and made her investments work for her. She didn't have any living relatives in the States except Mami and me, and although we didn't know her very well, she chose to include Mami and me in her living will, along with the friends she'd made along the years. She passed away while we still lived in New York. I hadn't lost anyone in my life before; hers was the first memorial service I remember attending. I remember twirling in my white-lace dress in the corner of the dimly lit funeral parlor all by myself. I felt pretty because Mami had curled my hair like I had begged her to. I hated my straight wave-less hair. Mami called me over to tell me this was a time to be sad. She walked me over to the casket and introduced me to Tía Adriana. She told me who she was and that she had been sick and passed away.

For ten years, from time to time, Mami asked me to call the lawyer who managed Tía Adriana's estate to ask him for the money before my eighteenth birthday. Any time our family was really hurting for money, or when she wanted to leave Papi, she asked me to call with a new reason. According to Mami, the attorney was a liar and was benefitting from holding onto the money until I turned eighteen.

On my eighteenth birthday, I started my first day of school as a freshman in college.

Alejandra offered to drive me to school and tag along on my first day. She hadn't made up her mind about life post-high school and had some free time on her hands.

During the air conditioning-free thirty-minute drive in Papi's red truck, we decided to grab a drink, as we were both thirsty and not used to the Carolina August heat.

"Let's stop and get a Coke," she said. I agreed. We continued to ride down the highway away from the big city and into a rural part of town toward my new college. We saw what appeared to be an old, locally owned gas station and decided to stop there.

Inside the small, obviously ancient, and dirty station, there stood an old, toothless clerk smacking his lips behind the counter as he scratched at his beard. We were being typical loud, obnoxious teens in our own little world, and walked over to the freezer to grab our Cokes and leave.

"This is the smallest gas station I've ever seen," said Alejandra.

I nodded. "I don't see any Coke in this fridge."

"Go ask the clerk if he has any. It's gotta be here somewhere." Alejandra continued to look in the fridge.

I walked over to the man and asked politely, "Hey, do you have any Coke?"

The man looked up at me, his gray eyes as serious as could be and replied in an accent I had only heard on TV, "I ain't got no Coke, I gots Cheerwine." His thick southern accent threw us off. We giggled out loud before we realized we were being rude.

I cleared my throat in attempt to get serious. "Um, what's Cheerwine?" I asked.

"It's a drank. Y'all want me to ring you up two of 'em?"

Alejandra and I looked at each other and shrugged our shoulders. *What the hell?* I thought. We had to embrace our new southern life. We walked out of there, laughing at the experience and sipping on the strange soda we had bought.

"Who doesn't sell Coke?" I asked. "Where have we moved to?"

I toured the campus for the first time on my first day of class. Alejandra accompanied me while I waited in all of the lines, figured out my schedule, and met some of my professors. When I came home that afternoon, Mami and I called the lawyer to give him our new address to mail the check. We needed the check to give the landlord a six-month advance and to buy food for the family until we landed on our feet. We stretched the almost thirteen thousand dollars (after interest and fees) for six months, which was just enough time for all of the adults in the household to secure stable jobs and steady income.

As we settled into our new lives in the south, I applied for jobs for Mami, Papi, and Tío Marcos. At this point, they could all speak English enough to get by, but couldn't write it and none of them knew how to use a computer. I created résumés, found positions they qualified for, filled out applications for them, and quizzed and prepared them for their job interviews. Papi got a job as a cook at a local, fancy hotel, and Tío Marcos got a job as a busboy at the same hotel.

I had convinced Mami that she didn't need to be a custodian anymore. She could get an administrative position and I would help her with the language barrier. I found her a secretary position at a local school and she got the job! This was a big deal. Mami could wear professional clothes and work daytime hours—what a privilege this was! Tía Sofia learned she was pregnant with their second child soon after our move, so she made plans to babysit a few children once we learned the ropes in our new town.

As a member of the household, I too was responsible for contributing financially and I had to figure out a way. As a college commuter, I first needed to find a way to get to school. When I'd applied to college, we didn't understand the college life system. We were all learning together for the first time as I was the first person in our family to go to college here in the States. All of my friends who had applied to college lived on campus, and the full extent of my understanding was that commuting cost less, and you did not live at school.

The thought of living at a college was strange to our family. Everyone is a commuter in Panamá and living on campus is not an option there. Mami told me tales of how early she would have to wake up to ride the bus to the one university in the city. She left home when it was dark and arrived back home after dark. A thirty-minute drive from our rental home to my new university was nothing compared to her day-long commute to get an education.

We didn't realize it until we arrived that public transportation in North Carolina was nothing like what we were used to while living in the north. The bus line ended about twenty-five miles away from campus and the only trains around were freight trains.

I wasn't able to get a car right away since I didn't have the money for it—or a driver's license. Mami never drove, despite her attempts to learn in the past. So, Papi and Tío Marcos took turns driving me to school, sometimes as early as 6 a.m. before work and picked me up very late, often well after midnight. I wouldn't be able to get a job until I figured out my transportation situation.

I spent time at the student center or clubhouse doing my homework, reading, or writing quietly while I waited for Papi or Tío to pick me up. I mostly daydreamed of moving far away from North Carolina. It became my priority, so much so that I applied to go to college in New York for that Spring semester without Mami's knowledge, and I actually got in. Alejandra had let me borrow money for my application fee with some money she had from a previous job. The two of us made plans to leave the crazy, quiet town we lived in and start our independent lives.

At school, I didn't go out of my way to initiate a friendly conversation with anyone. There was no point. I figured I wasn't going to live here for much longer anyway. I was reserved and ate alone as I sat and read in the student center. I didn't have a meal plan; therefore, I didn't eat in the cafeteria like most of the students did. I occupied my time in between classes by doing homework and writing poetry, a newfound hobby of mine. I'd thought a lot about Carlos after my big move.

An English teacher in high school had once given us an assignment to write a poem about someone special. I wrote a poem about Seli for that assignment, and found to really enjoy writing it. The summer I moved to North Carolina I picked up a pen and wrote my second poem—this time for Carlos. I missed him and needed to get it off my chest.

I love that smile you flash occasionally,
The way you tilt your hat so perfectly,
Those beady eyes when you look at me,
And that sexy birthmark on your cheek.
How you move your head when you hear music beat,
How when I lean against you I feel your heart beat,
How you grip my back and hold me tight,
I wish you could do that every night.
The way you kiss, of that I miss
The way you tugged at my bottom lip.
Talking to you clears my mind,
You are my therapist at times,
How open and comfortable I am with you,
And how you're like that with me, too.

I turned to writing poetry when I was hurting emotionally. I wrote about missing Carlos, my confusion about love, and my heartache. I wrote about my insecurity with the man who took my innocence when I was eight years old and the confusion and disgust I had every day I lived with him. I wrote about feelings I had about hurting myself, and how I would never do it because Mami would be too distraught and you four needed me. I wrote about missing our family in Panamá and wishing I lived there again when life was simple. I wrote about the curiosity and anger I had toward my biological father. I wrote, and wrote, and wrote. I wrote about everything I couldn't say out loud. I very often found myself writing poetry instead of notes during class. Poetry got my angry thoughts out of my mind and, in a way, shared them, even though no one read them or listened. Mami always reminded me not to tell anyone about *him*, so I wrote.

I missed Carlos. I missed Seli. I missed our old house, especially the layout of it. I hated the Newberry Road house. There were only two bathrooms. The one downstairs was the one Tío Marcos and his family used and was way too far from my bedroom. So we used the one upstairs, right across from mine and Alejandra's bedroom and next to Mami and Papi's room. The bathroom had two doors, one from the hall and one from the master bedroom. Two entrances and a window in the shower gave me too much anxiety. These were all ways he could get to me. I took quick showers while peeping behind the curtains and with towels on the small spaces under the doors. Getting dressed every day was an ordeal. I either had to take my clothes into the bathroom and get dressed very quickly or wrap myself in a robe and make a run for it to the bedroom. I wanted to get out of that house and away from Papi. Living with him was driving me crazy.

≈☺≈

One day while eating lunch by myself in the student center and writing quietly, a tall, young, southern gentleman walked over to greet me.

"Well, hello there, young lady."

I was so into my writing, I'd failed to see him approach me. His big, friendly smile shined brightly.

"Hi," I said timidly and smiled back. I closed my notebook immediately. No one had ever read my poems. I'd be so embarrassed if they did.

"I hope I'm not interrupting anything."

"Oh no, it's okay. I was just doing some homework." A little white lie wouldn't hurt anybody.

"Well, okay then…." he said, pausing.

I smiled at him for reassurance.

"I've seen you eat here by yourself for a couple of weeks. I don't know why such a fine young lady like yourself is eating alone. May I join you?" He spoke so proper and as if he was much older than me.

"Sure!" I made room for him at the table, even though he didn't have lunch. He sat with me and asked questions, wanting to learn a little about me. He was the first person I'd met in North Carolina who seemed to care. I answered his questions honestly. It kind of felt good to make a friend. He told me all about how much he loved our campus and how beautiful it was. I agreed. No matter how much I didn't want to be there, it truly was a beautiful school. He was genuine, charming, and something about him was so comforting.

His name was Austin and he played basketball. He knew and was loved by everybody—and I mean everybody. He knew just about every student on that campus. He knew the faculty; he knew the staff. He couldn't walk a full minute without greeting someone, patting them on the back, giving them a friendly handshake, or making a stranger smile. Every chance he got, he made the effort to introduce me to the people he knew around campus. His outlook and attitude was infectious. From that day forward, he always greeted me, and we became great friends. Without realizing it, he made me want to give North Carolina—and that small private university—a chance.

~ 9 ~

A few weeks into my commuter college life, I called Carlos with excitement. "Carlos! Guess what?" I nearly screamed over the phone.

"What?" he asked.

"I'm going up to New York in September!" I was so excited to tell him. I couldn't wait to buy my bus ticket.

"Oh yeah? What brings you here?" he said so uncaringly. I carried on with my excitement.

"You know how I applied to CUNY? I got in! I got the letter in the mail today. You're the first person I'm telling!" I didn't let him get a word in. I carried on, barely catching my breath. "Well, it's not like I can really tell anyone else besides Alejandra, but I got in! Aghhhhh!" I silently screamed in excitement while trying to keep my voice down. I couldn't let the family hear me.

"Oh, okay," he said indifferently.

His reaction was so disappointing. I was madly in love with this boy who determined my joy. When I felt helpless and defeated about my situation, I thought of him and it immediately made me happy. He was all I wanted to think about and I looked forward to our weekly talks. I wanted nothing but to reunite with him and feel his touch again. Just a hug or a kiss would suffice my yearning for him.

"When are you thinking about coming?" he asked, as if he was obligated to continue our conversation.

I quickly realized that my feelings for him weren't mutual. I could tell in his tone. I decided to downplay my visit. It was my only option to protect my feelings.

"Well, I want to go up there with Alejandra. We want to check out some places to see where we want to live. We may go visit our cousin, Nora… who knows?" I said. My tone was now casual.

I continued. "I just wanted to let you know just in case I had some time, maybe we could meet up." I sighed.

"Well, would we do what we did the last time we saw each other?" he asked, finally expressing some excitement.

"What do you mean, like have sex?" I asked, with disbelief.

"Well, yeah." he said.

I let out another sigh. He continued to let me down.

"I don't think I want to do that again. I don't know how I'll feel when I see you," I said.

"Well, Olivia… If we're not going to do it, then I don't think we should see each other," he said.

There was a long pause after he said that. I had no words.

The next thing I knew I felt steady teardrops falling on my thighs. I didn't want to let him know I was crying, but it was nearly impossible.

"Okay, like ever again?" I said, while trying to keep my voice steady.

"Yeah." He was so firm with his brutal words.

"Okay. Bye." I whispered.

"Goodbye."

We didn't speak on the phone after that and I tried to cope with the fact that I would never see him again. He wasn't interested in me. He was interested in my *body*. This felt like total rejection. I was completely heartbroken.

Alejandra and I ended up going on our trip to New York later that year, but we realized that living in New York was only a dream. We couldn't afford it. We weren't ready that year, but we made plans to simply defer it and not give up on it completely.

≈◎≈

A few weeks into school I met a man who was also a commuter during a meeting at school who offered me rides back and forth. Hank was an older white man, short, skinny, with thinning hair and a big mole on his scalp. He was kind and offered me free rides even though I'd offer him gas money, but he made me feel uncomfortable. He often complimented me on my looks. I don't think he intended to be as creepy as I found him to be, but after my previous experiences, all older men were molesters in my mind. His willingness to drive me for most of my freshman year of college allowed me to get my first legal, legit job near home, save money, and buy a car.

I got my driver's license the first day of my sophomore year and I drove my 1995 Nissan Sentra to class the remainder of my college career. I never spoke to Hank again. I hated that I dropped his friendship suddenly, but being friends with an older man was more than I could handle emotionally. Austin once asked me if Hank and I were dating, and the thought of it made me sick. I wondered how many other people believed the same.

College was a time during which I had to be very focused. I was on a mission to graduate in four years; the longer I stayed, the more expensive it would be and I couldn't afford that luxury. I got a job at a seafood restaurant during the second semester of my freshman year and also found other side jobs to help pay for my tuition. I was an adult living in the house, which meant I had to help pay bills. Juggling multiple jobs is what our family knew best. I gave Mami and Papi checks to help pay rent, gas money for their cars, groceries, utilities, etc. If any of you four needed anything for school, I bought it. If I needed anything for school, I bought that, too. I drove Mami to work before the one-hour commute to my eight o'clock class. Mami worked in the city, farther away from my school. Then in the afternoon, I left class, picked Mami up, took her home, went to work, then went home to do my homework. I slept very little, just enough to keep me going. If any of you had doctor's appointments, orthodontist appointments, afterschool activities, or so forth, I fit those into my schedule to make it work. Papi had multiple restaurant jobs that were important to maintain. Work was his main priority and as the primary breadwinner, his role and time was the most important.

At school, I made monthly visits to the big, fancy financial aid building that overlooked the gorgeous water fountain on our campus. I didn't appreciate how beautiful it was at the time. The building simply looked intimidating to me. I walked over every month with checkbook in hand as I paid for school.

One day while writing out my check, I engaged in conversation with a student who worked in the building. She took my check and wrote out my receipt while the full-time University staff member was on a lunch break.

I'll never forget how she asked so nonchalantly, "Why don't you just ask your dad to pay for your tuition?" I looked at her with the most bewildered look. She didn't know my life or our situation. She didn't even know if I had a dad. *She's so ignorant,* I thought to myself.

I hid my thoughts behind my smile as I said, "He can't."

When I left the building I immediately called Mami to tell her what had just happened. We thought it was so hilarious that someone would say that.

"Haha…" I laughed, "As if Papi could afford to pay my tuition…."

No one I went to school with knew our situation at home. They didn't know we fit twelve people into a four-bedroom house. They didn't know what it took to maintain our family. They had no idea that you four sometimes waited for me in the student lounge area while I was in class, because I had scheduled dentist appointments for you guys for the first break I got in my day. They didn't know the reason I fell asleep in class was because I only slept about four hours a night—if I was lucky. I fell asleep at the wheel on my way to school almost every morning.

My college social life was almost non-existent, though I got by just enough to feel like I got the gist of it all. I made a few friends along the way, but they didn't seem to get my life—our life. They invited me to events and parties and were disappointed when I couldn't go. Every minute of my day was planned. I have to admit I was a little envious of their lives. They went to school, played sports, went to parties, had lots of friends, had down time. I didn't have any of that.

Other students seemed to know more about college life than I did. I didn't know the difference between a subsidized loan vs. an unsubsidized loan, despite the financial aid staff who attempted to educate me. I couldn't even figure out how students got jobs on campus. It seemed like every time I asked, they were already taken up. An on-campus job would've been so convenient for me.

And how did students already seem to know what a fraternity or a sorority was? I had to get someone to explain it to me. How did people have time for all those extracurricular activities? Who was paying for their tuition? I had scholarships and *still* had to pay tuition. *And why in the heck would people toilet paper the school during homecoming?* What a waste of toilet paper! I felt so sorry for the janitors, I once helped them clean up the campus. Some of the students' actions honestly baffled me. How did the other students know about college things that I didn't? We were all in this together. I was smart and had the grades to prove it. Plus, at this point in my life, I had lived in the States longer than I had lived in Panamá. Why didn't information just come naturally like it seemed to come to them?

CHAPTER 16

Your Car
or Mine?

I t was my sophomore year in college and Austin invited
me to a party that his fraternity was hosting. He was
one of my closest friends and always tried to get me to
participate in school activities. This one was at the school's
gymnasium. I happened to be off work that night and I
decided to go. I thought I was hot stuff. I wore my white
capri pants, an orange and white Baby Phat brand tank top
that I bought at a discount store, and my white Skechers. I
curled my hair and tied it back in a tight ponytail like J.Lo
would wear and drove down to campus for the second time
that day.

I walked into the gym and found a young man sitting at the
six-foot wooden table just up ahead. The boy was thin under his
large, blue, Greek-lettered t-shirt, and loose-fitting jeans. He
had short, black hair that was combed forward and his eyes were
hazelnut brown and welcoming. His skin was my complexion
with a few freckles speckled over his nose and cheeks.

He quickly looked me up and down as I strolled toward him

continuing to take in his physique. He cracked a quick, bright smile at me in acknowledgement of the mutual attraction.

"Hi," I said confidently.

"Hey, how are you?"

"Fine," I said with a reciprocated smile.

He looked down at the small metal box on the table. I quickly realized he was charging for entry.

"What's the fee to get in?" I asked.

He looked back up at me and flashed his smile again. "Don't worry about it."

He reached for the marker on the table and held out his hand for mine. I extended my hand and placed it in his as he marked it and granted me access into the party. A warm feeling flowed through me as my hand laid in his.

"There you go," he said, smiling back up at me.

"Thanks," I replied and began to walk toward the loud music coming from around the corner.

"Hey! I'm Raymond. What's your name?" he called.

"Olivia."

"Nice to meet you, Olivia. Have a good time."

Raymond was *cute*—cute enough for me to look him up in the yearbook the next day and find out his full name: Raymond Elliot Carter. I was just curious and felt like I needed to know it, even though I never did anything with it. Though I *did* remember it, for some reason. It just kind of rolled off my tongue. I knew this handsome boy's name and that he was a senior, but I realized I would likely never see him again, and didn't throughout the remainder of my time in college.

༄ ༄ ༄

I dated two boys in college, each relationship lasting about two years. Michael was originally my rebound from Carlos.

He was from New York and reminded me of my home ties. He was nothing like Carlos. Michael was black and a running back for our school's football team. I was immediately drawn to his confidence and so were other women. We dated off and on in an unhealthy manner, mostly fond of each other's company and friendship.

I began my relationship with Reginald immediately after Michael and I ended things for good. I met Reggie at the seafood restaurant and spent almost every evening with him as we worked together. Reggie had a darker complexion and a muscular build. He played basketball and worked on cars in his spare time. Although Mami didn't like it, she understood that as a college student, it was okay to date. She didn't like any of my boyfriends, but liked Reggie the least as she felt he lacked ambition. Truthfully, I saw it, too. Still he was the sweetest boyfriend to me and I didn't mind that he didn't want to go to college.

≈ 9 ≈

After four hard years, the day of my college graduation finally came. Mami and Papi threw me a party that I put together. (I guess party planning has always been kind of my thing.) I found and secured the venue, sent out the invites, provided input on the menu, decorated the room with help from the four of you, and Mami and Papi cooked and footed most of the bill. I remember feeling so strange that morning. All of the family rode down to campus much later, after me. I drove myself and rode in complete silence for the full thirty-minute ride. I wanted to reflect on my college journey.

❦

My four years in college were the hardest working years of my life. There was always so much going on with our family. Mami had serious medical problems, two strokes, and countless seizures. Amelia had one surgery and lived with epilepsy. I worked several jobs while maintaining full-time student status in order to graduate in four years. Alejandra joined the army. Tío Marcos moved out of the Newberry Road home with his family. And Papi drowned himself in work and Bacardi.

Everything fell on Mami and me. Mami couldn't drive because of her epilepsy, so I drove the family around everywhere. She worked and used all of her energy to do the best she could. At night, I helped her by translating forms in her administrative role so she could take them back to work the next day.

Two weeks prior to my graduation, I quit all of my jobs. Over the course of my college career, I had been a shift manager at the seafood restaurant; an assistant manager at a video store; a teacher's assistant; a tutor; a baby sitter; a pet sitter; and I washed laundry for a local daycare center. I'm probably forgetting other odd jobs right now, but trust me when I say I was pretty busy. Somewhere along the way, I decided to save up enough money to live off of for a few months, so I could enjoy the summer before I joined what people called the "real world." I planned to work as hard as I could and take time off, starting in May of my senior year. Around the same time I quit all my jobs, I also ended my relationship with Reggie.

My drive to campus on that warm May day felt so strange. I felt so free. I hadn't been accepted into the one competitive psychology graduate program I'd applied to. I didn't have a job in my field lined up. I didn't have *any* job, but I wasn't worried. It felt so free for the first time in a long time.

I pulled into campus and parked in the gravel commuter parking lot for the last time. I walked alone to the designated area and stood in line, waiting to be given instructions. I watched other excited seniors in decorated caps and gowns standing in crowds with friends. They spoke of travel plans, moving out, graduate school plans, and jobs. In the parking lot, a bright red Chevy adorned with a big, yellow bow awaited a lucky new graduate, likely a surprise gift from the proud parents of a privileged adult child. I stood alone, in my plain black gown, waiting quietly by myself for my name so I could get the hell away from there.

Walking across that stage didn't feel like the beginning of my adult life. It wasn't joyous, exciting, or scary like the other graduates around me were describing. It represented the end of a bad era for me. I was angry. I felt held back. I felt tired. I regretted not taking full advantage of the college experiences the kids around me talked about and were already missing.

But maybe now, I could be free. I had done what I needed to do. I had made Mami proud by becoming a college graduate. She had always told me she would've become a psychologist if she'd been given the choice. Now here I was, a psychology major, wanting Mami to live that vicariously through me. My moment was finally here. My name was called, and I walked across that stage to get the expensive piece of paper that symbolized achievement, success, and progression. To me it symbolized a larger earning potential for our family. Now I could get a well-paying job, move out, and live on my own, but make enough money to still contribute to the family. But today and the next few weeks, I would enjoy freedom. No work, no relationships—just me, Mami, and the four of you.

The summer after college was a summer well-spent. I took two fun trips visiting my best friends—Saheli, and Austin. When I got back, you four and I had a blast and did fun things while Mami worked during the day. I bought our family season passes to the local theme park where we went to every day we could. We spent our days at the pool, and tried new restaurants together. Even getting ice cream was an adventure and a treat. I knew all of this freedom couldn't last forever, so I worked on my résumé and became proactive in looking for a job in my field. I sent out my résumé to twenty-one companies.

That same summer, hurricane Katrina hit the Gulf of Mexico pretty hard. It was devastating watching people suffer through that disaster from the comfort of our home. I felt guilty watching the pleas for help on television and so I followed my heart. I picked up the phone and volunteered to go down to Louisiana to help. Days later and against Mami's wishes, I left for three weeks. Luckily, I was still good friends with Michael and Reggie. Although they didn't know each other, they appreciated our relationship and the work I was being called to do. I left them my car keys, you guys' schedule, and a list of designated duties. While I was away, they took on my responsibilities of transporting Mami daily to and from work. They went grocery shopping and ran the errands you all needed.

When I got back after three weeks, I got a call for a job with a non-profit agency that worked with people with disabilities, and I took it. It was a clinical position where I would get to use my new degree. I was excited and welcomed the opportunity.

Everything seemed to be falling into place. All I had to do was tell Mami I wanted to move out and get my own apartment. When I told her, however, she told me I couldn't leave her. She was still unhappy and wanted to start a new life without *him*. We didn't need him anymore. We were U.S. Residents. The four of you understood Mami and Papi were unhappy and Mami and I both had well-paying jobs. All of the stars had aligned waiting for this very moment, so we began to devise a plan to move out without Papi's knowledge.

⇌ 9 ⇌

I had been working for the non-profit agency for three months, making good money but not enough to support our family of six if Mami was to really follow through this time. Against everything in my being, I asked for my job back at the seafood restaurant. I hated that I had to go back to working two full-time jobs, but I only did it for the four of you. Even though I hated working eighty-hour weeks, it was exactly where I needed to be since that's how I met Raymond Elliot Carter again.

I was back at the seafood restaurant, working to make the money for the apartment we never moved to when Raymond came into the restaurant. He was just as handsome as the day I met him in that gymnasium. I took his order. He was polite and friendly and he gifted me his cute, quick smile before he left. I wondered if he remembered meeting me years ago. He winked softly as he grinned to one side. His brown eyes were soft and gentle.

I smiled back.

Raymond came by frequently after that day. The girls I worked with noticed our flirty interaction and would always call me to take his order when they saw him walking in or heard his voice through the drive thru intercom system. They always pretended to be doing something else as they stepped back to watch Raymond and I engage in a quick, friendly conversation. I didn't mind. I enjoyed the rare attempt at privacy and the attention from the girls picking on me after he walked away.

After several weeks of harmless flirting, he reached out to me on MySpace, having come across my page through a mutual friend's—or so he said. He worked his full-time career as a booking agent during the day and a part-time job in the evening, similar to me. His part-time job was in the same shopping center as the seafood restaurant, which is why he often stopped by for dinner. We messaged each other back and forth and he invited me out to catch up.

We were supposed to grab a casual bite to eat on our mutual night off, but our casual meet up turned into dinner plans when a meeting I had got pushed back. We agreed to meet at his place since he lived on the way to where we were headed. I only agreed to meet him there because I knew he wasn't a serial killer. Austin had vouched for him.

I pulled my car into a parking space and texted him that I was downstairs. He came down and around the corner in his fitted, stonewashed jeans and black turtleneck. He also wore a gold rope chain with a letter 'R' charm hanging from it. As he walked over to me, I remember thinking his style was different from my ex-boyfriends, but that was probably a good thing. He greeted me with a big hug. This was the first time we had really seen each other without a counter space or a table in between us. His hug was comforting and felt right. It seemed long overdue.

"Do you want to take your car or mine?" he asked. He looked over at his 1993 Chevy Blazer and back at my newer 2000 Nissan Altima. My six-year-old car was the more reliable between the two. I had just recently upgraded from my Sentra only two weeks before our date. He almost seemed embarrassed by his older vehicle.

"Let's take yours," I said. I didn't care what kind of car he drove. So, we got in his truck and headed toward the restaurant we had chosen nearby.

As we were pulling into the restaurant, his truck shut off completely. It was parked at a forty-five-degree angle halfway into the space in the middle of backing it in. After several failed attempts to restart it, he sighed in embarrassment and asked if I would mind getting in the driver's seat and steering the truck while he jumped out and pushed it . I didn't mind.

We went inside and he called a tow truck. He assured me we would carry on with our evening after he secured a ride back to my car and he kept his word. We carried on our conversation and getting to know each other and before we knew it; the waiters and waitresses were waiting for us to leave. The chairs were on top of the tables around us and all had been cleared off and cleaned except ours. Neither one of us had noticed all of this going on around us. We were so into each other.

Raymond mesmerized me. He was confident, genuine, and was a true gentleman. He worked two jobs like I did to make ends meet. He was truly independent and wasn't living off his parents like many people I knew. He didn't judge me when I told him I still lived at home with our family. Rather, he acknowledged and respected my hard work. He was engaged in our conversation and heard every word I said to him. I felt comfortable enough to be myself. This wasn't something that was easy for me, it usually took time.

Raymond and I couldn't get enough of each other after that night. We spoke throughout the day, exchanged multiple e-mails, called, and texted after work. In the evenings, he would come visit me at work or eat dinner with me at the restaurant during my break. I would clock out for thirty minutes just to sit with him; this was a big deal because it was unpaid time. When I couldn't take a break, he would eat alone in the dining area just to be close to me. Sometimes I would call him to tell him I was going to take a break, and he would let me know he was already at the traffic light to turn into the parking lot of the seafood restaurant.

After work, I would come by to visit him at his condo. We were inseparable. I don't know how we weren't sick of each other. There was very little time we spent apart during our time off of work. The funny thing about it all is that although we both treated our relationship seriously, I was not willing to label it as such. Raymond asked me several times to be his girlfriend and I turned him down. I explained I was a busy person. I had to work to help our family, and our family depended on me. I didn't have time to be tied down to a boyfriend and it would be unfair to him. Unbeknownst to him, I was exclusive with him from the day we went on our first date. I called the few other people I had been casually spending time with and told them I wanted to pursue a relationship with a new person in my life. He had no idea I viewed us seriously, even though I didn't want a label.

I gave in one night after we both got off work. This particular night we both got off around the same time. I waited for him in the parking lot of the shopping center where we both worked and asked him to share a milkshake with me. We sipped on the cookies and cream treat and I asked him if he would be my boyfriend. He said 'yes' and introduced me to his mom the following weekend.

Raymond was raised by a single mother. She was the most significant person he could ever introduce me to. He had arranged for us to meet at the local Waffle House for breakfast that Saturday morning, one of their usual breakfast favorites. I wore a pair of nice fitted jeans, and a blue and black striped collared shirt. I wore my hair down and had blown it out myself. I nervously drove to the restaurant where they were waiting for me to arrive. I introduced myself to her and we hit it off great. We now laugh about that day and how I ordered a meal that came in three plates. The meal I ordered took up all the space at our table—I didn't hold back. I liked to eat and I didn't hide it. I wanted to be myself and be comfortable with her, too.

It was time to introduce Raymond to the big, crazy family I had been telling him about all along. I knew I couldn't introduce him to all of you at once. He grew up as an only child in an impeccable home, just him and his mother. Our family is chaotic and absolutely not what he was used to.

I decided to introduce him to our family in doses and started with the girls first. Do you girls remember that day? Carrie, you were about thirteen years old, Celeste, you were eleven, and Amelia, you were ten. I drove you to the park and asked Raymond to meet us there. It was a beautiful spring day, it was perfect. We played Frisbee. He liked you girls, and you all seemed to like him back. He got a good glimpse into the three of you because you were each yourselves. Carrie, you were sarcastic and skeptical. Celeste, you were full of energy and bombarded Raymond with questions. And Amelia, you were your usual intuitive and reserved self.

I took him back to the park on a different day, but this time to meet our brother, John. We brought a football this time. We played a game in which whoever caught the football had to tell a part of a story that we made up just for fun. We laughed at how silly our story turned out to be. John was comfortable around Raymond. He was twelve at the time and seemed to enjoy having another boy around, since the girls usually outnumbered him.

Mami and Papi were the next ones in line. Since Raymond and Mami worked only minutes apart from each other, I figured a lunch meet up was ideal. I planned to take a long lunch that day and I swung by Raymond's job to pick him up and then to Mami's job to pick her up. We arrived and went inside to surprise her. Mami loved him from the start and Raymond looked great that day. He had on khakis, a pale pink, tucked-in polo shirt, a chestnut leather belt, and matching dress shoes. He looked just as handsome as ever and gave an excellent first impression. Mami walked him around her office, proudly showing off her daughter's new boyfriend. She hadn't done this with any other boys I'd introduced her to before. Raymond was independent, educated, and a young professional. I knew she liked him and that I had done well. Raymond won her and her co-workers over with the smile that had captured my heart all those years ago in the gym.

I caught Papi off guard when I introduced him to Raymond. I brought Raymond by the house and he walked up to Papi, gave him a firm handshake as he introduced himself, and was respectful. Papi shook his hand back and carried on with his work on the car in the driveway. Papi liked to intimidate other boys I brought by the house. He didn't do this to Raymond. Raymond demanded respect with his mere presence. He was the alpha.

We fell fast and hard and we were in love.

CHAPTER 17

No Means No?

Mami chose to stay with Papi time and time again. Their relationship was one that I didn't understand at the time. She was unhappy and vocal about it. Fortunately, the rest of the world was oblivious to our dysfunctional household. For reasons I hope you understand now, I had to get out of that house when I did. April 16, 2006 was the last time I'd try to help Mami escape, or so I thought at the time. Exactly 139 days later, I chose *my* happiness. I moved in with Raymond. This was the first relationship I had been in that was mature and balanced. He brought me joy and I trusted him fully.

Raymond was in the music and entertainment business when we began dating and had been back before we met at the party in the university's gym.

Since graduating, event season for him meant working double shifts six days a week for seven months of the year. As an entertainment booking agent, the beginning of spring up until about the middle fall was the busiest time of year due to outdoor events. He planned events during the day and dropped in on them at night. He told me my company made work more pleasant for him. I loved Raymond, so I tagged along with him to every event I could in an effort to spend as much time with him as possible.

One day we were on our way to a summer concert series on the snooty side of town, about forty-five minutes away. About five minutes into the drive, I decided it was time to share my most painful memory with him.

"Can I tell you something?" I asked nervously.

"Sure, baby," he replied, focusing on the road.

"You have to promise not to say anything. Do you promise to keep it to yourself?"

Raymond looked worried. "Okay?" he replied curiously while still looking ahead at the road.

"My dad…" I began, "He hurt me. It was a long time ago…." I proceeded to tell him about the biggest worry of my life.

I blurted out my grief, sparing him the awful details. Mami was the one other person who knew *everything* I shared with Raymond that day. No other boyfriend before him knew anything. Not even Saheli knew everything. I trusted Raymond. For the first time in my life I felt like someone cared enough to protect me and my secrets.

To me, knowing my secret meant holding it and not acting on it. It meant understanding the complexity of our situation and not trying to solve my family's biggest worry. It meant keeping any judgment aside and understanding that Papi would continue to be in my life despite our past. These are the agreements I asked of him.

I didn't realize at the time that it was such a tall ask. But how could I have known this was a lot to ask for? This was my norm.

I had shared my biggest burden and I felt relief in sharing it with someone I loved and trusted. Raymond now carried that weight with me and he agreed to my terms. Still, something changed after I told him that story. It didn't happen immediately, but over time. Raymond was with me every time Papi was around me. He was present every Sunday when we spent time together as a family. Raymond held my secret and did just what I had asked of him that day, but he also took it upon himself to become my protector. And he did this in his own manner. Papi—as well as the rest of our family—knew that Raymond had my back and he wasn't going anywhere. With Raymond around, I felt powerful, strong, safe, and protected.

Life felt good for once. I had everything I wanted. I had graduated from college. I only had one job, my career. After April 16 had come and gone and Mami chose to stay with Papi, I no longer needed to work at the seafood restaurant. After moving in with Raymond, I kept my word to Mami about maintaining my responsibilities despite not living at home with you all.

≈◎≈

I now lived with my boyfriend who loved me and understood I had responsibilities outside of our relationship. Mami had to be at work at 7 a.m. and I had to be at work at 8 a.m. I'd wake up extra early to pick Mami up by 6:30 a.m. to drive into town and drop her off on time. I then drove back home, showered, and got ready to go to work which was only a ten- to fifteen-minute commute for me. Mami got off work at 4 p.m. just like me and she didn't mind waiting. I'd leave at 4 p.m. every weekday to drive into Uptown Charlotte to pick her up. I didn't want her to wait long. I always felt like her co-workers disapproved of me picking her up late, as if I were some lazy kid. I imagined them thinking, 'Here's this poor lady who works hard to support her kids and she can't drive because of her seizures, and to top it all off, her daughter is always late to pick her up.' They probably weren't thinking that, but I felt guilty about picking her up late anyway.

From there, I'd drop Mami off at home, then head to mine and Raymond's place and have dinner on the table by 6:30 p.m. when he walked through the door. My agenda planner was marked all over the place. I was determined to make everything work. I was determined not to miss a band concert, parent/teacher conference, field day, awards ceremony, open house, doctor's appointment, or anything for you four or for Mami. I would have dinner ready every day for my supportive boyfriend. I would pack him his lunch every day, too. And I was going to be home on the couch next to him by 8 p.m. with few exceptions.

Raymond knew from the beginning Mami and you four were my priority. So he made you guys his top priority as well. He came along to school events, graduations, and anything else where he felt I could use his support. He even offered to take Mami to work on mornings he noticed were difficult for me. If I were stuck at work or doing something for my church volunteer group, he would offer to take Mami to the grocery store or take you to buy a last-minute school item. I used to take John to get his haircut at the barbershop every two weeks and he offered to start cutting his hair to save me time and money. He even offered to cut Papi's hair too. Although he was disgusted by what Papi had done to me, he didn't let on to anyone about it. He pretended everything was normal, just like me, just *for* me.

Sundays at Mami and Papi's house became a thing. By this time, you all had moved to a new dream house on Fancy Road—the house Mami chose over the two-bedroom apartment I offered her. Raymond and I came over every Sunday. He would cut Papi and John's hair. I would straighten Mami and you girls' hair. I was jealous of all your curls, so Mami curled mine.

He understood my financial responsibility and knew that Christmas was about the four of you. He knew I bought your school supplies every year, and he knew birthdays and holidays were a big deal in our family. Raymond was the first person I ever dated who became invested in our family. He shared the work with me. We were a true team. He genuinely cared about you guys and he loved me. My responsibilities were *our* responsibilities. I didn't feel alone anymore.

"Why doesn't your dad help out more?" he would ask. He didn't seem to understand our family dynamic.

"He's working," I'd respond.

"But you work, too. What happens if you just can't drive them somewhere?" he wondered out loud.

"Well… My family wouldn't be able to go anywhere," I responded, as if it weren't obvious.

"I'm sure they would figure out another way," he said. And just like that, he planted a seed in my brain that what I was doing could be optional and not mandatory. What *if* I woke up and simply got ready for work without having to wake up extra early to drive Mami to her job? What if I came home directly from work and cooked dinner and spent time with my boyfriend before eight or nine o' clock every night? What if I didn't have to check in with Mami and you guys' schedule before committing to hours with my volunteer group? What if I could tag along to a networking event with Raymond or a concert that he had to attend for work without checking with all of you first? Was that even possible? And so, I tried it.

I'd never told Mami 'no' before the day I finally did. It began with small favors. "Olivia, can you take me to the grocery store?" she asked.

"Is Papi home?" I replied.

"Yes, but he's sleeping."

"Sorry," I said. "Maybe you can wait for him to wake up and take you. I'm not going to be able to."

Another time, Mami asked me to take her to the doctor. When I said 'no,' she responded with, "You know it's hard because he's working. You understand the doctor better than him or me. You ask the right questions, and I don't want your father there with me. I want you."

"I'm working too, Mami," I replied. "I can't. I'm sorry."

From that point forward, I occasionally told her 'no' if it didn't have something to do with you four and if Papi was available, especially if it was a matter that I felt was something a husband should be present for such as doctor's appointments, which were still frequent enough.

If it was about the four of you, however, my answer was always 'yes.' If there was an appointment, afterschool activity, volunteer at a school field trip, overnight camping trip, open house, parent/teacher conference, or one of you got sent home from school sick, my answer was always 'yes.'

Back then, Mami and Papi saw Raymond as a negative influence in my life at times, but that was just because I learned to say 'no' to them for the first time in my life. Raymond had my best interest at heart and I recognized it. He gave me something I'd wanted to feel for a long time: *confidence*. My power was taken from me at a young age and his love and support gave it back to me, little by little.

Raymond helped me to realize that Mami had chosen Papi. She *chose* him, but she still *wanted* me. Saying 'no' eventually became easier. I was still angry at her and I wanted the four of you to ask me for favors directly if you needed me. Carrie and John were in high school and Celeste and Amelia were in middle school at the time. You were old enough to know and tell me what you needed. If Mami called to ask me to do something for one of you, occasionally I'd be angry that the request came from her. I was angry that she always seemed to be in between us. I wouldn't say no to any of you. You four were my world. If anything, I had only survived because I wanted to keep you safe, and wanted to set a good example for you four. I owed you four my life. But Mami? I didn't owe her anything—I had already given her everything.

The crazy part was that my saying 'no' brought Mami and Papi together. They figured things out. Papi stepped up after some arguing and fighting against it, but he did it. He even started taking and picking Mami up from work on days when I wasn't available to do so. I slowly started to break free.

~⑨~

Working in the entertainment business, Raymond was often invited to events and networking opportunities. I became more comfortable accepting invitations from Raymond without feeling so obligated to our family for the first time in my life. I told you all to call me if there was something you absolutely needed or if there was a place you needed to be and Papi couldn't take you or you couldn't find a ride with a friend. I felt guilty about it at first, but freedom felt sweeter. Raymond had made arrangements with his schedule to always be there for me and our family, and I was finally able to bend my schedule to be there for him.

I still saw you all almost every day. If I wasn't there to give rides, Mami and Papi would cook and invite us over for dinner in exchange for a favor. Papi often asked Raymond for help with the computer or whatever piece of equipment he was struggling with. Papi liked to try to fix any appliance, car, or any gadget to cut costs from hiring a professional. And Mami still came home almost every day with work she couldn't complete as it required her to translate forms from Spanish into English and she didn't have the skill to do it. Eventually I began to ask her to start relying on you guys for this and I held her accountable to try to improve her English with classes I'd bring her to. The relationship between Raymond and I continued to blossom beautifully. He supported me and I supported him.

≈ 9 ≈

"Olivia, Mami won't stop crying, I don't know what to do!" Carrie sniffled over the phone one day.

"Where is she?" I asked

"She's in the living room, on the couch. Can you come over?"

I walked in to find Mami in the living room of the Fancy Road house. She was crying uncontrollably and was inconsolable. You three girls greeted me at the door with tearful eyes from watching Mami cry in pain from something unknown.

"No puedo mas con el," she wept desperately. "I just can't anymore."

I immediately knew it had to do with Papi and I grew angry. I wasn't angry at him, I was angry at *her.* She continued in Spanish, saying words that were hard to understand, as she couldn't catch her breath in between her cries.

And then our mother said words she had never said before in her life—and I knew she meant them.

"Me quiero morir, Olivia! Ya no lo aguanto mas."

The words stung deeply, as I had never before heard our mother beg for death. She couldn't stand him any longer. I knew she needed to leave.

I told you girls to go upstairs so I could talk to Mami privately. You didn't need to see her this way. Mami began to talk freely. She told me she had made a mistake in staying with Papi. She feared he was unfaithful even still and his drinking and smoking was bothering her more than before. She told me they argued that his smoking was affecting her health and they argued over it frequently because he wouldn't quit for her. They argued so much so, that Amelia had made him a no smoking sign and placed it on their bedroom door. She was the youngest and the boldest of us all. Mami vented more and at the end of the conversation, we agreed to go see a therapist.

Lately, during neurologist appointments, Mami had used her time as therapy sessions. Her neurologist referred her to a therapist because he feared she suffered from depression. Mami dismissed the diagnosis and said depression wasn't a real thing. She wondered how she could possibly be depressed now at this time of her life when she had endured so much more stress in the past.

I went with Mami to multiple appointments in which they assessed her state and officially diagnosed her. The doctors explained to me that Mami was not in the right state of mind to make the best decisions for her health. She agreed to always consult me before making health-related decisions, and I was also the appointed person to make decisions for her health in the event she couldn't be consulted, such as when she underwent medical procedures.

It was around this time that Mami decided family therapy may do her some good. We attended one session all together—do you guys remember that day? Papi drove all of you, and I met you guys there one weekday afternoon. The seven of us sat there in the crowded room to meet a tall, thin, brown-haired white lady. We were all there for Mami. Mami began to cry and say things that didn't make sense to anyone but Papi and me. She spat out that this was all her fault. In between sobs and snot, she explained that her seizures were due to stress and that we stressed her out. She said I was rude to her because I was angry about what happened to me a long time ago. The rest of us sat quietly watching Mami's breakdown. Papi removed you all from the room when instructed by the therapist.

Before I knew it, it was just the therapist, Mami, and me in the room, though it felt just as crowded with Mami's ambush of attacks. She told the therapist about what Papi did to me. She unloaded about what we didn't ever talk about and I didn't realize she carried it like I did. She'd never said a word before, not since it happened. Mami told her she always felt guilty and tried to please me in any way she could. She didn't understand why I took my anger out on her. She cooked me my favorite meals when she could, and tried to buy me things she knew I wanted when she could afford it. This was Mami's way of making it up to me.

I had constantly yelled at her, despite her sensitivity and health. The truth of the matter was that her poor health was what was keeping her in my life. I wanted nothing more than to get away from Mami and Papi both. Our most recent argument had been about John.

I was driving home from work when Mami had called and asked me to go talk to John. Mami complained about John getting a bad grade at school and asked me to talk to him and punish him. She couldn't get through to him and didn't have the energy. I heard her go on for about five minutes. She was being dramatic and I just started crying as I was driving and then I lost my patience. I started yelling frantically. You know that high-pitched, raspy yelling? The kind of yelling where you wonder later whether you made any sense or not? It was *that* kind of yelling.

"I just want to be their sister, Mami!" I shouted. "I can't do this anymore! I am *so* sick and tired of you calling me for everything. Why can't you and Papi just handle it? Leave me alone! I just want to go home. I had a bad day and all I want to do is go home to Raymond and cook dinner. Why can't Papi do anything? Tell *him* to talk to John!"

"John isn't going to listen to your dad," she said. "You know your dad is just going to say something crazy like, 'no TV for a year,' and John isn't going to take him seriously. I'm so tired from work. I don't feel well."

I continued yelling. I hated when she threw her illness in my face.

"Well whose fault is it that the kids don't listen to Papi?" I screamed. "You always taught us to hide things from him and lie to him. We always told him we had to pay for school lunch when we had free lunch, just so you could take his money and plan an escape you were too much of a coward to make. You always make faces when he talks, so we learned not to respect him. You always told us not to bother him or talk to him!"

I hung up the phone, made a U-turn, and headed to the house to punish my brother.

Mami always seemed to call me over Papi. We were a better team than she and Papi ever were. Whether John got called to the principal's office at school, or Carrie got bullied on the bus, Papi was never involved. Or when Celeste got into a fight with the neighbor's daughter, or Amelia required constant medical appointments and hospital visits and getting picked up early from school when she wasn't feeling well. It was never-ending and always something.

I barely said a word during that therapy session, but Mami was right. I was furious with her, I just wasn't prepared to talk about it. Not that day. Not even when I realized that we'd both wanted to end our lives, though at different times, all because of the same man. We'd uprooted our lives years ago for him and he made us hate our lives to the point we couldn't bear to live anymore. Things were never as they seemed for us. From the outside looking in, no one had any idea what was really going on.

Mami eventually stopped seeing the psychologist, as she never did believe she was depressed. I only became angrier with her when I learned she was skipping her medication. She would tell me that she couldn't afford it since she'd used the money to buy you all things she knew you wanted. She told me she had to buy things instead of asking me for them since I didn't want to help out the family anymore and "I only wanted to be your sister." She manipulated me and I saw right through her games. She felt like she was a good mother because she bought you what you wanted. Truthfully, she could have been a better mother if she'd just taken her medicine.

CHAPTER 18

Forgiveness and Proposal

During the Christmas of 2007, each of the four of you got an iPod and a brand-new computer to share along with other things you wanted and needed. Christmas was my excuse to spoil you. Raymond knew and expected it and enjoyed watching you open gifts maybe almost as much as I did that Christmas Eve.

On Christmas morning that same year, one year into our living together, Raymond proposed to me. He pulled out a diamond solitaire ring he had saved for and bought loan-free and promised to take care of me forever.

We'd sat on the living room floor at our condo beside our beautiful, six-foot, thin, artificial Christmas tree. Before his proposal, I'd opened gift after gift Raymond handed me: a casual bubble coat to keep me warm, two pairs of sweatpants, and a brown leather man's wallet. He had listened to me complain about needing comfortable loungewear and efficient ways to carry my money rather than in the big purses I hauled around. Raymond was a practical man and always wanted me to have what I needed. This is how he showed it.

The gifts kept coming. He had gotten my college diploma professionally framed and matted to match our school's colors. For two years, I had stored my diploma in the same folder given to me on graduation day and didn't display it proudly in my office, as I should according to him. Lastly, he handed me the blue digital camera I'd been eying to help me take better pictures for my scrapbooks. I loved every gift and he truly outdid himself.

I had only one gift for him that year and I was excited for him to open it. I had finished opening my gifts, so I thought, and handed him the big box that I'd stashed under the tree. In it was a new PlayStation 3 that he so badly wanted that year. It was the newest gaming system and he'd said he would buy it after the price went down. I wanted him to have what he wanted, so I bit the bullet and bought it along with the game he wanted.

His childlike excitement when he realized what was in the box was priceless. He tore open the box and quickly began to set it up in our living room. Moments later, he stopped and came back to me. Amongst the crinkled and torn wrapping paper and unassembled gift boxes was a small gift bag that I hadn't yet noticed. "There's still one more gift for you," he announced.

Raymond pulled a shiny burgundy box out of the bag and bent down on one knee.

As I stared down at the marquise-cut diamond ring in front of me in complete astonishment, he began to speak.

"Olivia, when you came into my life, I had no idea how much my life would change for the better. You've taught me how to love unconditionally and inspire me to be a better man every day. I love you and I want to build a life with you forever. Will you be my wife?"

"Yes!" I exclaimed.

I threw myself at him and bombarded him with kisses.

"C'mon, we have to go!" I shouted. I couldn't wait to tell you guys.

I threw on the new brown bubble coat and my new sweatpants over my pajamas and we rushed out the door.

I used my key to let Raymond and I in to the house. All of you were asleep. I had just seen you hours before for midnight mass and gift sharing. I ran up the stairs in excitement and couldn't figure out who to tell first, so I went with fair and square in age order. I ran to Carrie's room and woke her up, then woke up John, then Celeste, and Amelia. After I told all of you, I told Mami and Papi.

Raymond and I married eleven months later with a big wedding party that included all of you, Drew, Alejandra, Seli, Austin, and a few more of our closest college friends.

It was a gorgeous southern November morning, perfect for a wedding day. My twenty-five-year-old brain wasn't able to focus on the beauty of the day at the time. I had other things on my mind.

The morning of our wedding was full of as much chaos and chatter as a house with twenty people sharing two bathrooms could cause. We were all scheduled to be at the church by noon and the time constraint meant added pressure. Seventeen-year-old Carrie argued with me about not wanting to wear her bridesmaids dress. Forcing her to wear a dress was the worst thing I had ever asked of her in her dramatic teenage life.

I'd stayed the night at the Fancy Road house and was up at 5 a.m. to meet the hairdresser and bring her back to the house to do all of our hair. It was the first time I'd used the shower in that house and I looked up at the skylight. *Can he watch me from up there? No, crazy thought…* I shook my head and carried on. I showered quickly and hurried downstairs. The blow dryer was blaring loudly in the dining room and people were speaking over the noise. Mami's friend, Dana, wanted to French manicure my toes. I hadn't had a chance to get a pedicure earlier in the week and she insisted on making me look perfect that day. I was so annoyed with her for absolutely no reason. Getting a pedicure was the least of my worries.

In the kitchen, Papi made me breakfast. He cooked me a cheese omelet and handed me the paper plate. I reached for it out of mere politeness and sat at the table to try to eat it while trying to mask the ridiculous thoughts I associated with omelets. Did he not remember? How ironic that he would make me an omelet on my wedding day. I pierced it with my fork and embellished my wedding day stress and pending tasks before walking away from the table.

At this point, Papi and I were on speaking terms. We got along and did a great job at hiding our discomfort. Moving out of the house had done wonders for me. I was comfortable wearing a dress or shorts while visiting you guys at home, even when I knew he would be around. Usually when he was home, he was asleep or didn't hang around with us much anyway, but this confidence was a huge progress for me. I felt protected and safe when I was with Raymond. I knew Raymond would kill him if he ever hurt me or anyone I loved.

Papi and I would speak, joke around even but we never touched. Eye contact was minimal. When I looked into his eyes, all I could see was the same guilty glare he gave me outside the bathroom that day. But today, on my wedding day, we had to touch.

It was the one thing I dreaded for months. I didn't want Papi to walk me down the aisle and I had told Austin that I wanted him to walk me. The thought of touching his arm, accepting a hug or kiss from Papi as he gave me away, and giving him the *honor* of doing so completely repulsed me. It gave me anxiety all the months leading up to my wedding day.

Ultimately, Mami convinced me to give him the honor, because what would people say if he didn't? We couldn't let people wonder why Olivia wouldn't let the man who raised her give her away in marriage. *La ropa sucia se lava en casa.* She begged me to let him do it, and so, against everything in my physical and emotional being, I did it to make our mother happy.

When those doors to the sanctuary flew open and the wedding march began to play, I waited until the last possible moment to clasp my arm in his. I focused on the guests smiling at me as I walked and shook with every step. Mami had robbed me from the joy of awaiting my husband-to-be and replaced it with fear and disgust. I masked my discomfort well.

         ❧

It wasn't until about a year into my marriage that I realized moving away wasn't enough to release me from *him.* This thing that had happened to me still controlled me. It made me furious. My feelings weren't healthy and they were affecting my marriage and the happy life I was trying to live. I was away from him and Mami, but I was still carrying this darkness with me.

I didn't want to see a therapist about it. I believe in therapy, but in this case, I knew I needed more, something greater. This thing was so deeply rooted in me; I needed the greatest power I knew of to release me from it.

I was experiencing intimacy issues with Raymond and I wanted to be a good wife to him, so I prayed. My sudden piousness surprised me, because religion had always just been a practice of going through the motions. Catholicism was all I knew and though I prayed at church on Sundays, I typically didn't pray as a routine. Seeking prayer for me was a sign of desperation. But now I sought a higher power.

I prayed every day, every single day, for months. I put all my faith in God's hands to help heal me, help me forgive Papi, and allow me to be healthy and whole. I couldn't even imagine what feeling healthy would feel like, but I wanted so desperately to feel it. I'd finally come to grips with the fact that I was incapable of forgetting what he'd done that night when I was eight years old, and the way he'd looked at me when I caught him outside the bathroom door years later.

When Papi greeted me, he'd always look down at my chest. He thought he was discrete, but I always caught him. It repulsed me. I'd never forget what he did. He would always be in my life and I was sure Mami would never leave him. My only option was to forgive him. I was finally happy in my life and I refused to let him ruin this, too. This feeling became about choice, *my* choice.

≈◎≈

I don't know if any of you remember the day I stopped by the Fancy Road house to look for a bible. I didn't own one, but Mami had plenty. Amelia gave me hers. In the back of that bible, there are references for times when one is experiencing troublesome feelings. I referenced the suggested passages, sometimes reading the same ones over and over when I needed them. Prayer got me through it.

And then one day, I felt better.

There's something so beautiful about the moment you realize how far you've come. I don't know if I can do it any justice with words, but it really is amazing.

Today, I can talk about what happened to me without crying about it. I can wear what I want to wear around him. I can see him catch a glimpse of my chest without caving my torso forward to hide within myself. I can stand tall and feel confident and secure in my body at any time. I feel completely safe, powerful even. After that moment, after I knew I felt healed, I was completely free.

You all were getting older. Over time, I feared less that he could hurt you. You girls are feisty and mouthy and would never allow him to touch you. Even Mami and I were starting to see progress in our relationship. I was even learning to forgive Mami and trying to understand how much she loved him regardless of how much he hurt me.

Mami and I were in a comfortable emotional place, but as you know, this was only temporary. I was feeling strong and brave at the time and it led me to dive into the past to find what I much needed. Mami wasn't prepared for what came next, and neither was I, but I got the answers that changed my life forever.

CHAPTER 19

Trip to the Motherland

It wasn't until I was twenty-six years old that I got the terrible desire to visit Panamá after so many years, and I was determined to make it happen. I'd had the desire to go over the past twenty years, but never quite this badly. The burning urge that really pushed me to go was that I wanted to see my father. I wanted to see where I grew up, visit our family members who I loved and had kept in touch with over the years, and see the house I remembered so fondly. More than anything, though, my father was the missing puzzle piece in my life.

My biological father was always a mystery to me. I had very few memories of him that I held to tightly. His name was unspoken at our house. He was the enemy. I didn't really understand why his name was unspoken, just that, according to Mami, it would hurt Papi's feelings if his name were mentioned because Papi was my new dad. As a child, I took this as the truth and listened.

I had fantasized about mine and my father's reunion many times while growing up. I always daydreamed about how it would be. I pictured being at school and my father walking in to surprise me in a classroom full of people, or in the cafeteria as I was eating my lunch. Although I didn't know what he looked like, I'd instantly recognize him and I would faint dramatically at his sight. In these fantasies he somehow knew I needed his help, and so he was coming to my rescue.

I also thought about the more realistic possibility of me going to find him. I pictured myself going to Panamá and watching him from a distance; I'd hide behind a tree and just observe him. I would look for common characteristics and mannerisms we shared. I never wanted to say anything to him during my daydream episodes. After all, I didn't know what I would say and the last thing I wanted was to disrupt his likely very happy life.

I didn't know very much about him. Since he was a taboo subject, I'd tried not to ask. I can count on one hand the number of times I prompted a question wondering about my father over the course of twenty years. It was always when Papi wasn't around and it was almost always dismissed.

I have a handful of memories I've always quietly treasured. I remember skipping in the streets of our neighborhood while I held his hand and he walked beside me on a trip to the dentist. I don't know how he ever kept up with my skipping, but his walk beside me was effortless. He'd make a faint whistle sound with his mouth outside bathroom stalls to try to trigger me to pee that I can still hear in my head. When that didn't work, he'd turn the faucet on in the public bathrooms.

There was a time I remember faintly when Mami and Iban were still married and we were living in our apartment in Colón city. We played a game called 'Olivia sandwich.' They put me in between them on their bed and squeezed me in between their bodies. I laughed in enjoyment. Playing the 'guess the cloud shapes' game, while eating lime popsicles was the last memory I had of him.

All of these memories were pleasant and made me smile, and although I remembered specific moments, my father never had a face in any of them. The mental image of the man I once called my Papi was fading from my memory. All I remembered about his appearance was that he had lighter eyes and slightly darker skin than mine. I wondered if that was even true or if it was an image I had created for myself because I needed it.

Besides my few memories, I knew only what Mami had told me. I once got a wart on my hand and Mami said, "You get those from your father." When I became a teenager and began experiencing acne breakouts on my face, she would tell me, "Your father's side of the family has acne." The same applied when I wondered where I got the hair on my arms or my ugly toes. Everything associated with him was always negative. Sometimes when I was doing something like reading quietly or sitting alone for a moment, Mami would walk by me and tell me to stop sucking on my tongue. She said, "Your father used to do that, you look ugly when you do it!" I often did it when I didn't notice, but sometimes I started to do it on purpose just to reach for some sort of connection with him.

I often wondered where he was and what he was doing. I wondered if he had another family, and if they knew of me. Did he think about me? And why didn't he ever come looking for me? Didn't he love me? Mami had told me that he wanted to have a son and name him after himself. Maybe he didn't love me because I was a girl?

In the twenty years I wondered about him, I spoke to him two times. The first time I spoke to him was the first time Mami wanted to leave Papi and the man in the white van came to pick us up. The second time was when I was twenty-one years old. I was getting ready to graduate from college and Mamacela flew in to visit and attend the graduation. She brought with her a letter from Iban.

Mami handed me the medium-sized manila envelope with the handwritten letter from him. The envelope had clearly been tampered with. I had no doubts Mami read the letter before me. She was so protective over me.

"This is so ridiculous, he didn't need to write all of this!" she exclaimed as she handed me the envelope.

I was puzzled by her reaction but I agreed with her. I was on Mami's side over him—always.

I proceeded to read the letter. It was written in Spanish.

Dear Olivia,

It's nine o' clock in the evening here in Panamá as I'm writing you this letter. The truth is, it has been days since my first attempt at writing this letter, but I just don't know where to begin. These are the first words I share with you in a very long time. These words are from my heart, daughter of mine.

The reality is that I lost you. I lost you many years ago. I don't know who you are, how you think. I don't know of your achievements, dreams, what excites you. I don't know what your needs are. I don't even know what you look like anymore. The list goes on, but why continue?

Your grandmother, you know her as Mamacela, told me she is going to visit you. She told me that you're graduating from college in just a few short days. This is such a great accomplishment. I am so proud of you. I can't take credit for the woman you've become, this is a testament to the wonderful mother you have who raised you.

I think about you all the time. I know a little about you, but I hope to live to see the day I get to see you again and get to know you. I pray one day we can be friends.

If you ever find yourself in Panamá, I would love to
see you. I live in a house in Panamá City in the Balboa
neighborhood—house #345. My home telephone number is XXX-
XXXX and my cell is XXX-XX-XXX. I hope to hear from you.

I look forward to the day I get to talk to you, see
you, hug you, hold you.

Until that day,

Iban Batista

Your biological father

"Uggghh… I look forward to the day I get to talk to you,
see you, hug you, hold you," Mami mocked him.

"He wants me to call him," I said nervously.

"Do you want to talk to him?" Mami asked with a
disgusted look on her face.

I paused in complete intimidation. I was twenty-one years
old when I received this letter and completely influenced by
Mami. How embarrassing for me.

"I guess?" I stated as a question.

So, Mami and I called him together. She dialed the number
and asked for him. He was there. Right on the other side of
the conversation was the man I thought about and wondered
about for so many years. She handed me the phone.

I said, "Hello?"

"Olivia, is that you?" His voice was not what I imagined
it to be, but it was somewhat familiar.

"Yes," I responded timidly.

Mami pasted her head on the other end of the cordless
phone, trying to listen in. She made faces, ridiculing him,
and I could barely hear what he was saying. He passed the
phone to other people, but I didn't understand who I was
speaking to. I gave simple, single-word responses. I didn't

know what to say and the conversation didn't last long. Mami took the phone back and she hung up shortly after that.

I hadn't spoken to him since, if that conversation even counts.

Five years after that last conversation, I played the two encounters I'd had with him via telephone in my head as I contemplated my trip to Panamá. I definitely wanted to see him. After all, this would be my chance to do it. I didn't want to travel that far and regret not looking him up while I was there.

My biological father doesn't have a very common name, so, one day I thought, maybe I should do an Internet search for his name just to see what comes up. The thought came and went. I was too afraid of finding something. What would I do with the information?

Finally, one day while feeling particularly gutsy, I did it. I typed his first and last name into the search bar. I was feeling lucky. I searched through the insignificant pages that I knew couldn't tie me back to him or my country of origin. I didn't know anything about him, but I imagined he was still back home and none of the Google hits were about anyone in Panamá.

Finally, I came across a seventeen-year-old boy with my father's name who lived in Panamá. This seventeen year old with my maiden name had a profile page on a Spanish social media site called Sonico. I didn't know anything about this site, but I decided to join it just to see if I could learn more about this person. I crossed my fingers that it wasn't some crazy site I didn't really want to be associated with. Maybe this boy was related to me? Maybe he wasn't? I had to find out either way.

When I joined the page, I found out that the boy wasn't active on it. I didn't learn anything more about him and didn't even find a picture of him. I was hoping a picture would somehow mean something to me.

Full of nerves and disappointment of not finding any answers after all my research, I logged off the site and thought about my next steps for a few days. My mind went absolutely *crazy*. I couldn't stop thinking about it.

Should I send him a message? If so, what should I say? What if he's not family? What if he is*? What if he knows who I am? But even worse, what if he doesn't? What if he doesn't know who I am, and we're related, and I start stirring up trouble? What if I unintentionally disrupt their happy family? I have mine here. Maybe I need to leave them alone? Mami is going to kill me when she finds out I'm looking for trouble.*

Still, I couldn't stop thinking about the handful of memories I had of my biological dad, and decided to send this mystery boy a message after all. I didn't want to cause any problems, so I was very careful with my words. I typed in Spanish:

```
"Hello. My name is Olivia Batista. I live in the
United States and I think we may be related. If you
would like to contact me feel free to message me here,
or e-mail me at XXXX and I'm also on Facebook."
```

I sent it, made the sign of the cross over my face, blew a kiss up to Jesus in prayer, and logged off the strange, new social media site. To say I was nervous is an understatement. I experienced extreme anxiety, an emotional roller coaster. I checked my profile compulsively only to find an empty inbox.

A million thoughts ran through my head. Had he read my message? Had he not read my message? Is he my brother? Should I have worded my message differently? Had he read my message and asked our father who I was? Have I sparked some sort of argument or drama? Is my father married? Does his wife know of me? What if this person isn't related to me? What do I say if we're family? What do I do if they know who I am but want nothing to do with me? How would that make me feel? What have I done?

I needed to feel loved. I was scared and anticipated nothing but rejection. He hadn't fought to be in my life. He never came to rescue me when I needed him. Through his absence, I felt rejected by him already. I went into full protection mode and turned to find comfort and love where I had always received it: our mother.

I told her what I had done. I needed her love. She couldn't believe I had looked him up after all these years, considering what I had been told about him. She was anxious for a response just as much as I was and together we waited. Every single day seemed like painful eternity. I prepared for the worst—how to respond to this boy if he ever wrote me back, and how to cope if he never did.

One and a half long weeks later, I received a response. It read:

```
"Hello, I know exactly who you are.
You're my older sister. I've thought about you
       and I'm happy to hear from you."
```

My heart exploded. I had a seventeen-year-old brother, Iban Jr., and he knew about me? I had no idea he existed and yet he accepted me? I cried like a baby. Complete relief filled my soul and gave me life after the long days of anticipation. This young man on the other side of the computer screen had total control of my emotions and he brought me so much joy with his few words.

Iban and I exchanged private messages back and forth in which he explained that he lived with his mother. His mother and our father were not together, but he saw our father every fifteen days and would tell him about me the next time he saw him. He told me we had another brother and sister he had never met, though he had seen them from a distance once. He didn't know where our father lived and had never been to his house. Our father always came to see him at his house. Iban Jr. was so excited to hear from me and to meet me. We bonded instantly in our commonalities and I shared that I was planning a trip in the summer time. I told him to give our father my e-mail address, but not to tell him I was planning on visiting Panamá.

Iban Jr. did as I asked. He sent me a message after he saw our dad and told me he gave him my contact information. Apparently, our dad was shocked but happy. Still, I waited and waited and did not receive an e-mail from my father. *Who doesn't have e-mail these days?* I wondered. *Does he not want to talk to me?*

Days later, I received two friend requests on Facebook. The request was from two children, an eleven-year-old boy and a sixteen-year-old girl. I accepted their requests because their last name was "Batista." I wondered if these were cousins, or were these the brother and sister Iban had told me about?

I immediately visited their profiles and here he was. It was a picture of my father. The man had a face. It was him! He stood there with a woman who I could only assume was his wife. I clicked through all of my sister's pictures (she *was* my sister after all!), looking for more pictures of him. I saw him at his fiftieth birthday party. I saw him there with my sister at her quinceañera. I just *knew* that was him in those pictures.

I had missed his fiftieth birthday. He had missed my quinceañera.

When I got married, only two years before planning my trip to Panamá, I had asked Mamacela to bring me Mami's wedding album from Panamá. This was special to me because they were the only pictures I knew of that existed of my father. The once all-white album was a faded, cream-colored book, with brown spots on the outside edges. As I opened the book, there was a black circular music box that played "The Wedding March." On the first page, there was an invitation for the wedding, and as I flipped through the thick cardboard pages with the plastic securely stuck to the sheets, I saw the two of them. I saw my previously faceless father and our beautiful mother in her gorgeous wedding gown and veil. I saw something I didn't know or believe before. They were happy.

In all the tales I knew, they weren't happy. And yet there it was. This album confirmed it: once upon a time, my parents loved each other and that is why I was here today.

I recognized my father in the pictures on my sister's profile. It was the same man in the wedding album, twenty-seven years after those wedding pictures were taken. My sixteen-year-old sister then sent me a message in Spanish.

"Hello, sister," she said.

I responded, "Hello, how is everyone doing?"

Then I started wondering: Where was he? Where was my father? Why hadn't he said anything? He obviously told them of me.

My sister then told me our father wanted to chat with me. We scheduled a chat date and said goodnight.

What will I say to him? I wondered. *Do I want to know why he never looked for me? Mami said he knew how to find me. Why did he give me his contact info in that letter five years ago? Why did he put all the pressure on me? Why couldn't he make the call? What should we talk about? Maybe other family members? My grandparents? Is it silly to ask him about our family medical history? Doctors always ask me and I never know what to say when it's about his side of the family.*

After a lot of pondering back and forth, I decided I didn't want to ask him any of the questions I had immediately wondered. What I really wanted was to find our commonalities and get to know him as a person. *What are his hobbies? When is his birthday? How old is he now? What does he do for a living?*

The anticipation nearly killed me. I was frightened to talk to him. I turned to Mami for advice on what I should talk to him about. I could tell she was happy for me because clearly this was something I wanted, but she also became very protective of me. She could see that the process thus far had been very stressful and nerve wracking.

I logged on at the time I said I would, and there she was. My sister was logged on which meant my father was on the other end of the computer, thousands of miles away, waiting to finally talk to me.

The conversation went like this:

```
Me: Hello
Him: Hello, Olivia. How are you?
Me: Fine, and yourself?
Him: Very well.
```

...Minutes went by.

```
Me: How is the family doing?
Him: We are all well. You can ask me anything. I
    know you want to know about the past.
Me: I don't have any questions to ask you about
    the past.
Him: I am sure you're curious about a lot of things.
Me: When is your birthday?
Him: January seventeenth. Your birthday is on
    September fourteenth right?
Me: No, September nineteenth.
Him: Do you have any other questions for me?
Me: Do you suck on your tongue?
```

```
Him: No. Why do you ask?
Me: My mother told me that I suck on my tongue
    like you.
Him: Do you have any other questions?
Me: No.
Him: I have an early day tomorrow. Maybe we can
    talk again at another time.
Me: Okay, goodnight.
```

Our chat time was nothing like I thought it would be. I had anticipated this moment for *years* and it was nothing I could've guessed or imagined. He wanted me to question him about the past, but I purposely avoided it. I'd come to realize that I simply didn't care. I didn't care about what happened before that very moment. I just wanted to get to know him and find a connection to him, but he clearly had a different agenda than I did. He wanted to explain himself. He wanted to talk about the past, and I didn't allow him the opportunity.

I called Mami to tell her about our uncomfortable chat. She was angry and said negative things about him, which was nothing new to me. She told me she believed his wife was on the other end of the conversation. His wife probably wanted to see what I wanted and why I was trying to come into their life all of a sudden.

My father and I scheduled another chat date. We scheduled it for nine o'clock a few days later. I logged on at 8:59 p.m., but unlike the first chat, he was not logged on yet. I was excited about starting fresh with him and had even jotted down questions to ask, all unrelated to the past of course.

My questions included: How are my grandparents? How is my aunt? How is my godmother? What hobbies do you have? Have you ever been to the United States? I thought about asking him what memories he had of me growing up in an effort to prove our mother wrong about it really being his wife chatting with me.

I waited, and waited, and waited and he wasn't logged in. The anticipation and excitement turned into disappointment and heartbreak with every minute that passed. I began to cry. Where *was* he? He told me to log on at nine o'clock. I was emotionally fragile and I couldn't take any more disappointment from him. He'd already failed to meet my expectations. This was a man who for so long represented the possibility of a better life. He was my dream savior. He was supposed to love me and rescue me, and yet he couldn't even log on like he said he would. He didn't want to know me. I cried. I was so hurt.

"What games is he playing with me?" I cried to Raymond.

"Olivia, anything could've happened. Maybe he got tied up at work. Maybe he forgot. Give it a couple minutes." Raymond comforted me.

Twenty minutes later, I saw my sister's name pop up. The window had three back-to-back messages, questioning where I was. I responded as soon as I read the messages.

"I'm here," I typed furiously.

His response: "You said nine o'clock. You were not here."

I was offended. Here I was wiping tears off my face because he didn't log on at nine o'clock like we agreed, and he was questioning me? How dare he accuse me! I didn't do anything wrong.

After agreeing that there was a poor internet connection, we engaged in another chat that was almost as equally as uncomfortable as the first. He answered my questions, but not as warmly as I had hoped. He mentioned a memory of me that I had no recollection of, and when I told him the memories I had of him, he told me he didn't remember any of them.

Of course, I *wanted* to demand answers of him. Why didn't he come looking for me? Why did he let me leave so easily? Why didn't he initiate this reunion years ago? Why did *I* have to remind him he had a daughter? Why was I the one to put forth the effort? I swallowed the negative thoughts and moved onward with the conversation.

Although he didn't deserve to know, I decided to tell him I was planning a visit to Panamá six months from then. Even though he didn't meet my expectations, I still wanted to see him and meet my siblings. He told me to keep him posted on the details, but he didn't seem as excited as I was. Reconnecting with him was hard; I couldn't pin point it, but it seemed like he had built this emotional barrier between us. Still, I was willing to give us a fresh start, even if he wasn't ready to do the same.

≈·9·≈

As the date drew closer, my anxiety began to rise. I was excited to visit the land with which I associated so many wonderful memories. I was a mess of emotions—one minute excited, terrified the next. This trip was becoming real. It was surely going to be a beautiful experience, but it was still scary nonetheless.

My biggest fear with meeting the Batista family was rejection. I asked Mami if she could travel to Panamá when I went and she agreed. I needed her to fall back on. I needed her to love me when the Batista family rejected me. Although Raymond was going to go too, Mami had lived the past with me. She had been hurt by Iban Batista and his family. If anyone could relate, it would be her.

As the trip drew near, the truth began to surface.

"So, tell me the itinerary again. When am I going to see you?" Mami asked.

"Raymond and I fly in on Thursday," I said. "Iban, and my brother, Iban, Jr., and my Aunt Renee are greeting us at the airport."

"Are they taking you to your hotel? I told you that your uncle Manuel could take you. I don't want Iban to do you any favors," she said, with concern in her voice.

"No, Mother. I arranged for a shuttle to take us to our hotel. I don't want to depend on Iban. I don't want him to think I need anything from him."

"Okay, good! Because you don't!"

"Yes, Mami. I know," I sighed.

"So, what are the plans then?" she asked.

"I'm going to spend time with the Batista family on Thursday. I asked Iban if he could arrange for the whole family to get together for dinner at a convenient restaurant and I told him I would meet them all there."

"So, you're going to see your grandparents, your godmother, everybody?" She needed to know every detail.

"That's the plan."

"What's going on with your brother, Iban Jr.?" she asked.

"I don't know the whole situation, but I know he hasn't met any of the Batista family," I explained. "He only sees our father. He hasn't met our sister, Paulina or our brother, Sebastian. He hasn't met any of them. I asked our father if Iban, Jr. could come along to dinner, too and he hesitantly agreed. This is going to be new to us both, but at least we'll have each other."

"Okay. Well that's good," said Mami, being as supportive as she could. "So, when will I see you?"

"I'll be at Mamacela's house on Friday. I'll see you then and we'll go on with the rest of our trip."

Mami drifted quietly in thought and then quickly came back to me.

"Okay, so Thursday is the only day you'll be with them?" she asked. "You'll be with all of them and that's not a lot of time."

"Yeah," I sighed. "I just want to meet them. I can say I went to Panamá and I looked them up."

Mami always got so defensive whenever the Batista family came up in conversation. I had to be very casual about my feelings toward them. I had made the mistake of telling her how upset I was about my father disappointing me via chat, and she became very protective over me. I thought she might hunt him down and yell at him, and I didn't want her to come between us anymore. I just needed her to be my crutch, whether she knew the details or not.

It was during this conversation that I found out why she had always been so dismissive of any discussion about him.

"He's going to want to talk about the past," she warned, "and how I took you away from him without his permission and moved to the United States. And you're not going to want to hear any of that."

"I know, I kn—wait… *What?*" I was floored.

"I had to bribe someone to approve your passport to leave the country without Iban finding out," she continued, dropping this fact as if I'd known it all along.

For twenty years, I thought he'd known we were moving. I thought he'd known we were saying goodbye that last day I saw him. He never fought Mami on the idea. After all, he'd let me leave and didn't care to find me. And to think, our mother had taken me from the country without his knowledge. That changed everything. He didn't abandon me. We abandoned *him*.

"So, you *kidnapped* me? He didn't know where to find me? He didn't know where to look?" I asked, my face growing hot.

She raised her voice right back. "He always knew how to reach you. All he had to do was ask Mamacela, and she would've told him where we were!"

"But would she *really?*" I demanded.

I felt the anger rise within me, and I could feel myself turning red. Until now, this whole experience had brought Mami and I closer. I needed her love. I needed her to be my rock as I was riding this fragile train. I couldn't find words for her. Not right now. I was in complete disbelief. How could she be so capable of lying to me for all these years? How was making her daughter believe her father didn't love her better than the truth? I wanted to scream. I wanted to cry. All sorts of emotions ran through my mind. *Is she only telling me now because I've gathered the courage to look for answers?* I wondered. *Would she have ever told me the truth?*

All my life I had felt abandoned and rejected by my father. Would she have let me feel this way forever? And now she spoke so nonchalantly about it. In that moment, I wanted to hurt her.

I quickly realized there was nothing I could do at that exact moment. I couldn't hit her. And if I continued to yell at her, she'd probably have a seizure. So, I chose to keep my mouth shut. I didn't say anything. I didn't tell her how furious she made me. I didn't tell her how much it hurt me to believe one thing for so many years, and to only just learn the truth. I knew why she was telling me now. This was her worst nightmare. She knew I'd learn the truth, and she wanted me to hear it from her and not him.

I was no longer in the black hole. I was piecing my life together and felt powerful. I had Raymond's full support and it fueled me to keep moving forward and find my truth. Mami couldn't stop me from going on this trip.

~⑨~

Over the next few weeks, more and more truths began to spill out. Mami explained the argument she'd had with Iban the first time she called him from the yellow house. She had asked him for money because she wanted to leave Papi after Priscilla had shown up. She asked Iban for money, telling him I needed it for private school, although her intentions were to use it to move away from Papi. Apparently, he did not want to give her money, as she had left the country without notice. Iban believed she had left him for another man and that he could take care of us.

Iban hadn't wanted to divorce Mami. It was all her idea. She had fallen in love with Papi and Iban had fought for our family. As soon as he began to suspect something between them, he would show up to Mami and Papi's work to keep an eye on them.

All the stories Mami told me about him over the years flooded my brain. She had painted him to be such a horrible man. She told me he was violent. She told me had taken a knife out and threatened her. She told me she was scared for our lives. She told me he was crazy and often banged his head against walls. Were these lies, too? Why would she tell me all of this? Why did she tell me he only wanted a son? Why would she want to make me feel this way? How would my life be different if I had grown up with my father? He would've never hurt me the way Andrew did.

All I ever knew was wrong. I became a bigger emotional mess. Just when I was learning to forgive her for staying with Papi, she told me this? How could the one person who was supposed to take care of me, the person I needed to trust, hurt me more than she already had? How could she do this to me?

I used the months leading up to the trip to create a little distance between Mami and me. I needed time to think, but Mami didn't understand the distance. She wanted to make sure she didn't lose me to Iban. She constantly asked me about my communication with the Batistas, though sharing updates and news with her wasn't helpful. She still spoke negatively about them. She wanted to discredit them.

The more time I spent away from Mami, the better I felt. I needed the distance. At this time, I truly hated her. The time spent apart was helpful. It helped me realize I had only two options: I could be angry; never speak to our mother again; and resent her for the rest of my life, or I could use this information to make sense of my past; go on this trip; get to know my father and the Batista family; and just focus on the present and future.

Realizing my options didn't make my situation any easier. On one hand, I was elated to learn things and get to know my family. On the other hand, I feared rejection. What if they met me and didn't want to get to know me? What if they simply felt obligated to meet me? What if they thought I had ulterior motives? Finding them was so meaningful to me—especially now. Learning about them filled a void in me that I never knew I had. I didn't know I needed them. I was slowly piecing my story together and making sense of where I came from.

I'd always felt loved by the four of you. It was strange how suddenly learning I had family I'd never before known about filled a space I didn't know needed filling. Still, it was important to me.

Furthermore, I was excited to see my dear Mamacela, Papou, aunts, uncles, and cousins. I was an emotional mess as the days drew near and Mami continued to unveil the truth of our past. She too was going to see her father for the first time in twenty years. The last time they'd seen each other was the night we were packing to move to the U.S.. He had disagreed with her decision to move to another country with her married lover.

The day finally arrived. Raymond and I were flying into Panamá. Mami and all of you, had flown into Panamá the day prior so you could experience the country you'd heard of for so many years.

Raymond and I woke up early the morning of our big trip. We arrived at the airport at 4 a.m. for our 6 a.m. departure. I was more emotional than ever. In just a few short hours, I would meet a brother I'd learned about only six months prior, an aunt whom I played with when I was younger (she was just two years my senior), and I would finally see my biological father again. I would also see my grandparents for the first time in twenty years, and meet my other two siblings, and the entire Batista family.

I stared out the plane's tiny oval window that now revealed shades of greens and browns peeking through the clouds. I longed to see my beautiful Panamá, the land we left so long ago.

The pilot began to announce our landing. My heart sank to the pit of my stomach. I'm not a nervous flyer. I knew it was the anticipation of meeting my family. The moment had come. Raymond looked over at me, sensing my nerves. He had kept me steady throughout this process and was doing it again as he held my hand.

"Are you alright?"

"No... but I will be." I held his hand tight.

CHAPTER 20

The Batistas

As Raymond and I walked through the halls of the Panamanian airport, he looked at me for guidance and direction; he couldn't understand the Spanish signage. I walked in complete disbelief of where I found myself at the present moment. I had last been here twenty years before to say goodbye to my family and my entire world as I knew it to be. So much had happened since then. And yet, although I knew I was going to see my family as soon as I reached the baggage claim area, I was in no rush to face that awkward situation. I walked at a casual pace, studying the pastel colored walls and looking out the windows to my country. To our country.

Raymond seemed in more of a hurry than I was. He was so excited for my reunion. Whenever I'd been disillusioned over the last six months, he picked me up. He always re-focused me into seeing the positive out of the whole situation. When I was frantic and stuck selfishly in my own emotions, he pushed me to try to understand the other person's point of view. He felt Mami was doing what she thought best and that she never meant to hurt me. According to Raymond, maybe Iban was distant because he wanted me to feel safe with getting to know our family. Maybe Raymond was right. I was essentially a stranger to Iban.

At last we reached baggage claim to find my biological father, Iban, standing there to greet us. I recognized him immediately. He stood there in his green cargo pants, colorful striped polo shirt, and brown sandals. Beside him was my Aunt Renee wearing loose fitted jeans and a white polo shirt, with her hair tied back in a ponytail. Mami told me Renee was only two years older than me and that we looked alike as children. I examined her features and agreed with Mami.

Iban Jr. stood beside my father with a big smile on his face. I found comfort in his smile and gave him my first hug. I squeezed tight, hoping he would appreciate my gratitude. I wanted to say, "Thank you for responding to my vague message six months ago, and telling me about our father and two other siblings. Thank you for not rejecting me. Thank you for giving me the courage to make this trip. Thank you for connecting me to a family who was once a big part of my life. Thank you for wanting to get to know me. Thank you for taking the time to welcome me here today." I hoped my hug said it all.

I then hugged my Aunt Renee, and lastly, I hugged my father. At this point, he was a stranger to me, and yet just a little bit familiar. He gave me a tight embrace; I gave him a social squeeze. I backed away from the hug before he was done and cracked a straight- lipped smile at him. I didn't want to be disrespectful, but I wasn't able to reciprocate the emotions he was trying to express.

One of my biggest worries about meeting the Batistas was that they'd feel I was using them. I didn't want them to think I wanted money or that I was trying change or threaten the dynamic of their lives. I was hopeful they'd be welcoming toward me and hoped they would gradually get to know me.

I feared they would think of me as someone who wanted to take advantage of them. I was hopeful that this meeting would be as positive as possible and yet I needed to prepare myself for rejection and disappointment just in case.

I called Mami from the shuttle using my brother's phone just to let her know we had arrived. During our brief phone call, she asked me about my plans. I reminded her that I had plans with the Batista family that day. We would eat some lunch and walk around the mall to kill time before dinner at my hotel. All of the Batista family was coming to see me and meet my brother, Iban, for the first time. Before that, Mami planned on stopping by the hotel to drop off a cellphone for me.

"What mall are you going to?" she asked.

"Albrook Mall," I responded.

"Okay, I'll drop off the phone before the end of the day."

"Sounds good," I said.

"How are they treating you?"

"So far so good, Mami. 'Gotta go." How could she ask me these questions knowing I was with them? She made me uncomfortable.

We arrived at the hotel only to drop off our luggage and head out to lunch and an informal city tour in my father's car. The five of us were enjoying the car ride, when my brother's phone rang and he gave it to me. It was Mami.

"Hello?" I answered.

"I'm at the food court at Albrook Mall," she said. "Come get the phone from me."

"Mami, I'm not at the mall yet and I'm with people." I smiled at my audience to make it seem like all was okay.

"Come to the mall, I'm here with your family and they want to see you," said Mami.

"I'm with people, Mami. I can't just tell them to drive me around. I just met them."

"Come now," she practically shouted. "And you better not bring him! I don't want to see him! I'll see you when you get here." She hung up.

I laughed nervously.

"Is everything alright?" asked my father.

"Yes, ha ha ha… My mom is at the mall and wants me to get a phone from her so I'll have it in case of an emergency."

"Okay, let's go to the mall," my father said.

I translated what had just happened to Raymond who sat next to me. He rolled his eyes in annoyance. "Of course, we're on her time," he said.

Internally, I was having a panic attack and going through how everything was going to play out. My day wasn't going as planned, which already gave me some level of anxiety. Today was supposed to be about the Batistas. I wasn't supposed to see our De La Cruz family. Of course, I wanted to see them, but how long were we going to be at the mall? I didn't want to be rude to anyone. Respecting people's time was important to me.

All sorts of thoughts raced through my mind. *Oh my God! My parents are going to see each other for the first time in twenty years? How's that going to go? Mami doesn't want to see him. How am I going to make that work? Should I just tell my father to wait for me in the car while I run in? Yeah… I'll try that.*

The phone rang again and my brother, Iban, handed it to me.

"Are you here yet?" Mami asked.

"Mami, I just parked. You're being really annoying," I said, trying to keep my composure.

"We're by the big gorilla at the food court," she said, nonchalantly.

"Big gorilla?"

"You'll see it. *He's* not with you, is he? I want to see your Aunt Renee and I wouldn't mind meeting your brother, but don't you dare bring him!"

"You're stressing me out," I said. "I'll see you at the big gorilla." I hung up.

"Where is she?" my father asked.

"She's by the gorilla in the food court?" I said, baffled. "I'll just run in and be right back."

"Haha… nonsense," said my father. "There's no way I'm letting you go in a mall you've never been to before. You don't know your way around this city, let alone this country. I'm going with you."

"No, it's okay," I pled.

"I'm going with you," he insisted.

At this point I was in full panic mode. Raymond was annoyed that Mami found an opportunity to make this situation and beautiful reunion about her. I was clearly displaying stress signs as my father started to express concern for me.

He looked at me and said, "It's okay. Everything will be okay." He nodded at me for reassurance. "Do you understand me?" he asked. I had known him less than an hour and he didn't know how much Spanish I understood, yet he knew my language of distress.

I couldn't tell him she didn't want to see him. How awkward would that be? *Hey, I know I've only just re-united with you an hour ago and we want to move past history and all, but my mom hates you and refuses to see you.* Yeah… that didn't sound like it would come out well. I chose not to say anything, but nodded my head to let him know I understood what he was telling me.

We reached the food court and I took off looking for the gorilla. In my head if I ran fast enough I could get the phone, greet our family, and run back to the Batista family before they even made it to the gorilla statue. I was wrong.

I ran to Mami and immediately and rapidly under my breath apologized to her, "Sorry, they're all here." She tightened her face, sucked her lips, and just as quickly switched her face to fake joy as the De La Cruz family greeted me for the first time in many years. By this time, Raymond, along with the Batista family, had reached the gorilla and all of us. I knew Mami was mad at me, but I introduced Raymond to those who hadn't met him yet. It was all very pleasant—except the view directly across from me.

There they were, Mami and my biological father for the first time in twenty years. I couldn't imagine the last conversation they'd had was positive. *But surely,* I thought, *this time will be amicable. I mean, it's been twenty years and that's plenty of time to get over any hard feelings. Right?*

Not exactly.

Iban reached out his hand to shake Mami's hand and she rolled her eyes as she turned and walked away from him in true Mami fashion.

Have my eyes just played a trick on me? Did that really just happen? I thought as I continued to hug and kiss our family. I got the phone from Mami and told everyone I would see them the next day. I must've came off rude to you all, but I had to get them away from each other after what I had just witnessed.

After the mall, my father dropped Raymond and I off at the hotel. He was going to go pick up my grandparents and come right back for the big reunion dinner. Iban, Jr. left to run a quick errand. Raymond and I were running on four hours of sleep and at this point had been awake for about fifteen hours with no end in sight. We freshened up in the thirty minutes we had to ourselves before we were expected to be downstairs.

The dinner that night was a big deal and a long time coming.

We agreed to meet at the hotel's restaurant for the convenience factor and Raymond and I were naturally the first to arrive. We sat at the center of the table for twelve. My brother, Iban Jr., arrived alone and joined us as we anxiously waited for everyone else. We sat across from each other in awe of one another and grateful for the reunion ahead. We had little to say, but our smiles to each other said it all. He gave my hand a squeeze as I laid my other hand on top of his. We had each other.

Not much longer after his arrival, the rest of the group came in. I was greeted with tight hugs and kisses on the cheek. My grandparents palmed my face in disbelief. "It's really you," they said. They cried happy tears. They hugged Iban, too, as they were introduced to him. I masked the awkwardness with confidence in introducing Raymond to everyone and translating conversations to him throughout the night.

The family shared kind memories of Mami and me as we ate our dinner. Raymond and my grandpa bonded over who could keep up with whom on domestic beers. Grandpa spoke a little English and Raymond appreciated him for it. Among the rumble of chatter, I looked across the table at my brother Iban, laughing and talking with our brother, Sebastian, and sister, Paulina, or Lina for short. This very moment filled my heart with tremendous joy. Nothing in the past mattered, only now and how we all moved forward. Our night ended with real, tight, and meaningful hugs and hopes to see each other again really soon.

～◎～

If you all remember, Mami and I argued a lot during this trip. I had made every effort to plan our trip itinerary down to the hour, but all was derailed after the first night.

Raymond and I went to sleep on a high after that very special dinner. The following day, Friday morning, I had plans to meet with all of you at Mamacela's house. Mamacela and uncle Manuel would pick us up from the hotel and drive us to the countryside. We were going to have a big party and all of Mami's side of the family would stop by to visit. On Saturday, we would all head up to explore a small island ironically named 'Big Island' for the weekend.

When Raymond and I walked down for a quick breakfast before our ride arrived Friday morning, we were surprised to find my father in the lobby.

"Good morning," he said.

"Hi, how are you?" We greeted with hugs.

"I didn't want to wake you, but I wanted to see if we could join you for breakfast," he said pleasantly.

Behind him was a woman sitting with my brother Sebastian.

"This is my wife, Paulina," he explained. "She didn't get to join us for dinner last night, but she wanted to meet you and Raymond, and Sebastian skipped school to come eat with us. He doesn't miss anything, right?" he chuckled as he tapped Sebastian on the shoulder. Paulina stood up to greet me. We shook hands politely. Sebastian's timid smile parted his chunky brown cheeks. He was such a cute twelve-year-old. I was still feeling grateful from the night before and appreciated Iban introducing me to his wife; however, I was starting to feel the anxiety come back. My two worlds had not mixed well the day before. Today was supposed to be about spending time with Mami's side of the family and all of you. I thought maybe I had time for both.

"Sure, come join us," I said. "Mamacela should be here in about forty minutes to pick us up, though. I'm sorry we have to eat in a little bit of a hurry."

My father was so calm. "Any time I get to spend with you is valuable. I'm just grateful for this blessing." We walked over to the breakfast buffet and sat down to chat.

"So, tell me, what do you remember about Panamá?" my dad asked.

"I remember lots of things. I think because I was asked that question a lot growing up, the memories never left me." I continued on, sharing the memories I had. He smiled with what I interpreted as pride.

"What made you finally decide to contact me?" he asked, after a while.

"Well, I always wondered about you and the Batista family," I said. "I kept the letter you sent me five years ago."

"Letter?"

"Yes, the one you sent with Mamacela when I graduated from college," I said. "I saved it and still have it. It's really all I have from you and, well, I finally decided it was time to look for you." I smiled, hoping my answer was sufficient.

He looked puzzled with my response. "Did you say letter?"

"Yes. You don't remember writing it?"

"I do," he affirmed and he paused. "I wrote you several letters for years."

I instantly believed him. Why wouldn't I believe him? Of course he had written me. Mami likely kept the letters from me, but I couldn't think about that now. I couldn't explain where they had gone. So I simply responded with the truth.

"I only have the one," I said.

We continued to chat in the hotel courtyard as I got to know my father's wife. She was kind and welcoming. I was appreciative that she wanted to meet me and Raymond, and that my father felt comfortable sharing his world with me.

≈ 9 ≈

The last four days of our week-long trip were supposed to be spent exploring the country with the De La Cruz family. We were back on the mainland and had plans to do a Panamá Canal tour, then enjoy the resort and sightseeing. My time, however, became heavily devoted to the Batista family. First my father showed up at our hotel and asked to take us to my grandparents' house. Another day, my sister Lina visited, so we swam at the pool and ate lunch. Then my father wanted to show us where he works. He took us to the the Panamá Canal, where he is an engineer. He's so proud of his profession and achievements. During car trips, we'd talk and get to know each other. He showed us all of the places he'd lived and where he, Mami, and I used to live, as well as places we used to visit together. Iban took Raymond and I to visit his home, and he even took me to lunch at the place where he and Mami had their wedding reception. He wanted to show me where I was from, and show me his life and world. My father opened up to me naturally and at his own pace. We were finally able to make progress in our relationship and I was happy getting to know him.

Truthfully, I enjoyed every moment I spent with Iban and the Batistas. I didn't anticipate spending as much time with them as I did, but I accepted it because I truly enjoyed being with them. When we'd first connected with each other only six months earlier, my father had been apprehensive. He didn't know who I was or who I had become. He was now given the opportunity to get to know me and I wanted to get to know him just as much. We had been robbed of this time in the past and now had to make up for it in a very short span.

Meanwhile, Mami was upset. She had expected me to spend all my time with Mamacela and her side of the family.

In her defense, that's what was planned and expected. On the other hand, my father didn't want to let me go. Iban was greedy of my time, but he meant well. Mami continued to say nasty things about him and was clearly jealous. She'd call and ask me to tell her everything we talked about and everything we did. She wanted to keep me on the phone when she knew I was with him.

The morning before our flight, we found Iban in the lobby of our hotel. This was almost expected at that point. He said he had a surprise for Raymond before we left for the airport, and we agreed to go with him to see what it was.

Iban then drove us to his church. It was where he and Paulina were married and they still attended mass every week. Paulina walked inside the old cobblestone building. Iban led Raymond and I up the cracked steps and through the big wooden door. The sanctuary was quaint and special. Few people were scattered throughout. I knelt in the aisle, made the customary sign of the cross, and followed Paulina into the pew.

"Will you indulge me for a moment?" Iban asked.

"Okay," I agreed, wondering what he had in mind.

"Will you both kneel and say a prayer with me?" he continued. I interpreted for Raymond and we obliged.

As we knelt next to my father and his wife, I closed my eyes and began to pray. I'm not sure what Raymond prayed about, but I thanked God for our week together. It had been a whirlwind of activities, laughter, bonding, arguments, stress, lack of sleep, and happy moments. Although Mami was mad at me for missing some time with her family, I ultimately didn't regret it. I didn't miss out on family time; I was getting to know *other* family. I got to know my brothers and sister. I spent time with my grandparents, whom I hadn't spoken to in twenty years. I got to know my father and his wife. I ate with them at their favorite places. I witnessed my brother, Iban

Jr., spend time with our siblings and hoped their relationship would continue to grow. I felt incredibly fortunate to have had this opportunity. It was beautiful and unforgettable.

In the middle of our prayers, I felt something placed around my shoulders. Raymond and I opened our eyes. My father had placed a large strand of ivory colored rosary beads around the two of us to symbolize his blessing of our union. He prayed over us, as we accepted his blessing. When he was finished, he explained he had the same set of Italian marble rosary beads hanging on his bedroom wall. The blessing and prayer he shared with us was a ritual done at his own wedding. The beads hung on the wall above their bed as a reminder that God plays an essential role in their marriage.

After we left the church, Iban took us back to our hotel to catch our shuttle. He then followed us to the airport in his own car, walked us into the airport, and watched us check our baggage. He asked if we had time for one last meal and we all ate lunch together. When it was time to head to our gate, Iban first hugged Raymond and then me. This embrace was different than our first at this same place only a week ago. He cried and sniffled. His eyes were red and full of tears. He had completely taken down his guard. Raymond cried alongside Iban, wiping his tears with the back of his hand. I don't think I'd ever seen Raymond so touched from emotion.

"You're leaving me again," said Iban, his voice shaking. There was so much pain behind his voice. I mustered strength for the three of us and held him quietly. Our embrace was firm and heartfelt. I didn't find the words to comfort him; I couldn't jeopardize our relationship. Acknowledging the moment was too overwhelming, and I didn't want to face the reality that I was leaving my father whom I was just getting to know and actually *liked*. I hoped that my embrace said it all.

CHAPTER 21

Aftermath

In the blink of an eye, Raymond and I were on our way back to North Carolina. I was overcome with a burst of emotions and confusion that I didn't know where or how to place. I found myself in disbelief of the week-long experience in Panamá. I had developed a foundation for a relationship with family I didn't even know I had. This possibility hadn't existed only six months before the trip.

It was an overwhelming, almost indescribable feeling to have this new set of people in my life whom I'd never known I needed. I'd never imagined two more brothers and a sister. I never dreamed of having a new set of grandparents, or more people to call 'tía,' 'tío,' or 'cousin.' Never in my wildest dreams did I wish for more family. But somehow, I had them, and somehow, I needed them. My life now made more sense. My new family filled a void in my heard that I never knew existed. And just when I got to meet them, know them, like them, and even *love* them, I'd had to say goodbye.

When we got back, Mami and I didn't speak for months. She thought I was angry at her and had it in her head that Iban had told me their story and turned me against her. It was true that Iban had offered me the opportunity to ask him questions about the past, but I didn't want to ask him about their relationship. I solely focused on the present and forward. The past didn't matter to me. Everything I knew about their story was what I'd heard from Mami prior to the trip. Iban only confirmed what I already knew in comments here and there. He complimented me and told me he was proud of the woman I had become. He also complimented Mami on the job she had done in raising me.

The truth is, I wasn't mad at Mami at all, not anymore, not about that and not about anything. To this day, I've never even asked her about the missing letters. What would be the point? Instead, I used the time apart as a break from her. I needed the space in order to continue any kind of relationship. If she was going to be in my life, it would have to be on *my* terms. It would have to be a relationship *I* was comfortable with. I needed to have my own life with my husband, and I wanted to be there for Raymond when he needed me. I needed her to understand that. I needed her to figure things out with Papi, the man she *chose* to be with. And I needed Mami and Papi to be your parents, and not to rely on me so much.

I enjoyed a break from Mami's multiple phone calls to stop and help her respond to an e-mail; they'd always interrupted my workflow throughout my busy work days. I enjoyed not having to translate her paperwork after hours. I also enjoyed being present and available to Raymond, and to his new entertainment management business that was in the early stages of growth and that ran from the spare bedroom in our condo. My own career was demanding, as well. I still worked for the same company and I'd consistently received promotions and had new responsibilities. I was engulfed in my volunteer work through church and I loved my life. I wasn't as available as I once had been for you guys, though I thought about you all every day. I know this meant you were at doctor's appointments with Mami instead of me, and I'm sure you had to help translate the work she brought home. I'm sorry if you felt I wasn't there when you needed me, but trust me when I tell you this time was for the best.

Three months later, I called her at work. It was time.

"You've reached Marcela. How can I help you?" Mami asked. She sounded so sweet and I couldn't believe how much I'd missed her voice.

"Hi Mami, it's Olivia," I said earnestly.

"*Hija, cómo estás?*

And just like that, we carried on our conversation as if we hadn't skipped a beat.

CHAPTER 22

Thanks, but
no Thanks

It was New Year's Eve, the last day of 2011. It had been about a year and a half since our trip to Panamá. Our family gathered at the house on Fancy Road, playing games, eating, and waiting to ring in the New Year together as a family. The house was gorgeous, even more beautiful than the Pennsylvania home. The four of you, Alejandra and her new husband, Jacob, Raymond, and I were all in the living room when Mami walked in with an envelope. She handed it to Raymond and asked him to read it to the family.

Raymond quickly skimmed the letter and asked, "Are you sure you want me to read this? Shouldn't Andrew tell everybody?"

"Babe, what is it?" I asked, feeling a lump in my throat.

Papi was upstairs asleep or passed out from drinking, as usual. Raymond sighed and proceeded to read a final foreclosure notice from America's First Bank, where Mami and Papi owned their mortgage loan.

The room fell silent as we processed the words out of Raymond's mouth. Heads around the room bowed in disappointment. I grew angry with each word in that letter. All his life, Papi had one job—provide a roof for our family. I was furious at him for not taking care of you all. And I was angry at Mami for still placing all her trust in him.

Raymond read the letter down to the last line. After a short pause, Mami began to explain herself to the group.

"I'm sorry I haven't told you all before. I've been carrying this for months." She sniffled as she powered through her voice breaks. "We've received countless letters. Your father hasn't been paying the mortgage. At first, the bank was willing to offer us payment options, but he won't call them back. He won't pay them. He doesn't care. I didn't know what to do. We're going to lose the house."

Mami was in full tears at this point. Amelia started sniffling and immediately ran upstairs to her room, surely because she didn't want us to see her cry. Amelia is always a rock. She hardly shows emotion. The rest of you were in college at this point, but she was still a senior in high school and this news was hardest for her. She was going to lose her home. John got up and followed her; I don't think he was ready to hear what else she had to say.

"Why hasn't he paid the mortgage?" I accused.

Mami continued, "Well, as you know, he pays the mortgage and I pay utilities. The mortgage is solely in his name. He lost his job a few months ago and refuses to find another one."

Alejandra and I looked at each other. Papi had lost his job months ago and we didn't know it? This must've been stressful for you guys and I'm sure you knew before me. If Mami was anything like she was with me, I'm sure you were her most trusted friends and housemates. Her worries became your worries.

"At first, I thought it was strange he didn't get dressed to go to work with the clothes I laid out for him," Mami explained. "He dropped me off at work in casual clothes. He picked me up from work in the same clothing. His clothes were stained with food he'd made for dinner and he didn't care enough to change. He reeked of smoke and liquor—even more than usual. When I asked him about work, he'd tell me that he was using up his vacation time. It didn't seem strange to me because he never used his time. It was believable.

"By the third week," she continued, "I became suspicious so I called his boss. His boss was hesitant to talk to me, but he explained that your father no longer worked for the company. In so many words, he brought up his alcoholism."

"He told you Papi was fired for drinking on the job?" I interrupted. I was growing in anger. So many thoughts ran rapid through my mind. *Has Papi really been so bold as to show up drunk? Was he fired fairly? Or has his drinking gotten worse? Mami barely makes enough money to pay her portion of the bills. How am I supposed to support my family again? Surely not in this house....*

"His boss didn't want to tell me much," Mami continued. "I could tell that what he told me was only because he knows our family. He said your father had gotten into a sloppy altercation with another co-worker. He said Papi needed to find help for his disease."

Alejandra sat back, taking in the information; Jacob and Raymond sunk into the sofas; Celeste and Carrie listened intently; and I fell deeper into thought. *How could he do this to me? How could he do this to Mami and the kids? How could he be so irresponsible?* Something had to be done and it had to be done now. In order for me to get Papi to cooperate, I had to calm down.

Mami went upstairs to wake him and ask him to come downstairs. Alejandra, Raymond, and I sat with him, and in the privacy of his home office, we began to talk.

"Mami filled us in on your financial situation and we want to help," I began. "If we sit here with you, would you be willing to call America's First Bank to explain that you want to work with them?"

Papi was still half asleep and he huffed at us in frustration.

"If I call for you, will you talk to them?" I raised my voice at him.

"Yes, yes! Okay!" he replied.

I dialed the phone number on the letter and handed him the phone. Papi agreed to make a payment within two weeks and made arrangements for how to catch up with monies owed. The family rang in the New Year in sadness, but faithful things would work out. I made plans to begin to help Papi look for a new job the next day.

⋙ 9 ⋘

Two weeks later, Papi hadn't done as agreed. Mami called me daily, in a state of panic. She wanted to leave him for good this time, as she'd threatened ever so often.

I had heard this time and time again. She said it just to say it. Her words meant nothing to me. I knew that things weren't perfect between her and Papi lately, but really, when had they been? This was their norm. As for Mami and I, we were in a comfortable bubble at this point. The trip to Panamá had been over a year before. I was in a healthy emotional place with her and with Papi, and Mami didn't rely on me nearly as much as she used to.

Please know that I love and would do anything for our mother, but my efforts and involvement in the months to follow were for Amelia, not for Mami. Amelia was afraid the house would be padlocked any day as she counted down the days until college, and she was afraid she wouldn't be able to get any of her things. After days of discussing it with

Raymond, we offered for Amelia to come live with us, but she declined our invitation.

After a few more days, Amelia called to ask if she could change her legal address to mine and Raymond's for her school records; she wanted to make sure she got her diploma when it was time. She also asked if she could keep a box of things she found most valuable at our condo, as she wasn't sure how much longer they would live there.

The situation infuriated me. Although Amelia was strong, my heart broke for the situation and stress she was forced to endure. If Mami called me daily asking for help and support, I could only imagine the stress she was putting Amelia through. All she should have to worry about is graduating from high school and celebrating her accomplishment.

I'd reached my limit with our parents yet again. My blood boiled just thinking about the whole situation that could've been avoided.

One evening, three weeks after New Year's, I told Raymond I was going to visit the house and stormed out in a frenzy. Mami had called me at work earlier that day to vent and I couldn't hear her complain any longer. I tried to carry on with the remainder of the day, but I couldn't take my mind off it. I went home only for a bit to set my things down and left right after. I sped into the driveway of the Fancy Road house and let myself in. I scared Mami who was downstairs watching television in the dark and not expecting me.

"Where's Papi?" I demanded.

"He's upstairs, sleeping," she said, emotionless. I remember wondering how opposite my reaction was from hers. Mami was calm and composed. I was infuriated. Seeing her so battered and helpless fueled me more.

I scurried upstairs, turned on the bedroom light, and began to scream at him. I had to stand up for my family.

Mami's worries and Amelia's panic drove me to fury and I let him have it.

"I need you to do something about this! Your family may not have anywhere to live any day now. *What are you going to do about it?* Amelia is worried, your wife is worried, and you're not doing anything! You're not working—you're not even trying to work! Are you looking for a new place to live? Have you made *any* payments to the bank? Mami says they're calling again, and you won't talk to them! Did you do *anything* I asked you to do?" I was completely out of breath. Every bit of built up anger from the past two weeks had spilled out.

"Olivia, what do you want from me?" Papi muttered. He was still asleep as he sat up in bed. My words bounced off of him. His inconsiderate demeanor only made me angrier.

"I want you to take care of our family because if you don't, I will!" I threatened him through clenched teeth.

He sucked his teeth at me.

"Do whatever you want and get out of here," he hissed. He pulled the covers over his head, letting me know that the conversation was over. I had gathered the courage Mami didn't have to confront him and he'd dismissed me. How *dare* he? Did he think I couldn't do the job he was supposed to do?

"Just so we're clear, if you don't find a new place for the three of you to live in the next week, I'm going to find a place for Amelia and Mami without you. *Do you understand?*" I said very slowly and confidently. "I'm going to sell everything in this house, they're keeping the money, and they are leaving. Are we clear?" I added.

"Uh-huh." His tone was indifferent. He mocked me; he dared me with his carelessness.

I went downstairs and could barely say anything to Mami.

"What happened?" she asked.

"Start packing and setting things aside," I said, shaking my head. "I'm going to help you sell what you don't want or need anymore and I'm going to find you a place to live, okay?"

"Okay. Thank you, hija." Mami said, relieved and grateful. We hugged and said goodnight.

Just like that, I was in the middle of Mami and Papi's relationship again. I didn't want to be. I had tried to guide Mami without getting involved every time she called and she cried. She was destroyed. Mami found herself in a helpless situation and didn't know how to get out of it without me. We had talked about her finding a place to live with Amelia, but the two places she tried had denied her due to credit. She wasn't computer savvy and didn't know how to sell things online. She didn't even know how to begin. I *had* to take the reins.

Honestly, I'd known it on New Year's Eve. I just prolonged it, hoping she would take responsibility. She knew I wouldn't ever leave her.

The next month was absolutely critical. Time was of the essence. How to pack a five-bedroom home and prepare to downscale tremendously? And how would we do so while Papi was adamant about not cooperating? He was in complete denial of everything. He continued to sleep, drink, and ignore what happened around him.

Mami and Papi had been sleeping in separate beds for months now, and she and Amelia lived in daily worry of not being able to come home to their things—or shelter. Mami worked and Amelia went to school and then they both came home to pack and part ways with most of their belongings. I took pictures of all of the furniture, uploaded posts on Craig's List, and made arrangements with potential buyers. I advertised and helped prepare for a massive yard sale.

On the day of the sale, Papi walked in from running errands. He saw what we were doing and he did absolutely nothing. I invited him to take part in the yard sale, but he declined. Instead, he made himself a drink, went upstairs, and went to sleep.

During this same month, I began to look for apartments for Mami and Amelia. Every place wanted to run a credit check, which I knew Mami wouldn't pass. I finally found a two-bedroom rental right across the street from where Raymond and I lived that was willing to bypass the credit check.

"Mami! Promise me he's not coming with you," I said sternly.

"Olivia Rose! Of course, I promise. I don't want him to move in with us. He's the reason we're in this mess! After all he put me through?" She sounded sincere, though it was hard to believe her.

"I mean it!" I threatened. "I put a lot of work into finding this place. I had to explain your situation to the landlord in order to bypass the credit check and get a discount on the rent. I gave her my word that you would be a good tenant in our community."

"Thank you. I promise," she gratefully agreed.

≈◎≈

A month later, Amelia and Mami were secure and all moved in into their new home—without Papi. For as long as I could remember, Mami had talked about this day and it had finally arrived. It was unbelievable. I was really proud of her. She had been so unhappy for a very long time and she finally took the big step to do something about it. Amelia was at ease, as well. I took her to school in the mornings and picked her up most days when she couldn't find a ride home from friends. Mami had a home and she was away from *him*. All was right in the world.

Later that same year, Raymond landed a big client that propelled his business and gave us the ability to move out of the condo.

Raymond and I had discussed the possibility of moving for several years. We'd outgrown the space as Raymond ran his business out of our home. We explored our options and reached out to a friend who was a real estate agent. We learned we qualified for a healthy loan and looked into purchasing our family's home that would soon be foreclosed on. This would get Papi out of a terrible financial situation by not having to pay as much on his loan, as we would offer to pay a fair amount for the house. We also talked about allowing Papi to live in the house until he found a place to live, rather than letting him to come home to padlocked doors.

He was still our dad, despite it all.

After we discussed it with our real estate agent friend, we told Papi. He declined the offer and was upset with us for even bringing it up. He was adamant that this was *his* house and no one was going to kick him out of it. 'Not even the bank!' We didn't purchase the home as you know, but found another home right around the corner. He stayed in the home until the bank finally foreclosed.

During our parents' separation, while you guys were away in college, Mami and Papi both went through tough times. Mami was alone for the first time ever. She was separated from the man she had once run off with. She was madly in love with him, though she felt hurt. Still, now that she was alone, she wanted him back.

Papi was hurt by Mami's betrayal. He never thought she would leave him after all they had been through. Mami wanted him to suffer; she felt betrayed, too. She dangled the possibility of the two of them getting back together, intentionally causing him more pain. In her mind, he had caused this. He was irresponsible, drank away good jobs, and brought this financial debt upon himself. In *his* mind, she walked away from their marriage and left him alone.

When Mami and Amelia moved out, Papi fell into a more depressive state. The neighbors across the street called Raymond when they saw Papi walking down Fancy Road in his bathrobe, crying loudly and wearing one shoe on his foot. Raymond drove over to help calm him down and bring him back inside. Papi would call me and cry. He cried about feeling lonely. He cried about Mami being cruel to him. He often stopped by Mami's condo to visit her, but she refused to let him in.

They both called me every day and Papi often came to visit Raymond and me at our new house around the corner. We'd found a house one street over from Fancy Road and he'd come over to eat dinner with us. I'd often call on him to help prepare a dish as it gave him a sense of purpose. It made him smile.

It hurt so much to see Papi cry. His cries were painful, deep, raw. Despite how he hurt me in the past, he was the one who was hurting now. He was so weak, vulnerable, and depressed. I was whole and strong, and I had the ability to help him, even just a little. I'd seen Mami and Papi fight, argue, and get through some tough times. But this? This was the hardest thing Papi had ever been through.

Papi called me one evening during an emotional episode. He had been over earlier that night for dinner. He'd had three beers from my fridge as I sipped on wine. I was always conflicted about his drinking, however, now that Papi had a new restaurant job, his drinking was under control. He wasn't drinking on the job and only drank afterward. Drinking made him happy and he was fine when he left that night. Well, he must've gone home to drink more because when he called that night, he was *drunk*. He stuttered and mumbled his words together.

"It's your fault your mother left me," he slurred. "If you hadn't found a place for her to live, she would still be here. She would still need me. It's all your fault!"

His words pierced my soul. He was right. He was absolutely right.

Even months after he told me that, I gave myself a hard time about it. Their conflicts were always a struggle for me. I didn't want to intervene, but I wanted to be there for Mami and you guys. I didn't know what was the best thing to do. Should I get involved or should I let Mami and Papi be and just focus on my own marriage? In the end, I'd decided it was more important to help Mami out of her situation. Honestly, I don't think I could've turned her away.

I'd encouraged Mami to leave him. I helped her sell their furniture, their belongings, the things they'd worked hard to earn. I found a new home for her and Amelia. I moved her in on moving day. And I threatened her not to dare allow him to move in. I thought I was doing the right thing. I thought I had Mami's back.

Mami's heartache hit her worse when Papi met a woman at his new job. He started a relationship and moved her into the Fancy Road house, our parent's dream home, a year after Mami and Amelia moved out. That was the home where we'd celebrated birthdays and holidays. The home where we'd gathered every Sunday as a family to watch football and eat a good, home-cooked meal.

Mami was hurt that Papi had moved on without her. He got a new job and did so without her help. He made arrangements with the bank and made mortgage payments that allowed him to live in the house longer than expected. He claimed to have stopped drinking and invited the new woman in his life to move into the home that he and Mami had picked out.

When the news hit her, it drove our mother mad. She became obsessed. She had flowers delivered to Papi's job. She showed up at his restaurant just to see him. She pleaded for his love, but it was too late. He had moved on without her.

I was sound asleep one night when my cell phone rang on my nightstand. I sat straight up. It was 2:30 a.m. and Papi was calling; this couldn't be good news.

"What's wrong?" I said, rubbing my eyes.

"Come get your mother!" he shouted. I heard Mami yelling in the background. She was angry and demanding. "Olivia, come get your mother!" he repeated.

"Okay, okay. I'm getting my shoes! What's going on?"

Papi was trying to talk over her. "She just showed up at my house and started yelling. She told Franny to get out of her house. Just get over here before I have to call the police. She's pissing me off!"

Papi had told me about his new girlfriend. I'd actually run into them at the grocery store one day and he didn't really have much of a choice but to introduce us. I wasn't a fan of Franny. I had made an attempt to be friendly toward her since she did, after all, make our father happy and slowly pulled him out of his depressive state. Still, she was cold toward me and not friendly back. After that first meeting, I was done with it, though relieved she was taking care of him. Mami had found out about Franny from one of Papi's co-workers who spilled the beans.

"Don't call the police," I said. "I'm on my way."

Mami was hurting. She told me that night as I took her back home, that she didn't ever want to leave Papi, even when she did. She wanted me to find her and Amelia a place in hopes that Papi would come crawling back to her when he got evicted. She wanted to be there for him when he didn't have anywhere to go, hoping they would reconcile and carry on with their lives in the condo I had found for them. She never expected Papi to move on. She never expected him to have so much time before the home was finally foreclosed on.

As you know, Mami fell into a deeper state of depression. Her health took a bad toll. She wasn't able to work much longer as her seizures were almost daily and became a disruption to her work. Her doctors urged her to apply for disability as her health had spiraled. Her youngest children were all away in college. Her oldest daughter was no longer across the street. And her partner of twenty five years had moved on.

One day after we'd picked up her medication from the pharmacy, Mami tried to convince me to drive by the Fancy Road house. She often tried to talk me into it. I felt dwelling on Papi was unhealthy for her and usually told her I wouldn't do it, although when she begged me and pushed me far enough, sometimes I did.

This time I didn't. I drove her back to the condo in silence. She was unhappy with me. I hated having that control. I knew she wasn't able to drive herself, but I also knew it would only do her harm when we drove by and saw Franny's green Ford Taurus in the driveway. I couldn't do that to her. I couldn't let her do that to herself. I pulled into the parking spot at her condo to drop her off. I didn't have a lot of time. I had to get home and start on dinner.

"Do you know why I left your father after all those years?" she asked before she got out of the car.

Oh boy, where is this going? I thought.

"I don't know, Mami. Pick a reason," I said, sarcastically.

"I left him because of what happened between the two of you." She said it so certainly and with purpose. I refused to engage.

I let out a sigh and a gulp. I was not expecting to have this conversation.

She continued. "I did it for you." She gathered her purse and medicine and got out of the car. I watched her walk up the stairs to her front door and a million thoughts flooded my mind.

How could she say that to me? How could she put this heavy burden onto me? I'd never asked him to hurt me. I never provoked him. I'd wished with all of my being that nothing had ever happened. I had worked so hard to be normal after his abuse. I had attended counseling with my husband in order to have a healthy, intimate marriage. I had prayed to God to be able to live a normal life, all the while masking my insecurities and fear to portray the happy family I'd always desired. And now, *now* was when she decided to throw it in my face? She blamed *me* for their separation?

You're welcome, Mami. Both of you, *you're welcome.*

All I had wanted since I moved out was to take a step back from them and allow them to sort things out as a family. I wanted them to troubleshoot their own affairs. I wanted them to be a parental unit to the four of you, separate from me. I wanted them to be an example to what marriage should be. Instead, I'd done what I never wanted to do. I'd enabled her. I'd caused them both pain.

⋘☙⋙

Two years and one month after Mami and Amelia had moved out, Mami was served with divorce papers. Three months later, Papi married Franny in a small ceremony at the Fancy Road house. Mami found out through a mutual friend. Ever since Franny had come into Papi's life, we saw him less and less and heard from him even more scarcely. None of us were invited to the wedding. This new life without Papi was difficult for me to get used to. Our family had gone through so much together. How could he move on so easily?

CHAPTER 23

Full Circle

Mami and Papi's relationship is one I'm not sure I'll ever understand. During their separation period, they experienced all sorts of emotions. I was wedged in the middle of a lot of their arguments. I felt pulled in each direction as they each struggled for an ally, desperate for a friend. They'd call to complain about the other: "He's outside my condo. I'm not opening the door;" or "He usually calls me every day, and now he's not;" or "She walked away from me after all these years and left me when I most needed her. I didn't cause this on my own;" or "She turned my kids away from me." I heard it all.

They felt comfortable sharing their feelings with me because I was always in the middle. Throughout the years, I knew what they argued about; I knew their insecurities. Living in confined spaces, they didn't have the luxury of privacy.

I remember a time while I was still in elementary school and the two of them argued one morning. They yelled back and forth at each other. I decided it was a good idea to stand in between them and told them I wasn't going to go to school until they made up. I recall feeling so brave as I tried to outsmart them. It didn't work the way it played out in my head. They both turned on me and yelled at me to get out of the house and walk to school. I got to school even earlier than usual that morning. It's pretty funny now that I think about it.

Their separation makes sense to me. They had such a dysfunctional relationship that lacked partnership. How did it work out (kind of) for so long? The crazy thing is how much they still love each other. Through the heartbreak, the struggle, the stress, and all of us kids—they love each other. Their love is like no other.

They've come full circle. Mami now cleans houses for cash; it's not nearly as stressful as her office job was. Papi is a line cook at a local barbeque restaurant. They both circled around from their early professional careers in Panamá, to physically demanding jobs during our early years in the states, back to professional roles when they learned the language and moved up in their occupations, and now back to the same physically challenging jobs they had previously.

Mami made the decision to move to this country and follow her heart so many years ago. She was young and didn't know how things worked in a new country, but she took a big risk. (Which one of us would do that?) Mami and Papi came to this country with two suitcases to their names. They worked their asses off to support us, and, as a result, we live in a free country and have our education. We have roofs over our heads, shoes on our feet, and food on our tables. We never went hungry and we always felt loved. We can't take that for granted.

Because of you guys, I have all the love and support my heart can stand. I can't be angry at our parents or the past. Everything I have experienced has made me the person I am today—and I love me. For that, I thank them.

And I thank you.

CHAPTER 24

New Year,
New Life

I can't believe how quickly time flies. It seems like not that long ago, the five of us were playing school over summer breaks in the basement of our old house in Pennsylvania. I'm sorry for torturing you and making you study during your vacation time.

You guys are all so grown up.

Carrie, you're married and just bought a house. You're the only person I know who managed to graduate college without any student loans. You worked your butt off and were so independent from early on. You are wise beyond your years. You were always a quirky little girl, but you owned it. Who else swings one arm while standing in place to wind themselves up before they take off running? You're so brave. It took me so long to accept myself for who I am, but you always knew who you were and never let anyone steer you otherwise. I've always admired you for that.

John, you're a grown man. What happened to our little Cookie Monster? I can still picture you in your royal blue footie pajamas, devouring all the chocolate chip cookies in the pantry. You were so cute, and still are. I'm just glad you finally grew out of your biting phase. You're smart and have big dreams, like me. I can't wait to see you walk across that stage to get the degree you've been working so hard for, and then finally move on to the career of your choice. You've got some big ideas—go get 'em!

Celeste, stop growing up! It seems like just yesterday I was in the audience of your preschool show. All the students were following the teacher, singing along and gesturing after her. Not you. You sat there on stage in that gorgeous, frilly white dress in all your highness, and waited until your classmates completed the concert for you. You knew the song and the parts, but you never follow and no one tells you what to do. You do things on your own terms. You're a true leader and you amaze me every day. Now that you're a teacher, I hope you get a 'Celeste' in your classroom and smile at her royal attitude.

Amelia, you may be the baby girl but you've got an old spirit. There aren't words perfect enough to describe the strength you exemplify. You've gone through a lot and continue to face health challenges, and you handle it all so well. You're amazing and nothing stops you from doing everything you want to do. You're my little partner in crime. You're *everyone's* partner in crime! You're always there for us. And we need you! Don't ever move too far away from any of us. We wouldn't know what to do without you.

I'm so proud of all of you. Your love keeps my world turning, and each of you holds a special place in my heart. And Raymond, you all know how special he is to me and all of us. My heart overflows with love from all of you. I am truly blessed.

Raymond and I are going on nine years of marriage. We live in a big, beautiful home that I pray to one day fill with tiny versions of us that you guys will babysit, for sure. We work hard and smart. We play, laugh, and love. And we strive to be the best role models we can be to each other and the people around us.

Mami and I are in a better place emotionally. In fact, it's the best we've been in a long time. We have our space, we're open and honest with each other, and we accept each other for who we are. Neither one of us lets the past influence our relationship today, not negatively. Mami is focusing on her health, staying busy, and has built a support system beyond just me, which includes depending and relying a lot on you guys. The responsibilities are spread out now. Although she still has seizures, she doesn't let it stop her. She's the strongest I've ever seen her—and independent, too. We should all be proud of her.

I'm the healthiest I've been in a long time. For years, I felt miserable, trapped, and alone. I couldn't comprehend back then that I wasn't the only one who felt that way. I was stuck in my gloomy bubble with a desire to be independent, but held back by Mami's emotional and financial dependence on me—which only got worse after her first stroke. Her illness, to me, held the strings of her puppet mastery. I used to wonder how different would my life have been if she hadn't depended so heavily on me.

I also wondered what things would've been like had she not kept my Batista family from me. Would Papi have hurt me if Iban were in my life? Would I have felt so completely powerless and alone? These "what ifs" did me no good. Resentment is an ugly beast. It lived deep within me and made me imagine a better world without Mami or me in it. I struggled to view a world in which we co-existed.

As you know now, we've come a long way.

I'm now able to say that Papi is not a bad man. He did some bad things. He's your father; your only father, and the only father you're ever going to have. He's my Papi, too. And even though I have two dads now, he was the only dad I knew for most of my life. Sure, he's terrible at confrontation, he holds grudges, he doesn't know any of our birthdays, and he can't get our names straight half the time. He has nine children with four different women. He doesn't know how to say, 'I love you.' He avoids all of us because he knows we're angry at him—and with reason. But you know what else? In his own way, he loves us. He's living his own separate life away from us now, but I know he thinks about us. He has to.

He has to remember how Carrie used to claim him over all of us. Papi was *her* Papi and no one else's. She would tell us and clasp her hand into his. "He's *my* Papi," she'd affirm, as she kissed him on the cheek. He must remember carrying John like a football tucked in his forearm, and John loving it. He has to have memories of carrying little Amelia on his shoulders out in public and getting strange looks. Amelia was so fair-skinned, and Papi so many shades darker. No one believed he was her dad, but he didn't care. He carried her proudly. Celeste—he was so protective over you when you were little. You were so dainty. One day when Zoila's son pushed you, he actually pushed the baby back. He pushed his own grandson to the floor for you. That's our dad. Sure, unconventional, not always the best parenting skills, but he's our dad.

Papi loves his children—the four of you, Drew, Alejandra, Zoila, Dennis, and me. He may not have known how to be there for us. And yes, he made mistakes. He and Mami aren't married anymore, but he's still our father and, guess what? We're grown. We're adults now. We're independent and we can have our own separate relationships with him and Mami despite what he did to her, or how he hurt us each independently.

I have forgiven him for what he did.

Despite his faults, he worked multiple jobs to support his children and to make sure we had food on the table when we depended on him. Yes, some days he chose his Bacardi over milk and bread. He was an alcoholic—it's a disease.

Our family has been through a lot, but we've endured before and we'll do it again. We're going to keep going like we always do. Love will continue to fuel our family.

Afterword

"It's pouring out here! I can barely see the road, Mami!" I squealed. Our mid-afternoon errand run had turned treacherous. The charcoal colored clouds had arrived with little notice as the summer storm ripped through.

The sudden torrential, downpour muffled our conversation as I turned the radio dial from low to mute. My windshield wipers were waving as fast as they could go. Mami made the sign of the cross in the air toward me and then over her face and chest as I steered us through splashes.

"Where did this rain come from?" I added.

"God, please watch over us and our safety," she prayed under her breath while clutching the dainty Saint Christopher medallion that hung from her neck.

"Do you mind if we pull over?" I asked. "I need a break from these errands, anyway."

"I don't mind, hija."

"Are you hungry? There's a deli up ahead," I suggested.

"I could go for some soup," Mami agreed.

I found a parking spot at the storefront and we made a run for the door. Our fingers laced above our heads were worthless attempts at shielding the rain. *Where was my umbrella when I needed it?* We shook the dampness from our bodies as we stood on the black welcome mat inside. We walked up to the cashier and Mami asked what seemed like forty questions before she ordered a cup of the broccoli soup she always ordered. I ordered the cheddar potato soup—so many calories, but oh so good. We headed toward a seat by the window.

"What were we talking about in the car before that crazy storm hit?" Mami asked.

"Alguna mentira?" I raised my eyebrow amusingly at her. Mami chuckled. I smiled.

"I honestly don't remember," I replied.

Mami got quiet and drifted away in thought.

"Are you okay?" I asked.

She let out a loud sigh. "I want to tell you the story," she said, sounding relieved.

"Story? What story?"

"The story!" she exclaimed. "The story of your father and me."

"Oh God, Mami. We're good. We're past this. I don't care!"

"I know we're good, now," she explained. "I love that we have a good relationship now, but I still want to tell you the story."

"It's been *seven* years since our first trip back to Panamá! No offense, Mami, but I don't want to hear any more lies," I accused.

She squinted her eyes playfully, displeased with my comment. "It's really important to me that you hear my side of the story."

"You know that I only know *your* side of the story, right? Iban has never said anything negative about you, for the last time…"

She squinted her eyes again, this time in disbelief.

"I don't care, Mami," I said, much calmer and shook my head.

"I care!" she insisted.

"Fine! I give up. But if you tell me, I'm only willing to hear it if it's the truth," I said.

"I only want to tell you the truth."

CPSIA information can be obtained
at www.ICGtesting.com
Printed in the USA
BVOW08s1340270118
506489BV00001B/32/P